THE
BRIDGES
OF
CONSTANTINE

The Art of Forgetting

THE
BRIDGES
OF
CONSTANTINE

AHLEM MOSTEGHANEMI

Translated by Raphael Cohen

BLOOMSBURY
LONDON · NEW DELHI · NEW YORK · SYDNEY

First published in Great Britain 2013

Originally published in Arabic in 1993 as *Dhakirat al-Jasad* by Dar al-Adab, Beirut
First published in English in 1999 as *Memory in the Flesh* by The American University in Cairo Press

Bloomsbury Publishing plc
50 Bedford Square
London
WC1B 3DP

www.bloomsbury.com

Bloomsbury Publishing, London, New Delhi, New York and Sydney

A CIP catalogue record for this book is available from the British Library

ISBN 978 1 4088 4640 7

10 9 8 7 6 5 4 3 2 1

Typeset by Hewer Text UK Ltd, Edinburgh
Printed and bound in Great Britain by CPI Group (UK) Ltd, Croydon CR0 4YY

To my father

A son of Constantine who would say, 'There are cities where we live and others that live in us.' He made me fall in love with the city that lived within me and that I had not visited before writing this book.

The more than one million copies of this novel will for ever lack one reader: my father.

What use is our writing when there are no bookshops beyond the grave?

Chapter One

'WHAT HAPPENED TO US was love. Literature was all that did not happen.' I still remember the time you said that.

Now that everything is over, I can say: Congratulations to literature, then, on our tragedy. How vast the sweep of what did not happen, enough to fill several books. Congratulations to love, too.

What happened, what didn't happen, what will never happen – all so beautiful.

Before today, I believed we could only write about our lives once we had been cured of them. When we could probe old wounds with the pen and not feel the pain again; when we could look back without nostalgia, without going mad and, also, without bitterness. Is that really possible? We are never cured of memory. That's why we paint and why we write. And why some of us die.

'Would you like some coffee?' Atiqa's voice comes absently, as if asking someone else. Apologetic without apologising, like the sadness I haven't been able to shake off for days. My voice suddenly fails me, and I respond with a nod of the head. She goes out, only to return a few seconds later with a large copper tray bearing a coffee pot, cups, a sugar bowl, a phial of rose water and a plate of small cakes.

In other cities coffee comes pre-poured in the cup, with a spoon and sugar lumps on the saucer. But Constantine is a city that hates economy in anything. She always displays what she has, just as she wears all she owns and says all she knows. That's why even sadness could hold a banquet in this city.

I stack the scattered papers to make room for my cup of coffee, as though making room for you. The old drafts and blank sheets have spent days waiting for a few words – waiting for life to creep into them and turn them from paper into glory. Only words could take me from silence to speech, from memory to oblivion. Yet . . .

I put the sugar aside and sip my coffee – bitter, the way your love has conditioned me. I think of the strange sweetness of bitter coffee. At that instant, I feel able to write about you. I light a nervous cigarette and blow out clouds of the words that have been burning me for years. Words whose fire I have never once extinguished on paper.

Can paper extinguish memory when we leave the ash of nostalgia and the fag ends of disappointment on it? Which one of us snuffed out or fired up the other? I don't know, but before you I hadn't written anything worth mentioning. I will only start writing with you. Inevitably, I will finally find the words to write me. It is my right, today, to choose how I will be written, even though I didn't choose this story – a story that might not have been mine, if fate hadn't kept inserting you into every twist of the plot.

Where has this confusion come from?

How has the white rectangle of paper come to match the blank expanses of the canvases propped against the walls of my old studio? How have words abandoned me, just as colours did before them, turning the world into a black-and-white television showing a silent movie of memory? I have always envied artists who shift effortlessly between painting and writing, as if shifting from one internal room to another, as if moving untroubled between two mistresses. I should never have had only one mistress!

That would be the pen: more revealing and more wounding, skilled neither in toning nor shading, unable to give touches of colour to the wound on display.

These are the words I've been denied; naked, raw and painful, the way I want them. So why is my hand trembling fearfully, unable to write? Maybe it's only just dawned on me that I have exchanged my brushes for a knife. Writing to you is as fatal as loving you.

I sip your bitter coffee, this time with a dubious pleasure. I feel I am about to find the opening sentence for this book. A sentence with the spontaneity of a letter, as if I were to say, for example: 'I'm writing from a city that still resembles you and that I have come to resemble. The birds still hurry across these bridges, while I've become another bridge. Don't like bridges any more.' Or something like: 'Before a cup of coffee, I remembered you . . . Just this once you could have put a sugar lump in my coffee. Why such a large tray for bitter coffee?' I could have said anything.

In the end, novels are only letters and postcards we write not on special occasions, but to announce our inner news to those who care. That's why the most beautiful novels start with a sentence unexpected by anyone familiar with our moods and rituals – someone who might have caused all our turbulence.

A sudden flood of memory. I gulp down my coffee. I open

my window to get away from you, to retreat into the autumn sky, the trees, the bridges and the passers-by. To a city that has become mine once again, after I made a date with her for a different reason.

Constantine. Where everything is you.

Here you are, coming in through the window – as you did years ago – along with the familiar call from the minarets, the cries of the vendors, the footsteps of the black-clad women, the same old songs from the tireless radio: 'Apple, apple, tell me do/ Why the people fancy you.'

The naivety of the song breaks my reverie. It thrusts the nation into my face, unquestionably reminding me that I am in an Arab city. The years spent in Paris seem an epic dream. Is the singing of love songs to a fruit a peculiarly Arab thing? Or is it only the apple, with its taste of original sin, that is delicious enough to be serenaded in Arab lands? What if you had been an apple? But you weren't. You were the woman who tempted me to eat the apple, that's all. Instinctively you played Eve with me. But I couldn't renounce the several men inside me and be, with you in particular, as big an idiot as Adam!

'Hello *Si* Khaled. How are you today?' A neighbour calls out his greetings. His gaze has climbed the floors of my sadness and he seems surprised at how lost I look as I stand there. I vacantly follow his steps, and those of others who come after him, towards the neighbouring mosque. Indolent or in a hurry, all heading to the same place. The whole country is off to pray, while the radio extols the eating of an apple. Beside the minarets, rooftop aerials pick up the foreign channels that every evening on television suggest more than one – contemporary – way to taste forbidden fruit.

In fact, I don't like fruit, and the matter of the apple has no particular interest for me.

I loved you. Was it my fault that your love came in the form of a sin?

'How are you?' another neighbour asks on his way to pray. My lips give him a terse reply and proceed to ask about you.

How am I? I'm what you did to me, madam. And how are *you*? A woman whom my nostalgia has smeared with madness, until she has gradually taken on the features of a city and the contours of a nation where I live, oblivious to time, as though within long-locked vaults of memory.

How do you do? Like a mulberry tree decked in hereditary mourning for every season. You, Constantine woman in dress; you, Constantine woman in love, in joy, in sadness, in lovers. Tell me, where are you now? This is Constantine. With her cold limbs and feet, her hot lips, her bouts of insanity.

This is she. If only you knew how like her you are. Let me close the window.

It was Marcel Pagnol who said, 'Get used to considering ordinary things, things that may actually happen.' Isn't death, in the end, something ordinary? Just like birth, love, marriage, illness, old age, exile and madness? Until they happen, we expect so many commonplace things to be extraordinary. Things that we think happen only to other people. We think that life for some reason or another will spare us many of them, until we find ourselves before them.

When I examine my life today, I find that my having met you is the only truly extraordinary thing. The only thing I couldn't have foreseen or whose consequences for me I couldn't have anticipated. Because, at the time, I was ignorant of the fact that extraordinary things may also be accompanied by many ordinary ones.

Even so, and even after these years have passed, I still wonder where to place your love. Under the heading of ordinary things that happen out of the blue – like a medical condition, a twisted ankle or an episode of madness? Or should I file it where it began – as something extraordinary, like the discovery of a planet or an earthquake undetected by sensors? Were you a twisted ankle or a twist of fate?

I flip through a pile of recent newspapers searching for convincing explanations for an 'ordinary' event that changed the course of my life and landed me here. I browse our misery after all these years, the black ink of the homeland sticking to my fingers. You have to wash your hands after reading the newspapers here, although not always for the same reason. The ink of some of them stains, while the corruption of the glossier ones rubs off. Is it because newspapers resemble their owners that they seem to wake up daily like us, hitting the streets with haggard features and a sallow, hastily washed face? They don't bother to comb their hair, put on a matching tie or give us a winning smile.

Twenty-fifth of October 1988. Banner headlines. Masses of black ink. Masses of blood. Too little shame.

Some newspapers print the same front-page photographs every day. Only the suits are different. Others promote the same lies, but with less intelligence each time, or sell nothing less than a ticket out of the country. Since that's no longer possible, I'd better close the paper and go and wash my hands.

The last time the Algerian press caught my eye was a few months ago. By chance, I was leafing through a magazine when I came across a half-page picture of you alongside an interview about your new book.

My gaze was transfixed that day by that framed photo of you. I made a futile effort to decode your words. I read you in a state of confusion, stumbling over the words in my haste, as if it were me talking to you about myself, and not you addressing others about a story that might not have been ours.

What an incredible date we had that day! How – after all these years – had I failed to expect that, tucked between the pages of a magazine I don't usually read, you'd make a date with me.

It had to be the law of idiocy that by chance I'd bought a magazine I usually did not, just to turn my life head over heels.

Where's the surprise? Weren't you a paper woman, loving and hating on paper, leaving and returning on paper, killing and reviving with the stroke of a pen? Reading you had to be confusing. The electric thrill ran through my body again, firing my pulse, as though I were facing not your picture but you.

I went back to that picture from time to time, and would wonder how you had managed to waylay me after I had avoided every avenue leading back to you. How did you come back after the wound had so nearly healed? My heart that once brimmed with your memory had little by little emptied of you, you who had packed love's bags and taken off for another heart. You left my heart like a package tourist leaves a city. Everything pre-arranged, even the departure time; everything pre-booked, even the sights to visit, the play to see and the gift shop to buy souvenirs. Was your journey as tedious as that?

Stunned and confused, I was looking at a representation of you as though you were really present. I was surprised by your new hairstyle; what had you done to your hair, now short, hair that had embraced me in the loneliness of my nights? I gazed at your eyes, searching for the memory of my first failure with you. That day, your eyes outshone themselves in beauty. They held so much misery and so much joy for me. Had your eyes changed too? Or had my perspective changed? I continued searching your face for signs of my earlier madness. I barely recognised your lips, your smile or your new lipstick.

How had I once found an echo of my mother in you? I had imagined you in her burgundy dress, as you kneaded, hands with long, painted nails, the bread whose taste I had been missing for years. What insanity that was. What idiocy!

Had married life really changed your appearance and your childlike laughter? Had it changed your memory too, the taste of your lips and your dusky, gypsy-like skin? Had it made you forget the 'bankrupt prophet' whose Ten Commandments were stolen on his way over to you, so he only brought you an eleventh?

There you were before me in the guise of apostasy. You had chosen another path. You had put on another face that I no longer recognised. The face of an advertising model, made up in advance to sell something like toothpaste or anti-ageing cream. But perhaps you'd put on the mask just to promote a product in the shape of a book, which you'd entitled *The Curve of Forgetting*. A product that might be my story with you, the memory of my hurt, or the latest way you'd found to kill me all over again, without leaving your fingerprints on my neck.

That day, I remembered an old conversation of ours when I had asked you why you opted for the novel in particular. I marvelled at your answer. You said with a smile whose truth or deceit I couldn't gauge, 'I had to tidy up internally, get rid of some old stuff. Just like a house, we need to spring clean inside ourselves. I can't keep the windows shuttered on more than one corpse. We write novels for no other reason than to kill their heroes. To finish off the people whose existence has become a burden. Whenever we write about them, we get rid of them and let in the fresh air.' After a brief silence you added, 'Every novel that works is really a crime we commit against a certain memory or perhaps a certain person. We shoot them in public, with a silencer. They are the only ones who realise that the spray of words is aimed at them. Failed novels are just failed attempts at assassination. Authors' pen permits should be revoked on the grounds that they can't handle words. They might kill someone by mistake, and that includes themselves – after making their readers die of boredom!'

Why hadn't your sadistic tendencies raised doubts then? Why hadn't I anticipated all those crimes to come, where you used your other weapons? I never expected that one day you might take aim at me. That's why I laughed at what you said. Maybe my new fascination with you began then – in such cases we can't resist a crazed admiration for our killer.

Nevertheless, I expressed my perplexity. 'I thought the novel was a way for an author to relive a story they loved and grant immortality to someone they loved.'

My words seemed to surprise you, as though you saw in them something you hadn't taken into account, and you said, 'Maybe that's true as well. Ultimately, we only kill those we love. In compensation, we grant them literary immortality. It's a fair deal, isn't it?'

Fair? Who discusses justice with a tyrant? Did they argue with Nero the day he burned Rome out of pyromaniac love for her? Weren't you just like him, as skilled in arson as in love?

At that moment, had you foreseen my imminent end and were you trying to console me in advance? Or were you, as usual, just playing with words, noting their impact on me? Were you secretly relishing my constant amazement at you and your incredible capacity to forge a language that would match the scale of your contradictions?

Anything was possible. Perhaps *I* was the victim of your novel, the victim you sentenced to immortality and decided, as usual, to embalm with words. Perhaps I was only an imaginary victim, created by you to resemble the truth. In the end, despite my stubborn desire for the truth, only you knew the answers to all these questions that haunted me.

When did you write the book?

Before or after you got married? Before Ziyad left us, or after? Did you write it about *me*, or about him? Did you write it to kill me or to bring *him* back to life? Or to finish us both off with one book, just as you left us both for another man?

When I read the article a few months ago, I never expected you'd force your presence on me again and that your book would dominate my thoughts, a vicious circle in which I was caught alone.

After all that had happened I couldn't immediately go searching among the bookshops to buy a copy of my story. Nor could I ignore it and get on with my life as if I'd never heard of it and it had nothing to do with me. Wasn't I burning to read the rest of the story? Your story, which ended without my knowing the final chapters. Having been the main witness, I was now absent. Yet according to the same law of idiocy, I had always been both witness and victim in a story that only had room for one hero.

I have it now, your book. It would have been impossible to read today, so I've left it enigmatically closed on the table like a time bomb ready to ambush me. I turn to its silent presence for help in blasting open the quarry of words inside me and stirring up memory.

Everything about it has annoyed me today: its title, chosen as a clear deceit; your smile that seems to ignore my sadness; your calm gaze that treats me like a reader who knows little about you. Even your name. Perhaps that annoys me most. Its particular letters still strike the memory before they strike the eye. Your name isn't read so much as heard, like a melody played on a single instrument for an audience of one. How could I read it impartially when it was one chapter of an unbelievable story written by chance when our fates crossed?

A comment on the back of your book describes it as a literary event. I put a pile of drafts written at moments of delirium on top of it and think, 'It's time for me to write or remain silent for ever. These are incredible times.'

A sudden chill settles it. Constantine's night creeps towards me through the closed window of solitude. I put the top back on the pen for the moment and slide under the covers of loneliness.

Since realising that every city has the night it deserves, which resembles it and which alone exposes what is hidden by day, I have decided to avoid looking out of this window at night.

All cities unconsciously undress at night and reveal their secrets to strangers, even when they say nothing. Even when they bar their doors. Because cities are like women, some of whom make us wish morning would come soon. But . . .

'*Soirs. Soirs, que des soirs pour un seul matin.*' 'Evenings, evenings, how many evenings for a single morning.' Why do I remember this line by the poet Henri Michaux and find myself repeating it in two languages? Why do I remember it, and when did I memorise it? Perhaps for years I've been expecting such despondent evenings that will only ever have one morning. I search my memory for anything about the poem and remember it is called 'Old Age'.

My discovery frightens me, as if I had suddenly discovered I had new features. Does old age really creep up on us over the course of one long night, with an inner darkness that makes us slower in everything, ambling along in no particular direction? Are boredom, disorientation and monotony characteristics of old age or of this city?

Am I going senile, or is the whole nation having a collective mid-life crisis? Doesn't this country have a marked capacity to make us old and decrepit in a matter of months, a matter of weeks, even?

Before I didn't feel the weight of the years. Your love kept me young and my studio was an abundant source of renewable energy. Paris is an elegant city where one would be embarrassed to neglect one's appearance. But now the flame of my madness has gone out, and I have ended up here. Now we're – all of us – standing over the nation's volcanic eruption, and all we can do is fuse with the lava showers and forget our inconsequential fires. Nothing now warrants all that elegance and decorum. Our nation itself now struts shamelessly before us!

At an age when others have said everything they have to say, there is nothing more difficult than starting to write. Picking up the pen for the first time after the age of fifty is as crazy and lustful as reliving the passion of adolescence. It is exciting and foolish, an affair between an ageing gentleman and a virgin quill. While he is confused and in a hurry, she is chaste, unsated by the ink of the world.

I shall consider what I have written up to now as just preparatory, an overflow of desire for these sheets of paper that for years I have dreamed of filling. Maybe tomorrow I will begin writing in earnest. I've always liked to link the important things in my life with a particular date, in a nod to another memory. This idea seduced me again when I was listening to the evening news and discovered – having lost my relationship with time – that tomorrow will be 1 November. How could I not choose that as the date to start my book?

Tomorrow will mark the passing of thirty-four years since the firing of the first shot in the war of liberation. I'll have been here for three weeks, three weeks also since riots claimed the last martyred *shahids*, one of whom I came here to mourn and bury myself.

Between the first and the last bullets, hearts have changed and aims have changed. The country has changed. That's why tomorrow will be a down payment of grief. There will be no military parade, receptions or formal exchanges of congratulations. They will make do with an exchange of accusations, while we will make do with visiting the graves.

I won't visit that grave tomorrow. I don't want to share my grief with the nation. I prefer complicity with paper and its silent pride. Everything annoys me tonight. I feel I might finally write something great, not tear it up as usual. For, after all these years, an agonising coincidence has brought me back to this very place on the anniversary of the original memory to find the body of someone I loved waiting for me.

Tonight the past awakens bewilderingly inside me. It lures me into the labyrinth of memory. I try to resist, but can I resist my memory? I close the door of my room and open the window again. I try to see something other than myself, but the window looks back at me.

Forests of bay and oak stretch before me. Constantine creeps towards me, wrapped in her old cloak, with all the familiar woods, cliffs and secret passes that once surrounded her like a security cordon. Her branching pathways and dense forests lead to the secret bases of the fighters, as if explaining to us tree after tree, cave after cave.

All the paths in this ancient Arab city lead to steadfastness. All the forests and rocks here joined the ranks of the Revolution before we did.

There are cities that don't choose their fates. History and geography have condemned them not to surrender. So their sons do not always have a choice. Is it strange, then, that I resemble this city so much?

More than thirty years ago, I walked these paths. I chose these mountains as my home and clandestine school where I studied the only subject whose teaching was banned. I knew that there were no re-sits, and that my fate was confined to the space between freedom and death.

We chose a more enticing name for this death, so we could head towards it without fear and, perhaps, with secret desire, as though moving towards something other than our end. Why did we forget at the time to give freedom more than one name? Why from the outset did we limit our freedom to its original meaning?

Death in those days walked, slept and ate hasty meals with us, just as yearning, patience, faith and a vague happiness never left us. Death breathed in sync with us. The days grew ever harder, only different from those before in the toll of *shahids* whose deaths were mostly never expected. For some reason, their end – theirs especially – was never envisioned as so close, so devastating. That was the logic of death that I hadn't yet taken in.

I still remember them, those who we later got used to talking of en masse. They were not *shahids*, plural: each one of them was a *shahid* in his own right. As though the plural in this case in particular didn't abbreviate our memory of them, but rather diminished their claims on us.

One died in the first battle as though he'd come just for martyrdom. One fell a day before a stolen visit to his family,

14

having spent weeks working out the details and making preparations. One went to get married, then came back and died a married man. One dreamed of going back to marry, but never went back.

In war it isn't so much those who die who are miserable. The most miserable are those they leave behind bereft, orphaned, with wrecked dreams.

I discovered that fact early on, *shahid* by *shahid*, story by story.

At the same time, I also discovered that perhaps I was the only one to leave nothing behind except the fresh grave of a mother who died ill and in despair, an only brother years younger than me, and a father preoccupied by the demands of his new young wife.

The popular proverb has it right: 'The death of a father doesn't an orphan make. Only the death of a mother.'

I was an orphan and intensely aware of it, all the time. Hunger for tenderness, a frightening and painful feeling, eats away at you inside until it crushes you in some way or another. Did I enlist with the Front at that time in an unavowed effort to find a more beautiful death – one untainted by the unhealthy feelings of resentment gradually overtaking me?

The Revolution was entering its second year, and I was entering my third month as an orphan. I can no longer remember now exactly when the nation took on maternal features and unexpectedly lavished me with ambiguous tenderness and an extreme sense of belonging.

Perhaps *Si* Taher's disappearance from our neighbourhood in Sidi Mabrouk some months earlier played a part in resolving the matter and helped me to reach that surprising decision so quickly. It was no secret that he had moved to a hidden place in the mountains around Constantine to help establish one of the first cells in the armed struggle.

Where has *Si* Taher's name come from tonight, to add to my confusion? Which one of you led me to the other? Where has it returned from, and was it really absent, when only two blocks away from me lies a street that still bears his name?

There is something called the power of a name. There are names the memory of which makes us sit up straight and put out our cigarette. As soon as we talk about them, it's as if we were talking to them with the old respect and admiration.

Si Taher's name is still sacred to me. Habit and familiarity haven't killed it. Being in prison together and the years of the struggle haven't turned it into the ordinary name of a friend or neighbour. Symbols always know how to put up an invisible barrier that divides the ordinary from the exceptional, the possible from the impossible, in everything.

Here I am, remembering him during a night that I haven't set aside for him.

As I take a drag on a last cigarette, the minarets announce the dawn prayer. From a distant room comes the crying of a baby whose voice has awakened every corner of the house. I envy the minarets. I envy infants. They alone have the right and ability to scream, before life tames their vocal cords and teaches them silence. Who was it who said, 'Man spends his early years learning to speak, and the Arab regimes spend the rest of his life teaching him to be silent!'

Silence could have been a blessing this night in particular, just like forgetting. On such occasions memory doesn't come in instalments, but overwhelms me in torrents, sending me tumbling down unknown slopes. At that moment, how can I stop it without crashing into the rocks and being crushed in a landslide of memory? Here I am, out of breath, chasing after a past I've never really left behind, after a memory I live in because it is my body. A disfigured body, no less.

There are those who race from podium to podium on some pretext or another to condemn the history they were part of. Perhaps to jump on to the new wave before the flood sweeps them away. All one can do is pity them. How wretched for someone just emerging from the swamp to keep wet clothes on instead of waiting quietly while they dry!

Si Taher appears silently. Silently, like the martyrs. Silently, as usual.

I am embarrassed before him, as usual.

The fifteen years between us had always seemed greater. They were a lifetime in their own right, a symbol of a man who combined an eloquence of speech – which marked out all those who mixed with the Association of Scholars and studied in Constantine – with an eloquent presence.

Si Taher knew when to smile and when to be angry. He knew how to speak, but also how to remain silent. His face was always dignified, with its vague smile that constantly suggested a different interpretation of his features. 'Smiles are punctuation marks. But only a few people still know how to punctuate correctly,' wrote Malek Haddad.

My first partisans' meeting with *Si* Taher took place in Kidya prison. A meeting charged with extreme feelings and shock, the rawness and fear of a first detention. *Si* Taher drew me into the Revolution day by day. He knew he was responsible for my being there. Perhaps he secretly pitied my sixteen years, my truncated childhood and my mother. He knew her well and understood what my first spell of detention might do to her. But he concealed his pity from me, repeating to those willing to listen, 'Prisons were built for men.'

At the time, Kidya prison, like those throughout eastern Algeria, was suffering from a sudden influx of men. This followed the demonstrations of 8 May 1945 when the cities of Constantine, Sétif and their environs made the first pledge of Revolution in the form of a few thousand martyrs who fell in a single demonstration and the tens of thousands of prisoners who crammed the cells. This made the French commit their stupidest mistake, as for a few months they mixed political and criminal prisoners in cells that at times held more than twenty inmates.

In this way, they helped the Revolution spread among the criminal prisoners, who seized the chance to acquire a political consciousness and cleanse their honour by joining a Revolution for whose sake many of them would subsequently fall as *shahids*. Some of them are still alive today, enjoying respect and veneration as veteran leaders of the war of liberation, after history restored their criminal records to their original spotless state. As a result of colonial stupidity, political prisoners took the opportunity to get to know each other, and had time on their hands to discuss affairs of state and to plan the next stage.

Today when I remember that experience, which for me lasted only six months, its intensity and shock make it seem longer than it actually was. I was released along with two others on account of our youth, and because others were of more concern than us.

I went back to Constantine secondary school, having fallen a year behind. I found the same classes and the same works of philosophy and French literature waiting for me.

Some schoolmates were absent, either in jail or *shahids*. Most of these were students in the top stream, which was supposed to produce the top rank of Gallicised Algerian intellectuals and civil servants. It was a matter of honour for them when some ventured to call them traitors simply for choosing French secondary schools and culture in a city where it was impossible to ignore the authority of Arabic and its esteemed place in people's hearts and memories.

Was it surprising that many of them were to be found among those imprisoned and tortured after the demonstrations? By virtue of their Western culture, they enjoyed an early political awareness and were full of nationalism and dreams. When World War II ended in victory for France and the Allies, they realised that France had used Algerians to fight someone else's war, sending thousands to their deaths in battles that did not concern them, only for the survivors to return to slavery.

The coincidence of sharing a cell with *Si* Taher was the stuff of legend. A taste of struggle that accompanied me for years and perhaps went on to alter my destiny. Meeting some men is like meeting one's destiny.

Si Taher was exceptional in all things, as if he had been preparing himself all along to be more than a man. He was born to be a leader. He came from the stock of Tariq ibn Ziyad and Emir Abdelkader, of those who could change history with one speech. The French, who imprisoned and tortured him for three years, were well aware of this. But they did not know that *Si* Taher would take his revenge years later, becoming the man most wanted after every military operation in eastern Algeria.

What a coincidence that fate came full circle after ten years and placed me with *Si* Taher in another experience of struggle, this time armed.

In 1955, September to be precise, I joined the National Liberation Front, the FLN. My comrades were starting a decisive academic year. In my twenty-fifth year, I was beginning my other life.

I remember that I was surprised at the time by *Si* Taher's reception. He didn't ask for any details of my life or studies. He didn't even ask why I had decided to join the Front, or how I had found him. He kept looking at me and then embraced me passionately as though he'd been waiting for a year.

He said, 'You've arrived!'

'Yes, I've arrived,' I replied with a mixture of joy and vague sadness.

Si Taher could be like that. Terse, even in joy. In my sadness, I was equally terse with him.

Then he asked about my family, Mother in particular. I told him she had died three months previously. I think he understood the whole thing. While patting my shoulder and with half a tear sparkling in his eyes, he said, 'God have mercy on her. She suffered a lot.'

He became lost in thought, far from me at that moment.

Later, I envied that sudden tear in his eye, which elevated my mother to the rank of *shahid*. I only ever saw *Si* Taher cry over his men who had been killed. For a long time afterwards, I wished to be laid out as a corpse before him and enjoy, even from beyond the grave, an irrepressible tear in his eye.

Was it for all this that my family was suddenly reduced to this man? I devoted myself to demonstrating my heroism to him, as if I wanted to make him a witness to my manhood or my death. I wanted him to witness that I no longer belonged to anyone except this country, that I had left nothing behind except the grave of a woman who had been my mother and a younger brother for whom my father had already chosen a new mother.

I hurled myself at death every time, as if in defiance, or desiring it to take me rather than my comrades whose children and families awaited their return. But death decided to reject me, and I returned every time while others fell.

After I'd taken part in a few victorious battles, *Si* Taher came gradually to rely on me for difficult missions. He would assign me the most dangerous ones, those that demanded direct confrontation with the enemy. After two years he promoted me to lieutenant so that I could command some battles on my own and take military decisions as circumstances required.

Only then did the Revolution start to turn me into a man. As if my rank certified that I had been cured of my memory and my childhood. I was happy at the time, having finally achieved the serenity that only comes with peace of mind. Little did I realise then, but my ambitions weren't to be. At the very time I believed that my sadness had become a thing of the past, fate was lying in wait.

The fierce battle on the outskirts of Batna turned everything upside down. We lost six fighters, and I was one of the wounded. Two bullets hit my left arm and the whole course of my life suddenly changed. I was among the wounded who had to be transferred quickly to the Tunisian border for treatment. As the bullets were impossible to remove, my left arm had to be amputated. There was no room for discussion or hesitation. The only question was the safest route to Tunis, where the rear bases were situated.

I was facing another reality.

Fate expelled me from my only refuge, the life of night battles. It brought my clandestine world into the light and set another dimension before me, not of life or death, but one of pure pain that would be my lookout post over events on the battlefield. *Si* Taher's words made it clear that I might not return to the Front.

On that last day, *Si* Taher tried to maintain his normal tone. He said goodbye in the same way as he had done before every new battle. But this time he knew he was steeling me for my battle with fate. He was unusually brief. Maybe because no special orders are given in such cases. Maybe because he had endured the loss of ten of his best men, dead or wounded, in a single battle. He knew the value of every fighter and, with the Revolution beset from all sides, the need for every single one of them.

I didn't say anything to him that day. For an obscure reason, I felt that I had been orphaned again. A tear froze in each eye. I was bleeding, and the pain in my arm was gradually spreading to my whole body. It settled in my throat as a lump of pain, disappointment and fear of the unknown.

Events were racing past me and my fate took a new turn every hour. Only the voice of *Si* Taher giving final orders reached me. It formed my only connection with the world.

Even so, I still remember perfectly his coming to inspect me an hour before my departure. He put a piece of paper and a few banknotes in my pocket, bent over me and said, as if telling me a secret, 'I've left my family's address in Tunis in your pocket, and a little money.' Then he mumbled, 'If you make it there, I hope you'll visit them when you've recovered. Give the money to *Amma* to buy a present for the little girl. I'd also like you to register her birth if you can. It may be a long time before I can visit them.'

A few moments later, as though he had forgotten something, he added, half embarrassed as he uttered it for the first time, 'I am naming her — —. Register her when you can, and kiss her for me. And send *Amma* all my regards.'

That was the first time I heard your name. Bleeding between life and death, I heard it. In my coma I fixated on its letters, like someone delirious from fever might fixate on a word. Like a prophet grasps a commandment he fears he might lose. Like a drowning man grasps at a lifeline. Between the letter A (for agony) and the letter M (for pleasure) your name was spelled out. Dividing them was the letter H (for heat) and the letters L and A, the Arabic word *la* (for warning). I failed to heed the warning of your name, born as a small flame in the first fires of the war. I failed to heed the warning of a name that starts with 'ah', the antonymic cry of both pleasure and pain. I failed to heed the warning of this noun, which means 'dreams', both singular and plural, like the name of this country, which means 'islands', and realise from the beginning that plurals are always created to be split up.

Today, between smiling and sadness, I recall that command-ment, 'Kiss her for me,' and I laugh at fate, at myself and at strange coincidences. Then I'm shamed by the gravity of his voice, and the rare sign of weakness surrounding his words. He always wanted to seem imposing to us, unconcerned by anything except the nation, and with no family but his men. But he had confessed his weakness to me. He pined and longed, and maybe even cried, but within the limits of decency and always in secret. Symbols have no right to cry from longing. He did not talk much about your mother, for example. Didn't he miss her? A bride whom he had enjoyed for a few stolen months and whom he had left pregnant.

Why the sudden haste? Why didn't he wait a little while, arrange a few days' leave and register you himself? He had waited six months, why not a few weeks more? And why me? What twist of fate brought me together with you? Whenever I asked myself these questions, I was confounded and found myself believing in destiny.

Despite his responsibilities, *Si* Taher could have escaped to Tunis for a day or two. Crossing the well-guarded border with its patrols and checkpoints wouldn't have frightened him. Nor would breaching the electrified and landmined Morice Line that stretched the length of the border between Algeria and Tunisia, from the coast to the desert, which he subsequently crossed three times – a record number, given the dozens of corpses of fighters left strewn along it.

Was it *Si* Taher's love of discipline and respect for rules that made him feel so anxious after you were born? He'd discovered that he'd been a father for months, and the child was still unregistered, officially nameless. Having awaited you for so long, was he worried that he might lose you if he didn't have your existence and affiliation to him officially signed and sealed? Did he have a bad feeling about your legal status, and want to register his *ahlam* – his dreams – at the town hall to ensure her reality? So that fate wouldn't come and snatch her away. Ultimately, after a first failed, childless marriage, he dreamed of being a father like other men.

I don't know if, deep down, *Si* Taher wouldn't have preferred a baby boy. But I did learn later that he had tried to outwit fate and had chosen a boy's name before his departure – ignoring the possibility of a girl. Maybe this was the unconscious result of a military mindset and nationalist obsession. I often heard him begin his military speeches and plans with, 'We need men.'

So *Si* Taher seemed happy and optimistic about everything in that period. The hard man suddenly changed. He became less rigid and more fun when off duty. Something inside him was changing, bringing him closer to others, more sympathetic to their personal circumstances. He granted passes more readily for snatched home visits, yet denied himself one. Late fatherhood, a ready symbol for a brighter future, changed him.

A small miracle of hope. That was you.

* * *

Morning dawns.

The day surprises me with its usual din. Against my will, the sudden sunshine floods me with light. I feel it stealing something from me. At that instant I hate the inquisitive, shaming aspect of the sun. I want to write about you in darkness. My story with you was like undeveloped film. I am scared that light will expose it and ruin it, because you are a woman who flowered in a secret part of me and whom I possessed with the legitimacy of secrecy. I should only write about you after drawing all the curtains and shutting the windows of my room.

Even so, I'm happy at the sight of the paper stacked in front of me. I filled the sheets in a night of frenzy. With a tasteful cover, I might dedicate them to you as a book. I know, I know you hate overly tasteful things, and that you're very selfish. In the end, you care for nothing outside of yourself and your body.

A little patience, madam.

In a few more pages I'll have laid my other memory naked before you. A few more pages are needed before, in vanity and desire, regret and madness, I'll fill you out. Like love's feasts, books also need starters. Although I admit that writing the foreword is not as immediate a problem as finding where the story starts.

Where do I begin my story with you when your story with me had so many beginnings? It began with unexpected endings and upheavals of fate.

When I speak about you, whom do you think I am talking about? The baby who once crawled at my feet; the young woman who twenty-five years later turned my life upside down; the woman on the stylish cover of a book entitled *The Curve of Forgetting* whose scant resemblance to you makes me wonder if it really is you?

What name should I give you?

Maybe the one your father wanted, the one I myself registered in his stead at the town hall. Or your original name – Hayat – the one you bore for six months while awaiting another legal name. That's what I'll call you. It is just one of your names but it is the name *I* will use for you, as it was the name I knew you by, the name that only I know. The name that is not on people's tongues, not written down on the pages of books and magazines, nor in any official register.

The name you were granted so that you might live – God grant you long life. The name I killed one day when I gave you another, official name. It is my right to bring the other back to life, because it is mine, not used by any man before me. Your name as a child lingers on my tongue, as though you were still the you of decades ago. Whenever I say it, you come back as a child sitting on my knees, playing with my things, saying words I don't understand. At that moment I forgive all your sins. Whenever I say it, I slide back to the past and you come back as tiny as a doll. As my daughter.

Should I read your book to know how this little girl became a woman? But I already know you'll never write about your childhood, your early years. You fill the empty holes in memory with words. You get over the wounds with lies. Perhaps that was the secret of your attachment to me. For I know the missing links in your life. I knew the father you only saw a few times in your life, and know the city where you lived but that does not live in you – whose alleyways you treat without affection, trampling over its memory without paying attention.

You grew attached to me to discover what you didn't know. I grew attached to you to forget what I did know. Could our love last?

26

Si Taher was a third character in our story from the outset, even when we didn't talk about him. Though absent, he was present between us. Did I need to kill him again to be alone with you? If only you knew how heavy the burden of a last wish had been, even after a quarter of a century. How painful a desire confronted by its impossibility and by principles that ultimately only make it more appealing.

From the very beginning the question was how I would erase *Si* Taher from my memory, his life from mine, to give our love the chance for a natural birth. But what would be left if I excised you from our shared memory and turned you into an ordinary girl?

Your father was an exceptional comrade and an exceptional leader. He was exceptional in life and in death. Could I forget that?

He wasn't one of the fighters of the last battles of 1962 who, to guarantee their futures, joined the last wave. He wasn't an accidental *shahid*, surprised by death during carpet bombing or hit by a stray bullet. He was made of the same stuff as Didouche Mourad, Larbi Ben M'hidi and Mostefa Ben Boulaïd. They sought death instead of waiting for it to come to them.

Could I forget that he was your father when your constant questions restored his glory, in life and in death?

The heart that loved you to the point of madness has grown confused. The echo of your request remains present: 'Tell me about him . . .'

I will tell you about him, my darling. There is nothing easier than talking about martyrs. Their history is ready-made and known in advance, like their finale. Their ending absolves them of any sins they might have committed.

I will tell you about *Si* Taher.

27

Only the history of *shahids* can be written. Another history follows, appropriated by the living. This will be written by a generation that doesn't know the truth, but will deduce it of its own accord. Some signs cannot be misread.

Si Taher died *taher*, pure, at the threshold of independence. He had nothing in his hands but his weapon, nothing in his pockets but a few worthless notes, nothing round his neck but the honour of martyrdom. Symbols acquire their value at their death. Those who act on their behalf acquire their value from ranks and medals, and quickly line their pockets with the proceeds of secret accounts.

His murderers carpet-bombed the besieged town of Dachra for six hours so that they could put a photograph of one of the rebels France had vowed to destroy on the front page of the next day's papers, as proof of their crushing victory. Was the death of this simple man really a victory for a great power which, in a matter of months, would lose all of Algeria?

He was martyred in the summer of 1960 and did not enjoy the fruits of victory. He gave everything for Algeria, which did not even give him the chance to see his son walking beside him. Or see you fulfil his dream and become a doctor or teacher.

That man loved you so much! With the passion of a father at forty. With the great tenderness of one whose severity concealed much tenderness. With the dreams of one whose dreams had been confiscated. With the pride of a fighter who, when he sees his firstborn, realises that he will never completely die.

I still remember the few occasions he stole visits to you all in Tunis for a day or two. I would race to see him, desperate to hear the latest news from the Front. At the same time, I would restrain myself so as not to steal the few precious hours that he had risked his life for, so that he could spend them with his small family.

I discovered a different man from the one I knew. A man in different clothes, with a different smile and words. He sat so you could easily sit in his lap for him to play with. He lived every second to the full as though he were squeezing every drop of happiness from the meanness of time, stealing in advance hours of life that he knew would be few, and giving you in advance a lifetime's supply of tenderness.

I saw him for the last time in January 1960. He had come to witness the most important event in his life and meet Nasser, his second-born child. It was a secret wish of his to be blessed with a boy. That day, for some reason, I studied him closely, but spoke little. I preferred to leave him to his delight and his stolen happiness. When I went back the following day, I was told he had returned to the Front in a hurry, saying he'd definitely be back soon for longer.

He didn't come back.

The generosity of that miser fate came to an end. *Si* Taher was killed a few months later without seeing his son again. Nasser was eight months old at the time, and you had just turned four.

In the summer of 1960 the nation was a volcano, dying and being born every day. More than one story crosses paths with its death and its birth, some painful and some amazing. Some came late, like my story that one day crossed paths with you. An offshoot of a story, written in advance, that changed the course of my life after a whole one had ended, by the action of what might be called fate or mad passion. It came out of the blue, surprising us both and overwhelming our principles and values. It came later on, when we were no longer expecting anything, but it turned everything in us upside down.

29

Today, now that time has burned the bridges of communication, can I resist the insane desire to combine these two stories together in writing, just as I lived them, with you and without you, desiring, loving, dreaming, hating, jealous, disappointed and with tragedies to the point of death?

You loved listening to me, turning me over and over like an old notebook full of surprises.

I have to write this book for your sake, to tell you what I didn't find the years to say. To tell you about those who, for various reasons, loved you and whom, for other reasons, you betrayed. Even to tell you about Ziyad. You wouldn't admit it, but how you loved talking about him. There is no need for evasion any more. Each of us has chosen our fate. I'll tell you about this city that was a party to our love, and that went on to become a reason why we split up and where the beautiful scene of our destruction played out.

What would you have talked about? Which man did you write about? Which one of us did you love? Which one of us would you have killed? To whom were you faithful? You who exchanged one love for another, one memory for another, one impossibility for another.

Where do I rank on the list of your loves and your victims? Perhaps I'm in first place, because I'm closest to the original version. Perhaps I'm the fake copy of *Si* Taher, one not transformed by martyrdom into a replica. Perhaps I'm a fake father figure, or a fake lover. You – like this nation – are the expert in faking and turning the tables without effort.

Henry de Montherlant said, 'If you are unable to kill someone you claim to hate, don't say you hate him. That is to prostitute the word.'

Let me admit that right now I hate you and that I write this book to kill you. Let me try out your own weapon. Perhaps you were right, novels are just pistols loaded with words. And the words are bullets. But I won't use a silencer as you do. A man who's carrying a gun at my age can't take so many precautions. I want your death to resound as much as possible. I'm killing more than one person along with you. Someone had to be daring enough to shoot them one day.

Read this book to the end. Afterwards, you might stop writing fake novels. Review our story afresh. One shock after another, one wound after another. Our meagre literature has known no greater story, nor witnessed a more beautiful ruin.

Chapter Two

THE DAY WE MET was extraordinary.

Fate was no extra. Right from the beginning it played the lead. Didn't it bring us together from different cities, from another time and another memory, for the opening of an art exhibition in Paris?

I was the artist that day; you were a visitor, curious in more ways than one. You weren't exactly a young art lover, nor was I a man who felt threatened by younger women. What brought you there that day? What made me stare at your face? Admittedly, I was drawn to faces, because only our faces reveal us and give us away. I could love or hate because of a face.

Even so, I am not fool enough to say I fell in love with you at first sight. Let's say I was in love with you before first sight. There was something familiar about you, something that attracted me to your features. I was already disposed to love them, as if I had once loved a woman who looked like you, or had always been ready to love a woman just like you.

Out of all the other faces, yours haunted me. As your white dress moved from picture to picture, my incredulity and curiosity also turned white. The gallery, filled with visitors and colours, became completely white.

Could love be born from a colour we have not necessarily loved?

White suddenly drew near and started talking in French with another young woman I hadn't noticed before. Perhaps when white has long black hair, it obscures other shades.

Looking at one of the paintings, White said, 'I prefer abstract art.'

The colourless one replied, 'Personally, I prefer to understand what I'm looking at.'

In preferring to understand all she saw, the stupidity of the colourless one didn't surprise me. Only White surprised me – how uncharacteristic to prefer the obscure!

Before that day, I had never been partial towards the colour white. It had never been my favourite colour. I disliked categorical colours. But at that moment, I inclined towards you without thinking and found myself saying to that young woman, as though continuing a sentence you had begun, 'Art is not necessarily what we understand. It is what stirs us.'

The two of you looked at me in surprise. Snatching a glance before you said anything, you spotted the empty sleeve of my jacket, the cuff tucked into the pocket in shame. It was my card, my identity papers.

You stretched out a hand in greeting and said with a warmth that took me aback, 'I'd like to congratulate you on the exhibition.'

Before your words could register, my gaze was caught by the bracelet adorning your bare wrist. With its plaited yellow gold and distinctive engraving, it had to be a piece of Constantine jewellery. One of those heavy bands that in the past were always part of a bride's trousseau and were for ever found on the wrists of women in eastern Algeria. Without completely taking my eyes off the bracelet I took your hand. My memory instantly travelled a whole lifetime back to my mother's wrist, which was never without such a bracelet.

I was seized by an ambiguous feeling. How long had it been since I'd seen a bracelet like that? I could not remember. Maybe more than thirty years. With considerable adroitness you withdrew the hand I had been gripping, perhaps unconsciously, as though I were holding on to something you had suddenly brought back.

I lifted my gaze for the first time, but our eyes only half met. You smiled at me. You were looking at my missing arm, while I contemplated the bracelet on your arm. Both of us carried their memory on the surface.

That might have been the end of our acquaintance. But you were an enigma made even more mysterious by such details. I took a gamble on discovering you. Fascinated and confused, I examined you. It was as though I already knew you whilst also just making your acquaintance.

Your beauty wasn't of the dazzling, frightening or disconcerting kind. You were an ordinary girl with an extraordinary aura and a secret hidden about her face. Perhaps it was your high forehead, the natural arch of your thick eyebrows, the mysterious smile on your lips that were painted a pale red, like a covert invitation to a kiss. Or perhaps it was your wide eyes and their changeable honey colour. I already knew these details. I knew them, but how?

You spoke in French, interrupting my thoughts. 'It makes me happy to see such a creative Algerian artist.' You went on, a touch embarrassed, 'Actually, I don't really understand much

34

about painting, and I only go to art exhibitions once in a while. But I can give an opinion about beautiful things, and your paintings are superb. We need something new like this, with a taste of modern Algeria. That's what I was saying to my cousin when you came up to us.'

With that, the young woman came forward to shake my hand and introduce herself. Perhaps she thought she would join in the conversation from which she felt excluded – I had, without realising, ignored her from the beginning. Introducing herself, she said, 'Miss Abdelmoula. Pleased to meet you.'

The name shook me.

I looked in amazement at this girl who was shaking my hand with a warmth not lacking in arrogance. I gazed at her as if only just noticing her presence, then went back to considering you. Perhaps I was seeking an explanation for my amazement in the features of both your faces. Abdelmoula. Abdelmoula. My memory went searching for an answer to this coincidence.

I knew the Abdelmoula family well. There were only two brothers: *Si* Taher, who had been martyred more than twenty years before, leaving behind a boy and a girl, and *Si* Sharif, who had married before independence and might have had several sons and daughters by now.

Which one of you was *Si* Taher's daughter? She whose name I was commanded to carry from the front, back to Tunis, and whose father I represented when registering her birth at the town hall? Which one of you was the baby I had kissed, cuddled and spoiled as her father's stand-in? Which one of you was *you*?

Despite some features in common between you, I felt that *you* were you, not her. Or so I hoped, dreaming prematurely of a certain bond between us. I was astounded by this coincidence and suddenly found the reason why I was already attracted to

35

your face. You were the image of *Si* Taher, but more alluring. You were a woman.

Could you possibly be that little girl I had last seen in Tunis in 1962, right after independence, when *Si* Sharif had called me from Constantine and asked me to sell *Si* Taher's house, which was no longer needed? He had bought it a few years previously as a refuge for his small family after the French had exiled him from Algeria in the 1950s, once he had spent a few months in prison for political incitement. So I had gone as usual to check you were all fine and to keep an eye on the arrangements for your return to Algeria. How old were you then? Could you possibly have changed this much, grown up this much in twenty years?

I gazed at you again, unwilling to admit your age – maybe my own, too, and the man I had become since those bygone days.

What brought you to this city and this gallery on this day in particular? A day I had awaited, for a reason unrelated to you. A day for which I had made a thousand calculations that had not included you. In which I had expected all surprises except you.

I was stunned, afraid to meet those eyes of yours that were following my confusion with some astonishment. I decided to turn the question around and continue my conversation with the girl who had just introduced herself. I knew that if I found out who she was, the puzzle would be solved, and I would automatically know who you were. One of you had a name that I had known for twenty-five years. I just needed to learn which one. I asked her, 'Are you related to *Si* Sharif Abdelmoula?'

As if realising I was interested in her, she answered gaily, 'He's my father. He couldn't come today because a delegation just arrived from Algeria yesterday. He's told us so much about you. We were so curious to meet you that we decided to come to the opening in his place.'

Despite the spontaneity of what she said, it provided two answers. First, she wasn't you. Second, it explained why *Si* Sharif hadn't come. I had noted his absence and wondered whether it was for personal or political reasons. Or whether he was avoiding being seen with me.

I knew our paths had diverged years ago when he had entered the corridors of politics. His only goal was to reach the leading ranks. Even so, I couldn't ignore our being in the same city. He had been part of my childhood and youth, part of my memory. Because of this, and for purely sentimental reasons, he was the only Algerian personality I had invited.

I hadn't seen him for a few years, but news of him had always reached me since his appointment, two years previously, as an attaché at the Algerian embassy. Like all postings abroad, this required serious connections and a power base. *Si* Sharif could forge a path to such posts – and more important ones – by means of his past alone and by his name, which *Si* Taher had immortalised with his own martyrdom. Yet it seemed that the past alone was not enough to guarantee the present. To make progress, he had to adjust constantly to the way the wind was blowing.

All of this occurred to me as I tried to absorb the emotional shocks that had rocked me in the last few moments. It had started with my wanting to say hello to a pretty girl who was visiting my exhibition, nothing more. Then, suddenly, I was saying hello to my memory.

I returned to my initial surprise at you: to all the details that caught my eye and the particular picture that you were standing in front of for so long. It was more than coincidence, more than fate, more than destiny.

Was it really you? In a gallery looking at my paintings. Studying some and pausing before others, turning to the catalogue in your hand to find out the names of the pictures that most caught your attention.

Might it be you lighting up each painting that you passed? The spotlights directed at the paintings seemed to point at you, as though you were the genuine work of art.

Yes, you. You paused before a small painting that no one else had stopped at. You scrutinised it, moved closer and scanned the list for its name. At that instant a dark shiver ran through me, the curiosity of the mad artist piqued.

Who were you, standing in front of my favourite painting? Confused, I watched you studying it as you talked to your friend out of earshot. What made you stop before it? It wasn't the most beautiful painting in the show. It was just my first painting, my first effort. Yet, despite its simplicity, I had insisted this time that it be included in the exhibition – my most important to date – because I considered it my little miracle. I had painted it twenty-five years ago, less than a month after my left arm had been amputated.

It wasn't an attempt at creativity or designed to go down in history. I was just trying to live, to escape despair. I had painted it like an art student taking an exam in which the assignment is to paint the scene closest to who you are. That was what the Yugoslavian doctor had told me to do. He had come to Tunis with other doctors from the socialist states to treat wounded Algerians and had taken charge of amputating my arm. Afterwards, he had kept an eye on how I was doing, physically and mentally.

He had noted my continuing depression and, each time I saw him, he had asked if I had any new interests. I wasn't ill enough to stay in hospital, but neither was I whole enough to begin my new life. I was living in Tunis, a local and a foreigner at the same time, both at liberty and confined, happy and miserable. A man rejected equally by death and by life. A tangled skein of wool. How could the doctor find the end of the yarn and unravel all my complexes?

On one occasion he asked me, as he was inquiring about my education, whether I liked writing or painting. I seized hold of his question as if grabbing at a straw that might save me from drowning. I realised immediately the prescription he had in mind for me.

He said, 'I've carried out the operation that you've had dozens of times on those who've lost limbs in war. The operation is the same each time, but its psychological impact differs from person to person, depending on their age, job, social status and, especially, on their level of culture. Only an intellectual reconsiders himself every day. He reconsiders his relationship with things and with the world whenever anything in his life changes.

'I've come to realise this over the course of my experience. Yours isn't the first case I've come across, and I think that losing your arm has upset your relationship with what's around you. You have to build a new relationship with the world through writing or painting.

'You must choose which you prefer and then sit and write down everything that's on your mind, without inhibition. The kind of writing isn't important, nor its literary quality. What matters is simply writing as a means to get it all out and rebuild yourself internally.

'If you prefer painting, then paint. Painting can also reconcile you to things and to a world you see differently. You've changed now that you see and feel it with only one hand.'

My reflex answer would have been that I loved writing. It was certainly closest to me, seeing as I had done nothing all my life except read, which naturally leads to writing. I could have replied that my teachers had always predicted a glowing literary future for me – in French. Maybe that was why I answered without thinking or, as I discovered later, with the response that was already deep inside me, 'I prefer painting.'

My terse answer did not convince him, and he asked me if I'd painted before. 'No,' I replied.

'So, start by painting the thing that is closest to you. Paint the thing you love most.'

With the wryness of a doctor tactfully admitting they can do no more, his parting words were, 'Paint, then perhaps you won't need me again!'

I hurried back to my room, wanting to be alone between its white walls that were an extension of the whiteness of the Al-Habib Thamir hospital, which at the time was the place I knew best in Tunis. Unusually for me, I started staring at the walls and thought of all the paintings I could hang on them: portraits of those I loved, all the alleyways I loved, everything I had left behind.

My sleep was troubled that night. Perhaps I didn't sleep at all. The doctor's voice, in his broken French, kept waking me up as he said, 'Paint!' I saw him in his white coat, as he shook my hand in farewell and said, 'Paint!' A mysterious shudder passed through me and in my half-sleep I remembered the first revelation of the Qur'an, when the angel Gabriel, peace be upon him, came down to Muhammad for the first time and said, 'Recite!' The prophet, trembling in dread, asked, 'What should I recite?' Gabriel responded, 'Recite in the name of your Lord the Creator,' and went on to complete the first *sura*. When this was over, the prophet went to his wife, his body trembling in terror at what he had heard. As soon as he saw her he shouted, 'Wrap me up, wrap me up!'

That night I shivered with feverish chills, due perhaps to nerves and my anxiety after the meeting with the doctor, which I knew would be the last. There was also the thin blanket – which was all I had to cover me in the depths of the freezing winter, and which my mean landlord would not supplement.

I could have screamed when I remembered my childhood bed and the woollen blanket I always had against the Constantine cold. I almost screamed in my night of exile, 'Wrap me up, Constantine, wrap me up.' But I said nothing. Not to Constantine, not to the mean-minded landlord. I kept my fever and chills to myself. It was hard for a man just back from the Front to admit, even to himself, that he was cold.

I waited till early morning to buy, with the little money I had left, the supplies needed to paint two or three pictures. Crazily, I stood and painted Constantine's suspension bridge.

Was that bridge really the thing I loved most, for me to stand there and paint it of my own accord, as though about to cross it as usual? Perhaps it was just the easiest thing to paint. I don't know. I do know that I painted it again and again afterwards, as if every time remained the first time and it was the thing I loved most.

Twenty-five years: that was the age of the painting I had called, without much thought, *Nostalgia*. A painting by a twenty-seven-year-old in all his loneliness, grief and desolation.

There I was, lonely again, with my other grief and desolation. Just an extra quarter of a century full of personal disappointments and defeats and the odd triumph. By then I was one of Algeria's major artists, perhaps the biggest of all – so said the Western critics whose testimonials I included in large type on the invitation to the opening.

There I was, a minor prophet who was struck with inspiration one autumn in a mean room on Bab Sweiqa Street in Tunis. There I was, a typical prophet in exile. And why not, when a prophet is never honoured in his homeland? There I was, an artistic phenomenon. And why not, when the disabled can become a phenomenon, an artistic giant? As I was.

Where was that doctor who recommended that I paint and whose prophecy that I would no longer need him came true? He was the only person missing from the vast space where no Arab before me had ever held an exhibition. Where was Dr Kapucki to see what I'd done with my one hand? (I never asked him what he did with the other!)

There was *Nostalgia*, my first painting. Beside the inscription, 'Tunis '57', at the bottom of the picture, was my first signature. Just as I signed beneath your name and date of birth when I registered you at the town hall in that autumn of 1957.

Between the painting and you, which one was my child? Which my beloved? Questions that didn't occur to me that day when I saw you standing before the painting for the first time. A painting the same age as you. Officially, you were a few days older and it was actually a few months younger. A painting that marked my beginning twice: once, when I picked up a brush and first started to paint; the other, the day you stood before it and I began my adventure with fate.

In a diary full of insignificant dates and addresses, I circled that date in April 1981 as though I wished to single it out. There had been nothing throughout the previous years worthy of mention. My days, like the pages of my diary, were all rough drafts. Usually I would write something simply so as not to leave the page blank. White sheets of paper always frightened me.

Eight diaries for eight years, with nothing remarkable in them.

Together they formed a single page of exile whose years, by a process of false accounting, I tried to condense into eight diaries. That was all. They were still stacked in my cupboard, one on top of the other. They hadn't been kept according to any calendar, but counted off the years of my voluntary emigration.

I ringed that date as if locking you within, as if fixing you and your memory in my spotlight for ever. It was in anticipation that this date would be a turning point in memory, my rebirth at your hands. At the time I was well aware that being reborn through you, like reaching you, would be no easy matter. The fact that your phone number and address weren't on that page was proof enough. Ultimately, only the date was recorded. Was it reasonable to ask for your phone number at our first meeting or, rather, our first chance encounter? What possible justification or pretext did I have for that? Any reason would have seemed contrived – a man asking a pretty girl for her phone number.

I felt a need to sit with you, to talk to you, to listen to you. There was a chance I would encounter that other version of my memory. But how to convince you of that? How to explain in a few minutes that I – a man you were meeting for the first time – knew a great deal about you? You were even talking to me in a formal French, as if to a stranger. I had no choice but to respond in the same formal way.

The words got caught on my tongue that day, as though I were speaking to you in an unfamiliar language, a language that didn't know us. How could I, after more than twenty years, have shaken your hand and asked in neutral French, '*Mais comment allez-vous, mademoiselle?*' You responded with the same coolness, '*Bien, je vous remercie.*'

My memory was on the verge of tears; this was the memory that knew you as a crawling baby girl. My one arm was almost shaking in an effort to resist the unruly desire to embrace you and ask in the Constantine accent that I so missed, '*Washik*? How are you?'

Ah, how are you, my little one who grew up out of sight? How are you, strange visitor who no longer knows me? Baby girl, wearing my memory and my mother's bracelet on her wrist.

I gathered in you all those I loved. I contemplated you: your smile and the colour of your eyes brought back the features of *Si* Taher. How beautiful that the martyrs lived again in your face. How beautiful that my mother lived again in the bracelet around your wrist. Your appearance brought the homeland back to life. How beautiful that you should be *you*!

'When people encounter something extremely beautiful, they want to cry,' Malek Haddad wrote.

Encountering you was the most beautiful thing that had happened to me in a lifetime.

How could I explain all of this to you in one go as we stood there, surrounded by eyes and ears? How could I explain to you that I longed for you even without knowing? That I had been waiting for you without believing it? That it was inevitable we would meet?

To sum up that first meeting: fifteen minutes or thereabouts of talking, most of which I dominated, a stupid mistake that I regretted afterwards. I was actually trying to keep you there with words, neglecting to give you more of a chance to speak.

I was happy to discover your passion for art. You were ready to discuss each painting at length. With you, everything was up for debate. For my part, at that moment I only wanted to talk about you. Your presence alone made me want to talk.

Because there was no time then to tell you the chapters of my story that overlapped with your story, I made do with a word or two about my old relationship with your father and your early childhood, and about a painting you said you liked and which I told you was your twin.

I chose concise, clever phrases. I left pauses between them so you would feel the weight of the silences. I didn't want to play my only card with you too hastily in a single day.

I wanted to arouse your curiosity to know more and to ensure you would come back. When you asked me, 'Will you be here for the duration of the show?' I realised I had passed the first test with you and that you were thinking of meeting me again. But I said in a normal voice, betraying no sign of the turmoil inside, 'I'll be here most afternoons.' Then I added, thinking that my answer might not encourage you to visit in my absence, 'But most likely, I'll be here every day. I have plenty of meetings with journalists and friends.'

There was an element of truth to this. But I didn't actually have to be at the exhibition all the time. I was just trying not to make you change your mind for some reason.

Suddenly you spoke to me as if we were old friends. 'I'll come and see the show again next Monday. I don't have classes that day. I only came today out of curiosity and I'd be pleased to talk some more.'

Your cousin intervened, as if apologising, and perhaps disappointed not to be part of that meeting. 'That's a shame. It's my busiest day. I won't be able to come with you, but I'll come back another day.' Then she turned to me with a question. 'When does the exhibition end?'

'On the twenty-fifth of April, in ten days' time,' I replied.

'Great,' she exclaimed. 'I'll have a chance to come back.'

I sighed deeply. What mattered to me was seeing you on your own. After that, everything would be easier. I steeled myself with a last look at you as you shook my hand before leaving. There was an invitation to something in your eyes. They held a vague promise of a story and delicious submersion, and perhaps a look of apology in advance for all the catastrophes that would befall me as a result.

At that moment, when the whiteness had turned its back, gathered up its shawl of black hair and gradually moved away to mix with other colours, I was aware that whether or not I saw you again, I loved you. It was settled.

You left the space as you had arrived, the glittering passing of a dazzling radiance, pulling rainbows and unfulfilled dreams in its wake.

What had I found out about you? Afterwards I went over the two or three things a number of times. This was to convince myself that you weren't just some shooting star on a summer's night. One that flares and vanishes before the astronomers can turn their telescopes on it, and which the old astronomical dictionaries term 'escaping stars'.

No, you weren't going to escape me so easily and disappear into the boulevards and side streets of Paris. At least I knew you were studying for a degree at the Ecole Supérieure, and you were in your final year. You'd been in Paris for four years and had been living with your uncle since his posting to Paris two years before. Risible details, but still enough to find you again.

The time between Friday and Monday seemed interminable. The moment you left the space, I started a countdown.

I counted the number of days in between. At times I reckoned it was four, then I'd try again and exclude Friday, which was almost over, and Monday when I would see you, and the time would seem more bearable. Just two days, Saturday and Sunday.

46

Then I'd count the nights. I reckoned it was three whole nights – Friday, Saturday and Sunday. Anticipating how long they would be, I wondered how to spend them. A line of poetry came to mind that I had never found credible before: 'I count the nights, night after night/having lived an age of nights uncounted.'

Does love always begin like this? We start to exchange our own standards for others mutually agreed upon. We enter a phase of life that has no relation to time.

That day I was happy to see Catherine come into the exhibition space. As I expected, she was late and elegantly turned out, fluttering like a butterfly inside a soft yellow dress. She kissed me on the cheek and said, 'Sorry I'm late. It's always busy at rush hour.'

Catherine lived in the southern suburbs, and at the end of the week the roads leading to the city centre would get busier as Parisians headed to the countryside for the weekend. But this wasn't the only reason she was late. I knew she disliked public gatherings or, I inferred, disliked being seen with me in public. Perhaps she was embarrassed at the thought that someone she knew would see her with a one-armed Arab ten years her senior.

She loved to see me, but always at my house or hers, discreetly, out of view. Only then did she seem happy and relaxed. Simply going out to eat at the local restaurant was enough to make her seem embarrassed and strained, her only concern being for us to go home. When I knew she was coming I would buy enough food to last a day or two. I no longer argued with her or made any suggestions. It was much easier for me that way. Why bother arguing?

Holding on to my arm and looking at the paintings, all of which she knew, Catherine said in a slightly louder voice than usual, 'Bravo, Khaled. Congratulations. It's great, darling.'

I was a little taken aback. The woman was speaking as if she wanted others to know she was my friend or girlfriend or the like. What had suddenly caused her behaviour to change? Was it the sight of the crowd of artists and journalists who had come to the opening? Or had she discovered that she had been sleeping with a genius for two years without realising, and that my missing arm, which annoyed her in other circumstances, had now taken on a singular artistic dimension unconnected to the norms of aesthetics?

I realised that for the twenty-five years I had lived with one arm, it was only at exhibitions that I ever forgot my handicap. For the brief moments that people's eyes were on my paintings, they forgot to look at my arm. Perhaps this was also the case in the first years of independence, when fighters were venerated and the war-wounded were regarded as sacred. They evoked respect more than pity. There was no need to explain or tell their story. They carried their memory in the flesh.

A quarter of a century later, I was ashamed of the empty sleeve of my suit. So I would tuck it into my jacket pocket, as though hiding my own memory and apologising for my past to all those who had no past. The missing hand unsettled them. Disconcerted. Made them lose their appetite.

The time well after the war – the time for sharp suits, luxury cars and stuffed bellies – wasn't for me. So I was often ashamed of my arm as it kept me company in the Métro, at a restaurant or café, on a plane or at a party. I felt every time that people were waiting for me to tell them my story. All eyes were agog with the one question that was too shameful to articulate: 'How did it happen?'

Sometimes I was saddened when I took the Métro and clung on to the strap with one hand. Above some of the seats was a sign: 'Reserved for the war-wounded and pregnant women.' But those seats were not for me. Some vestige of pride and honour made me prefer to stay standing, holding on with one hand. They were seats reserved for other fighters, whose war wasn't my war, and whose wounds perhaps I inflicted. My wounds weren't recognised there.

I was confronted with a strange contradiction: I lived in a country that respected my talents but rejected my wounds, and belonged to a nation that respected my wounds but rejected me. Which one to choose when I was the person and the wound at the same time? When I was the disabled memory of which this disabled body was only a façade?

Questions I'd never asked myself before. I would evade them by working, by continuous creation. Something inside me never slept. Something that kept painting as if spurring me on to reach this space where I would exist for a few days as an ordinary man with two arms or, to put it better, as an extraordinary man. A man who with one hand mocked the world and recast the features of things. That's who I was in that gallery. My madness hung on display on the walls. Eyes examined it and mouths freely interpreted.

I could only smile when the contradictory comments reached my ears. I recalled a witticism of Edmond de Goncourt: 'A painting in a museum hears more ridiculous opinions than anything else in the world!'

Catherine's voice was low, as though addressing only me this time. 'Wonderful,' she said. 'I'm seeing these paintings as though I didn't know them. They seem different here.'

Continuing an earlier line of thought, I almost replied, 'Paintings also have moods and feelings. They're just like people. They change as soon as you put them in a gallery under lights!' But I merely said, 'Pictures are feminine in that way. They like the bright lights and dress up for them. They like us to spoil them and dust them down, sweep them off the ground and remove their covering. They like us to display them in large rooms for all to see, even if people don't like them. They hate to be ignored, that's all.'

She thought for a moment, then said, 'What you're saying is right. Where do you get these ideas? You know, I love listening to you. I don't understand why we never have time to talk when we see each other.' Before I could give her a convincing answer, she added, laughing and with a familiar intention, 'When will you finally treat *me* like a painting?'

Laughing at her quick wit and boundless appetite, I said, 'This evening, if you'd like!'

Catherine took my house keys from me and fluttered towards the door like a butterfly inside her yellow dress. 'I'm a little tired. I'll go on ahead,' she said, as if she suddenly felt jealous of all those paintings hung with care on the walls which some people were still looking at. Was she really so tired? Had she suddenly become possessive? Was she jealous of me, or had she been hungry when she arrived? As usual, I didn't try to understand her too deeply.

I just wanted her help to forget. I was happy to shorten a day or two's waiting with her. Waiting for you! I needed a night of love after a month of loneliness running around to prepare for the exhibition.

I caught up with Catherine an hour later. I was tired for many reasons. One of them was my incredible meeting with you and the emotional turmoil I had been through that day. She said as she opened the door, 'You didn't wait very long . . .'

I said playfully, 'I had an idea for a painting, so I came home quickly. Inspiration doesn't wait long, as you know.'

We laughed.

There was a certain physical complicity between us that made us happy together, a secret unrestrained happiness legitimised by madness.

She sat on the sofa opposite me watching the news and eating a sandwich she had brought with her. I felt that she was a woman perpetually on the verge of becoming my true love, and this time – once again – she wouldn't. A woman who survives on sandwiches is a woman with too little emotion and too much ego, unable to give a man the security he needs. That night I pretended not to be hungry. In truth, I was unable to adapt to the sandwich age. Nevertheless, I tried not to dwell on these details that irritated the Bedouin in me from the outset.

Since getting to know Catherine, I'd got used to not looking too hard for areas of difference between us and I respected her way of life. I didn't try to make her into a clone of me. Maybe I actually loved her because she was so completely different. There's nothing more beautiful than meeting your opposite. Only that can make you discover yourself. I confess I was indebted to Catherine for many of my discoveries. In the end, the only things that got me together with this woman were mutual desire and a shared passion for art. That was enough for us to be happy together.

Over time, we became used to not annoying each other with questions or musings. In the beginning I found it hard to adjust to this type of emotion that had no place for jealousy or possessiveness. Then I found there were many good things about it. Most importantly, freedom and no commitments to anybody.

We would meet once a week, or a few weeks might pass without us seeing each other. But we always met with shared longings and desire.

Catherine would say, 'We mustn't kill our relationship through habit.' So I made an effort not to get used to her. Just to be happy when she came by, and to forget she'd been there once she'd left.

This time I wanted to get her to spend the whole weekend with me, and was happy that she was eager to accept. In fact, I was afraid to be alone with the clock on the wall, waiting for Monday. Although Catherine stayed with me till Sunday evening, it seemed a long time, perhaps longer because she was there. All of a sudden I started hurrying her to leave, as if then I'd be alone with you.

I was only thinking about one question. What would I say to you when we were alone together on Monday? Where would I begin the conversation? How would I tell you that incredible story of ours? How would I seduce you to return, to hear the rest of it?

On Monday morning, for our potential date, I put on my best suit, picked a matching tie, dabbed on my favourite cologne and headed for the gallery at around ten o'clock. I had plenty of time to drink a morning coffee in a café nearby. You wouldn't come any earlier – the gallery didn't even open until ten.

I was the first person to enter the gallery that morning. There was a vague hint of depression in the air. The spots weren't directed at the paintings, and the ceiling lamps were unlit. I glanced rapidly at the walls. My paintings were waking up like a woman – unadorned, without make-up or restoration in the naked truth of morning – a woman yawning on the walls after a boisterous night.

I went over to the small painting *Nostalgia* and inspected it closely, as if inspecting you. 'Good morning, Constantine. How are you, suspension bridge? You, my sadness, suspended for a quarter-century.' The picture responded with its usual silence, but with a slight wink on this occasion. I smiled conspiratorially. We understood each other, me and the painting – kinfolk understand at a wink, as they say. It was a kindred painting, proud and authentic like its painter, understanding at half a wink.

I then distracted myself with some tasks put off from the day before – another way to gain time and be free for you later. During this, an inner voice reminded me that you were coming, and stopped me concentrating. She will come, she will come, repeated the voice for an hour or two, or more. Morning and afternoon went by, but you didn't come.

I tried to occupy myself with meetings and everyday things. I tried to forget that I was there waiting for you. I met one journalist and spoke to another without taking my eyes off the door. I was looking out for you at every step. The more time passed, the more desperate I grew. Suddenly the door opened and in came *Si* Sharif.

Hiding my surprise, I stood up to greet him. I remembered a French song that starts, 'I wanted to see your sister, but saw your mother as usual.' He embraced me and said warmly, 'Hello my good man. Long live the one who sees you!' I admit that despite my disappointment, I had never felt so happy saying hello to him.

Before I had asked him his news, he presented the mutual friend who was with him. 'See who I've brought with me?'

This was an additional surprise. 'Hello *Si* Mustafa,' I exclaimed. 'How are you? It's good to see you.'

Si Mustafa embraced me in turn and said with affection, 'How are you, sir? If we didn't come to you, we'd never see you or what?' Out of politeness, I asked him in turn for his news. I

53

took the fact of *Si* Sharif's accompanying him and excessive praise for him as proof of the rumours that he was up for some ministerial post.

Si Sharif scolded me with an affection I found genuine. 'My brother, is it conceivable that we both live in this city and you don't even once think of visiting me? Two years I've been here, and you know my address.'

Half-serious and half in jest, *Si* Mustafa intervened, 'Do you think he's boycotting us? How else to explain his absence?'

I answered honestly, 'Never! It's just that it's not easy for someone living in exile to pack up their things and come back. As they say, exile is a bad habit that people pick up. I've acquired several bad habits here.' We laughed, and the conversation moved politely on to other subjects.

As they toured the exhibition, it was only when they stopped in front of one of the paintings that I realised *Si* Mustafa had come because he wanted to acquire a picture or two. He said, 'I want to keep something of yours as a memento. Don't you remember that you started to paint when we were together in Tunis? I can still remember your first paintings. I was the first person you showed your work to in those days. Have you forgotten?'

No, I hadn't forgotten. But how I wished right then that I could have. I felt quite embarrassed as he tried to take me back to that period.

Si Mustafa was a mutual friend of *Si* Sharif's and mine from liberation days. He was part of the group under *Si* Taher's command, and one of the wounded transferred with me to Tunis for treatment. He spent three months in hospital there. Then he returned to the Front, where he remained in the liberation army until independence, rising to the rank of major.

Once upon a time he had honour and believed in the struggle. I had a lot of respect and affection for him. Gradually, his balance with me dwindled, while his other balances ballooned by various means and in various currencies. He was just like those before him who had made it to lucrative positions, which they shuffled among themselves in a studied division of the spoils.

Yet he in particular interested and saddened me. He had been a comrade in arms for two whole years. Lots of minor incidents had linked us in the past, and memory, despite everything, couldn't ignore them. Perhaps the most moving was when I was leaving the hospital in Tunis. A nurse gave me his clothes, the blood newly dried on them. In the pocket of his jacket I came across his identity card, which was barely readable through the bloodstains. I kept it to give back to him later. But he returned to the Front without knowing I had it, or perhaps without even asking after it. After all, where he was going there was no need for an identity card.

In 1973 I came across that card by chance among my old papers. I was packing up my things at the time in preparation to leave Algeria for Paris. I wavered between keeping it and giving it back to him, for I knew that this identity was not really his any more. I wanted to confront him with memory, but without saying anything. Being on the verge of exile, perhaps I wanted to end my relationship with the ID card that since 1957 had accompanied me from country to country. By placing him and his things outside memory, it was as though I was ending my relationship with the homeland.

Si Mustafa got a shock when, after sixteen years, I took the ID card out of my pocket and handed it to him. Was he more confused that moment or was I? As I was handing it over, I suddenly felt I was giving him something lodged in my chest: a part of me, my other arm perhaps, or anything that had been mine, that had been me. I found consolation in his delight. He embraced me with the same old fervour, a reward for memory and for the mistaken belief that his other personality might be restored.

Here was *Si* Mustafa, years later, contemplating a painting of mine as I contemplated him. The other man inside him had died. How had I once put my faith in him? At that moment, the only thing he was interested in was owning one of my pictures. He might have been willing to pay any price. He was renowned for not counting the cost in such cases. He was like other politicians and nouveaux-riche Algerians who had been bitten by the art-collecting bug for reasons that mostly had nothing to do with art, but rather with their being acquisition-minded and obsessed with joining the elite.

Perhaps he was more generous with me for the very reasons that made me reject him further. He had decided to exchange that tattered identity card for an aquarelle painting he could show off. Can blood be equated to watercolour, even after a quarter of a century?

Later, I was happy to have gotten rid of him and *Si* Sharif without offending them and without abandoning a principle that has caused me to go hungry. I simply cannot stomach tainted bread. Some people are just born with a sensitivity to filth. Actually, I was in a hurry and wanted to be over and done with them, fearful that you might arrive while they were still there.

Caught between the feelings evoked by *Si* Mustafa after so many years and the exhausting obsession with your visit, I was nervous and unsettled. But you didn't come, neither then nor later.

Where did all that subsequent depression come from? Downcast, my two legs led me heavily home after having carried me there on wings of overwhelming desire.

What if I was never to see you again? If the exhibition closed and you didn't come back? What if your talk about coming back had just been politeness, which I had taken seriously? How then would I chase your fleeting shooting star?

Only the card that *Si* Sharif gave me when saying goodbye left room for hope. At last I knew the secret numbers to reach you. I fell asleep planning how to justify a telephone call that might join me with you. But when love comes, it does not seek justification or make a date. As soon as I entered the gallery the next day and sat down to read the newspaper, I saw you come in. You were coming towards me and time stood still in wonder. Love, which had often ignored me before that day, had finally decided to give me its maddest story.

Chapter Three

S O WE MET.

You said, 'Hi. I'm sorry. I'm a day late for our date.'

'Don't be sorry. You came a whole lifetime too late.'

You said, 'How much do I owe to be excused?'

'The worth of that lifetime!'

A jasmine sat down opposite me.

Oh, jasmine flower that has quickly opened, less perfume, my beloved, less perfume. I didn't know that memory also has a perfume. The perfume of the homeland.

Confused and embarrassed, the homeland sat down and said, 'Do you have any water, please?'

Constantine welled up in me.

Drink from my memory, my lady. All this nostalgia is for you. Leave me a seat here opposite you.

I sipped you at leisure, the way Constantine's coffee is sipped. A cup of coffee and a bottle of Coke in front of us, we sat. We might not have thirsted for the same thing, but we had the same desire to talk.

In apology you said, 'I didn't come yesterday because I heard my uncle on the phone arranging to visit you with someone. I preferred to put off my visit till today so as not to see them.'

Looking at you with the happiness of someone who finally sees his shooting star, I replied, 'I was afraid you wouldn't come at all.' Then I added, 'But now I'm happy I waited another day for you. The things we want always come late!' Perhaps I said more than I should have at the time.

There was a brief, uneasy silence at this first confession. Then, as if to break the silence or arouse my curiosity, you said, 'Guess what? I know lots about you.'

Happy and surprised I said, 'What do you know, for example?'

Like a teacher trying to confuse a pupil, you answered, 'Lots of things that you may have forgotten yourself.'

I said, with a hint of sadness, 'I don't believe I've forgotten anything. Actually, my problem is I never forget!'

You answered with an innocent admission. 'Well, my problem is I do forget. I forget everything. Imagine, yesterday, for example, I forgot my Métro ticket in my other handbag. And a week ago I left my keys at home and had to wait outside for two hours till someone came to let me in. What a disaster.' At the time I wasn't aware of what all this would mean for me.

I said sarcastically, 'Thanks for remembering this appointment.'

With the same sarcasm you replied, 'It wasn't an appointment. Just a possible appointment. You should know I hate certainty. I hate to fix anything or stick to it. The most beautiful things are born as possibilities and maybe stay like that.'

'Why did you come then?' I asked.

You looked at me and your eyes lingered over my face as if in search of the answer to an unexpected question. With eyes laden with promises and seduction you said, 'Because you might possibly be my certainty!'

I laughed at this way of putting it, loaded with shameless feminine contradiction – at the time I didn't know this was your signature. Your eyes had charged me with masculine pride and arrogance, and I said, 'Well, I hate possibilities, so I'm determined to be your certainty.'

With a woman's insistence on having the last word, you said, 'It's hypothetical, a certainty like that!' We laughed.

I was ecstatic, as if I hadn't laughed for years. I had anticipated different beginnings for us and rehearsed many lines and ideas to try on you at this first meeting. But I confess I hadn't expected it to be like this. Everything I had prepared vanished when you arrived. I became tongue-tied at your language and I was at a loss as to how you'd acquired it.

There was something light-hearted and lyrical about you. A spontaneity and simplicity verging on the childish that didn't dispel the constant presence of a woman. You possessed an extraordinary ability, after one meeting, to level our ages. It seemed I'd caught your youth and vitality.

I was still under the influence of your previous statements when your words took me by surprise. 'Really, I wanted to study your paintings that day, not share them with crowds of people. When I like something, I prefer to be alone with it!' That was the most beautiful proof of appreciation for an artist, the most beautiful thing you could have said to me that day. Before I could get lost in my joy or say thank you, you added, 'Apart from that, I've wanted to get to know you for ages. My grandmother sometimes talked about you when she reminisced about my father. It seems she loved you a lot.'

I asked you eagerly, 'How is *Amma* Zahra? I haven't seen her for years.'

With a hint of sadness you said, 'She died four years ago.

Afterwards my mother moved to live with my brother Nasser in the capital. I came to Paris to study. Her death changed our lives to some extent. She was the one who actually raised us.'

I tried to forget that news. Her death was another thorn plunged into my heart that day. She had something of my own mother, her secret perfume, her way of tying her silk headscarf to the side, her concealing a silver locket in her full bosom. She had that reflexive warmth that our mothers exude, those words that in one sentence give you enough tenderness for a lifetime. But this was no time for sadness. You were with me at last. This was time for joy. I said to you, 'God rest her soul. I loved her a lot too.'

Perhaps at that moment you wanted to staunch the wave of sadness that had taken me by surprise, fearful that it would sweep us away towards memories we weren't yet ready to leaf through. Or did you just want to keep to your plan when you suddenly stood up and said, 'Can I take a look around the pictures?'

I stood up to accompany you.

I explained some of them and told you what occasions had made me paint them. Then you switched your gaze from the paintings to me and said, 'You know, I really like your style of painting. I'm not saying this to be nice, but I think if I were an artist, I'd paint like you. I feel that we both share the same sensibility. I rarely feel that about Algerian work.'

What confused me most at that moment? Your eyes, which had suddenly changed colour under the lights and were looking at my features as if contemplating another one of my paintings? Or what you had just said, which I felt was an emotional confession, not an aesthetic impression? At least that's what I hoped or imagined. My attention paused at the words 'we both'. In

French they take on a singular emotional tone. It's even the title of a soppy magazine for the remaining romantics in France: *Nous Deux*.

I hid my confusion with a naive question. 'Do you paint?'

'No, I write.'

'What do you write?'

'I write stories and novels!'

'Stories and novels!' I repeated, as if I didn't believe what I was hearing.

As if you sensed an insult in the hint of disbelief or doubt in my voice, you said, 'My first novel was published two years ago.'

Moving from one shock to another, I asked you, 'What language do you write in?'

'Arabic.'

'In Arabic?!'

My scepticism annoyed you. Perhaps you had misunderstood when you said, 'I could have written in French, but Arabic is the language of my heart. I can write in nothing else. We write in the language we feel with.'

'But you only speak French.'

'That's habit.' You resumed looking at the pictures before adding, 'What matters is the language we speak to ourselves, not the one we use with others!'

I looked at you in shock, trying to put my thoughts in order. Could all these coincidences meet together in one giant coincidence? Could all my fixed ideas and my first nationalist dreams come together in one woman? A woman who was you, the daughter of none other than *Si* Taher? A more astonishing meeting in my whole life was unimaginable. It was more than coincidence that our paths should cross after a quarter of a century. It was wonderful destiny.

Your voice brought me back to reality: you were standing in front of a painting.

'You don't paint many portraits, do you?'

Before giving an answer, I said, 'Listen! We're only going to speak Arabic. I'll change your habits as of today.'

In Arabic you asked me, 'Will you be able to?'

'I can,' I replied, 'because I'll also change my habits with you.'

You answered with the secret happiness of a woman who, I discovered later, loved orders. 'I'll obey you because I love that language, and I love your insistence. Just remind me if I should forget.'

'I won't remind you, because you won't forget,' I said.

I had made a most beautiful blunder. I had turned the language that I was romantically involved with into another player in our complex story.

I asked you in Arabic, 'What were you just saying?'

'I was surprised that there's only this one portrait of a woman in your exhibition. Don't you do portraits?'

'There was a time when I painted portraits, then I moved on to other subjects. In painting, the older and more experienced you are, the more confining it is. You have to find other means of expression.

'In fact, I don't paint the faces I really love. I only paint something that strikes me about them, a look, the wave of the hair, the hem of a woman's dress or a piece of jewellery. Details that stick in the mind after they've gone. Things you hint at without revealing entirely. A painter isn't a photographer chasing reality. His camera is inside him, hidden in a place he doesn't know himself. He doesn't paint with the eye, but with memory, imagination . . . and other things.'

You were staring at a woman whose blonde hair dominated

her portrait. There was no room left for another colour except the red of her less-than-innocent lips. 'This woman,' you said, 'why did you paint her so realistically?'

I laughed. 'This is a woman who can only be painted with realism.'

'Why did you call her portrait *Apology*?'

'Because I painted it as an apology to the subject.'

You suddenly spoke in French, as if anger or hidden jealousy had revoked our earlier agreement. 'I hope the apology convinced her. It's a beautiful painting.' With a hint of feminine curiosity you then added, 'It all depends on the sin you committed against her!'

I had no desire to tell you the story of that painting on our first date. I was afraid it would have a negative effect on our relationship or your view of me. So I tried to evade your remark, which might have tempted me to say more, and pretended to ignore you as you remained stubbornly standing in front of the painting. Can one resist the curiosity of a woman determined to find something out?

I gave you an answer. 'That painting has quite a funny story behind it. It reveals aspects of my psychological problems and traces of the old me. Perhaps that's why it's here.'

For the first time, I told the story of that painting. I had friends who taught at the College of Fine Arts, and they would invite me and other painters to life classes to paint and meet the students and amateur painters. The subject one day was a female nude. All of the students were absorbed in painting this body from their different perspectives, while I was stunned at their ability to paint a woman's body with a purely aesthetic gaze and without sex rearing its head. It was as if they were painting a landscape or a still life of a vase or statue.

Evidently I was the only person in the class feeling uncomfortable. It was the first time I had ever seen a naked woman in daylight. She shifted her pose and revealed her body without inhibition or shame before dozens of pairs of eyes. Perhaps to hide my embarrassment, I started painting too. But my brush carried vestiges of the complexes of a man of my generation and baulked at painting that body – out of shame or pride, I don't know. It started painting something else, which turned out to be the face of that young woman as it appeared from my angle. When the session finished, and the girl, who was just a student, had put her clothes on, she walked around to see how everyone had depicted her. She got a surprise when she saw my painting, since I had only painted her face. In a tone of mild reproof, as if she deemed this a slight on her feminine charms, she said, 'Is that all the inspiration I gave you?'

To be polite, I said, 'No! You inspired a lot of wonder, but I'm from a society where the soul still lives in the Dark Ages. You're the first woman I've seen naked in daylight, even though I'm a professional artist. Please forgive me. My brushes are like me. They also hate to share a naked woman with others, even in life classes!'

You were listening bewildered, as if by surprise you had discovered another man in me whom your grandmother hadn't told you about. There was suddenly a strange new look in your eyes: wilful seduction. Perhaps it came from a woman's jealousy at an unknown rival who had once caught the attention of a man who until that moment hadn't meant anything to her.

I took pleasure in the unintended situation. I was happy that jealousy should suddenly make you go silent, cause your cheeks to flush slightly and make your eyes widen in suppressed anger.

I kept the rest of the story to myself and didn't tell you that it went back two years and concerned none other than Catherine. And that afterwards I had to apologise again to her body. Winningly, too, it would seem, as she hadn't left me since!

Today I remember with some irony the sudden turn taken by our relationship after I told you about that painting. The world of women really is incredible. I expected you to fall in love with me when you discovered the secret link between you and my first painting, *Nostalgia*. A painting as old as you and with your identity. But you fell for me because of another painting of another woman that impinged on memory by accident!

Our first date ended at noon. I had a feeling that I'd see you again. Perhaps the following day. I felt we were at the beginning of something, and that we were both in a hurry. There were a lot of things still to say – we hadn't even really said anything. We seduced each other with potential speech. Out of innocence, or being clever, we were each playing the same game. So I wasn't terribly surprised when you asked me as you said goodbye, 'Will you be here tomorrow morning?'

As happy as someone whose bet's come in, I replied, 'Of course.'

You said, 'I'll come back tomorrow then, around the same time. We'll have more time to talk. Today went by really fast without us noticing.'

I made no comment. I knew that time had no measure except our two hearts. That's why it only races with us when the heart races too, from one joy to another, from one shock to another. Your words held an admission of a shared, secret joy that I hoped would be repeated.

I remember saying to you as you left that day, 'Don't forget your book tomorrow. I'd like to read you.'

Surprised, you said, 'Is your Arabic perfect?'

I said, 'Of course. You'll see for yourself.'

'I'll bring it, then.' With adorable feminine wiles, you smiled and added, 'If you still insist on getting to know me, I won't deny you the pleasure!'

The door shut behind your smile, without me understanding exactly what you meant.

You left shrouded in mystery just like you had arrived. I stood at the glass door, watching you melt into the crowd and disappear again like a shooting star. Quite stunned, I wondered, 'Did we really meet?'

So we had met.

Those who say that mountains never meet are wrong. Those who build bridges between them, so they might greet each other without stooping or diminishing their pride, know nothing of the laws of nature. Mountains only meet in massive earthquakes. Even then they don't shake hands, but turn into dust.

So we had met.

The unforeseen tremor happened; one of us was a volcano and I was the victim.

Inferno of a woman, volcano that swept away everything in your path and incinerated my last strongholds, where did you get all those blasting waves of fire? Why wasn't I wary of the ash that burned like the lips of a gypsy lover? Why wasn't I wary of your simplicity and false modesty? Why didn't I remember that old geography lesson: 'Volcanoes do not have peaks; they are mountains with the modesty of a plateau.' Could a plateau have done all that?

Popular proverbs warn us about the tranquil river that tricks us with its calmness and which, when we cross, swallows us, and about the twig we don't pay attention to that blinds us. More than one proverb tells us in more than one dialect to beware of what seems safe. But all her warning signs didn't stop us making yet more idiotic mistakes. The logic of desire is crazy, ridiculous. The more we loved, the more ridiculous we were. Wasn't it Bernard Shaw who said you know you're in love when you start acting against your own interest?

My prime folly was to act with you like a tourist visiting Sicily for the first time: he runs up Mount Etna, praying that the dormant volcano will lift one sleepy eyelid and engulf the island in fire in full view of the stunned, camera-wielding visitors. The corpses of the tourists are turned to soot to attest that there is nothing more beautiful than a yawning volcano spewing fire and rock and swallowing up vast regions in seconds. A spectator is always mesmerised by the hunger of flames and he is drawn towards those rivers of fire. He stands stupefied and in shock as he tries to recall all he has read about Judgement Day. In his lover's swoon, he forgets that this is his own day of judgement!

The destruction that surrounds me today bears witness that I loved you to death, that I desired you until the final pyre. I believe Jacques Brel when he said, 'Scorched fields can give more corn than the best of Aprils.' I bet on a spring for this parched life, an April for these blighted years.

Volcano! You swept everything around me away. Wasn't it insane to go further than deranged tourists and lovers, than all those who loved you before me? I moved my house into your shadow, set my memory at the foot of your volcano and then sat in the midst of the flames to paint you.

Wasn't it insane to refuse to listen to the weather forecast and disaster warnings? I convinced myself that I knew you better.

68

But I forgot that logic stops where love begins. What I know about you has no relationship with logic or knowledge.

So the mountains met, and we met.

A quarter-century of blank white pages unfilled with you.

A quarter-century of monotonous days spent waiting for you.

A quarter-century since the first meeting between a man who was me and a small baby playing on my knees who was you.

A quarter of a century since I had kissed you on your child's cheek, standing in for a father who hadn't yet seen you.

I was the crippled man who had left his arm on forgotten battlefields, and his heart in forbidden cities. I never expected you to be the battlefield where I would leave my corpse, the city where I would exhaust my memory, the blank canvas where my brushes would quit to remain virginal and mighty like you, holding all contradictions in their colours.

How did all of this happen? I don't know any more.

Time raced with us from one date to another. Love trans ported us from one gasp to another. I submitted to your love without argument. Your love was my destiny. Perhaps it was my end. Could any power withstand destiny?

We met almost every day in the same gallery, but at various times. Chance wished my show to coincide with the Easter holiday. You had enough time to visit me every day as there was no university. All you had to do was deceive others a little, your cousin perhaps a bit more so she didn't come along for one reason or another.

Every time, as I said goodbye to you and repeated reflexively, 'See you tomorrow,' I wondered whether it wasn't utterly absurd that we were growing more attached to each other with every passing day. Perhaps because I was older than you, I felt that I alone was responsible for the abnormal emotional situation and our rapid and terrible slide towards love. In vain I tried to withstand the torrent rushing me towards you with the crazy force of love in my fifties and the hunger of a man who had not known love before. With its youth and vigour, your love swept me to reason's nadir, the point where desire almost touches madness and death.

As I slid down with you into the labyrinths inside me – secret recesses of love and hunger, cavernous spaces never before entered by woman – I felt that I was also gradually sliding down the scale of moral values. Unconsciously, I was denying the passionate ideals that I had spent my whole life refusing to compromise. For me, moral values were indivisible. In my dictionary there was no difference between political morality and any other kind. But I was aware that with you I had begun to deny one to convince you of another.

I often asked myself at that time whether I was betraying the past by sitting alone with you at half-innocent meetings in a space furnished with paintings and memory.

Perhaps I was betraying the dearest man I knew, the most valiant and steely, the bravest and most faithful. Perhaps I would betray *Si* Taher, my leader, comrade and lifelong friend, sully his memory and steal from him the sole rose of his life. His last testament.

Could I do all of that in the name of the past, while speaking to you about the past?

But was I really stealing anything from you at those meetings when I talked at length about him? No, it didn't happen. The glory of his name was always present in my mind. It joined me to you and kept me from you at the same time. It was a bridge and a barrier.

My only pleasure then was to hand over the keys to my memory, to open the yellowed notebooks of the past and read them to you page by page. As I listened to myself narrating this for the first time, it was as if I were discovering it with you.

In silence we found that we complemented each other frighteningly. I was the past of which you were ignorant; you were the present, which had no memory and where I tried to deposit some of the burden of the years.

You were as light as a sponge. I was as deep and weighty as an ocean. Every day you filled yourself more with me. I didn't know then that whenever I grew empty, I replenished myself with you. Whenever I gave you some piece of the past, I turned you into a replica of me. So we carried a shared memory, shared streets and alleyways, shared sorrows and joys.

Both of us were war-wounded. Fate ground us down without mercy, and each emerged with their wound. Mine was visible, yours was hidden in the depths. They amputated my arm; they severed your childhood. They ripped a limb from my body and took a father from your arms. We were war's human remains. Two smashed statues in elegant clothes, nothing more.

I remember the day you asked me for the first time to tell you about your father. You confessed, with some embarrassment, that you had come to see me in the first place with just that design. Your voice had a touch of uncompromising sadness, a touch of bitterness that I had not seen in you before.

You said, 'What's the point in naming a main street after my father, of me carrying the burden of his name, which pedestrians and strangers repeat in front of me all day long? What's the point of that if I know no more about him than they do? And if not one of them can really tell me about him?'

I said in surprise, 'Doesn't your uncle talk about him, for example?'

'My uncle doesn't have time,' you said. 'If he should mention him when I'm there, it sounds more like a eulogy addressed to strangers to boast of his brother's glorious deeds. He doesn't make it relevant to me and talk about the man who, before anything else, was my father.

'What I want to know about my father isn't the ready-made words in praise of heroes and martyrs. That's what's said on every occasion about all of them. It's as though death suddenly made all *shahids* identical, copies of one template.

'I'm interested to know what he thought, the minor details of his life, his good and bad points, his secret ambitions and failings. I don't want to be the daughter of a myth. Myths are a Greek invention. I just want to be the daughter of an ordinary man with his strengths and weaknesses, his victories and defeats. Every man's life contains disappointments and setbacks that might have spurred him on to success.'

A brief silence fell. I was contemplating you and probing the depths of my soul. I was seeking the boundary between my defeats and my victories. At that moment I was no prophet, and you were no Greek goddess. We were just two ancient statues with smashed limbs trying to restore their parts with words. I listened to you as you repaired the ruin in your depths.

You said, 'At times, I feel that I'm the daughter of a statistic, one among a million-and-a-half others. Perhaps some of them were bigger or smaller, perhaps the names of some are written in bigger or smaller letters than others, but they all remain statistics in a tragedy.

'That my father left me a big name means nothing. He left me a tragedy as weighty as his name, and left my brother with a constant fear of failure, obsessed with not living up to expectations. He's the only son of Taher Abdelmoula. He has no right to fail at school or in life. Symbols don't have the right to fall apart. As a result, he gave up university when he realised it was futile to pile up qualifications when others were piling up millions. Perhaps he was right. Qualifications are the last thing to get you a decent job these days.

'He saw his friends who graduated before him going straight into unemployment or into jobs with limited pay and limited dreams. So he decided to go into business and, even though I share his view, I'm sad that my brother in the prime of his youth has turned into a small businessman running a small shop with a van given by Algeria as a privilege to the son of a martyr. I don't think my father expected his future would be like that!'

I interrupted you in an effort to alleviate your litany of complaint. 'He didn't expect a future like this for you, either. You've surpassed his dreams and inherited all his ambitions and principles. Science and knowledge were sacred to him. He loved the Arabic language, and dreamed of an Algeria that had nothing to do with the superstitions and worn-out traditions that had exhausted his generation and finished them off. You don't know how lucky you are today to live in a country that gives you the chance to be a cultured young woman who can study and work, and even write.'

You responded somewhat sarcastically. 'I might be indebted to Algeria for being cultured or educated, but writing is something else. Nobody gave me that. We write to bring back what we have lost and what has been stolen from us by stealth. I would have preferred to have an ordinary childhood and life, a father and family like others – not shelves of books and a pile of diaries.

73

But my father is public property in Algeria. Only writing is mine alone and no one is going to take it away!'

Your words stunned me. I felt a conflicting mix of emotions. Sadness yes, but not pity. An intelligent woman does not provoke pity. Even in her sadness, she always arouses admiration. I was impressed by you, by the defiance in your hurt, by your provocative way of challenging the homeland. You were like me, who painted with one hand to restore the other. I would have preferred to remain an ordinary man with two arms doing everyday things and not have been turned into a one-armed genius with nothing but drawings and paintings.

I didn't dream of being a genius, a prophet or an artist – rejecting and rejected. I didn't struggle for that. My dream was to have a wife and children, but fate chose another life for me. So I became father to other people's children and the partner of exile and the paintbrush. My dreams were amputated too.

I said to you, 'Nobody will take writing away from you. What is deep inside us is ours and nobody can touch it.'

You said, 'But there's nothing deep inside me except a void filled with newspaper stories, news broadcasts and artless books that have nothing to do with me.'

Then you added, as if entrusting me with a secret, 'Do you know why I loved my grandmother more than anyone else? More than my mother, even? She was the only person who found time to talk to me about it all. She would go back to the past unbidden, as if she refused to leave it. She wore the past, ate the past and only enjoyed hearing songs from the past.

'She dreamed of the past when others dreamed of the future. So she often told me about my father without me having to ask. He was the most beautiful thing about her fading past as a woman. She never tired of speaking about him, as though she brought him back and made him present with words. She did it with the grief of a mother who refuses to forget she's lost her firstborn to eternity. But she didn't tell me more about him than a mother would say about her son. Taher was the most beautiful, the most wonderful, the good boy who never said a single word to hurt her.

'On Independence Day my grandmother wept like she'd never wept before. I asked her, "*Amma*, why are you crying when Algeria's just gained its independence?" She replied, "In the past, I was waiting for independence for Taher's return. Today I've realised that I'm not waiting for anything any more."

'The day my father died, my grandmother didn't ululate with joy like in the made-up stories of the Revolution I read later. She stood in the middle of the house, racked with sobbing, trembling with her head uncovered, and repeating in primal grief, "Ah, black day of sorrow! Taher, my love, why have you gone and not me?"

'My mother was crying silently and trying to calm her down. I was watching them both and crying, not fully understanding that I was crying for a man I had only seen a few times. A man who was my father.'

Why did your memories of *Amma* Zahra always stir unaccountable emotions in me? Before that day, they had been warm and beautiful, but they suddenly became painful to the point of tears.

I still remember the features of that dear old lady who loved me as much as I loved her. I spent my childhood and adolescence between her house and ours. That woman had only one way to love. I discovered later that this was common to all our mothers. They loved you with food. They cooked your favourite dish, came after you with delicacies, and plied you with freshly made sweets, bread and pastries.

She belonged to a generation of women who devoted their lives to the kitchen. For them, holidays and weddings were banquets of love. There they made all their overflowing femininity and tenderness into gifts, along with the secret hunger that found no expression outside of food.

Every day they fed more than one tableful, more than one sitting on the terrace. Then every night they went to sleep without anybody noticing their age-old, inherited hunger. I only discovered that fact recently, when I found myself – perhaps out of loyalty to them – unable to love a woman who lived on fast food and whose only banquet was her body.

As I fled those painful memories of my distant childhood, I asked you, 'And your mother? You've never told me about her. How did she manage after *Si* Taher's death?'

'She didn't talk about him much,' you said. 'Perhaps inside she blamed the people who had arranged the marriage. They married her to a martyr, not a man.

'She already knew about his political activity. She realised that he would join the FLN after they got married and begin a clandestine life, sneaking home from time to time, and might return a corpse. Why marry, then? But the marriage was inevitable – there was the sniff of a deal in the air. Her family were proud to become linked in marriage with Taher Abdelmoula, a man with a name and money. It was fine for my mother to be his second wife, or his next widow. Perhaps my grandmother understood that he had been born to be a martyr, and so she visited the tombs of the holy and the good to beg in tears for her son to have children. It was just the same when she was pregnant with him, pleading that her newborn be a boy.'

I asked you, 'Where did you hear all these stories?'

'From her. From my mother, too. Imagine, as soon as my grandmother fell pregnant with my father, she didn't stop visiting the tomb of Sidi Mohamed of the Crow in Constantine. She almost gave birth to him there. So she called him Mohamed Taher in his honour. Then she called my uncle Mohamed Sharif, also in honour of him. Later, I found out that half the men of the city have such names. Its people ascribe a lot of importance to names, and most of them bear those of prophets or holy men. She almost called me Sayida in honour of Sayida Menoubia, whom she'd visited in Tunis, always with a candle, a prayer mat and invocations. She'd move between Sayida Menoubia's tomb and that of Sidi Omar el-Fayash. Perhaps you've heard of him – the saint who lived divested of everything. He made the Tunisian authorities chain his legs to stop him leaving his house naked. So he lived in chains, walking screaming around an empty room. Empty except for the women who scrambled to visit him. Some to honour him, others merely to see his manhood on display, or out of the curiosity of women wrapped in *sefsaris* pretending to be shy!'

Laughing, I asked you, 'Did you visit him?'

'Of course,' you said. 'And I visited with every one of the women individually afterwards. I also visited Sayida Menoubia, whose name I would have got had my mother not spared me that disaster. She decided to call me Hayat until my father, who had the final say, came back.'

My heart stopped at that name. Memory raced backwards. My tongue tripped as it tried to utter it after exactly a quarter of a century. 'Would you be happy if I called you Hayat?'

My question surprised you, and in astonishment you said, 'Why? Don't you like my real name? Isn't it nicer?'

'It is nicer,' I said. 'I was amazed at the time how your father thought of it. When I heard it for the first time there was nothing in his life to inspire such a beautiful name. Still, I'd like to call you Hayat, because I'm probably the only person apart from your mother who knows that name now. I want it to be like a password between us, a reminder of our remarkable relationship. That you're also somehow my child.'

You laughed and said, 'You know, you've never left the days of the Revolution. You feel a need to give me a codename, even before you love me. It's as if you were signing me up for a secret mission. I wonder what it is?'

I laughed in turn at the startling accuracy of your observation. Maybe you had begun to know me that well. 'Listen, my budding revolutionary,' I said. 'There has to be more than one test before we entrust someone with a guerrilla operation. I shall begin with your initial training to assess your level of readiness!'

At that moment, I felt the time was finally right to tell you the story of my last day at the Front. The day *Si* Taher spoke your name to me for the first time as he was saying goodbye and entrusted me to register you, if I made it to Tunis alive.

That night, feverish and with a bleeding arm, I crossed the Algerian–Tunisian border. In my delirium I kept repeating your name. In the midst of exhaustion and loss of blood, it became the name of *Si* Taher's final mission for me. I wanted to fulfil his last request of me, pursue his fleeting dream and grant you an official, legal name unconnected with superstitions and saints.

I remember the first time I knocked on the door of your house on Toufiq Street in Tunis. I remember all the details of that visit as though my memory had read in advance what fate had written and kept a space for it. That autumnal September day, I waited in front of your green iron door for what seemed like hours until *Amma* Zahra opened it.

I still remember her double-take, as though she had been expecting someone else, not me. She stood bewildered before me, taking in my sad grey overcoat and my pale, thin face. She lingered over my one arm holding a box of sweets and the empty sleeve of my coat which, for the first time, was tucked into a pocket out of shame.

Before I said a word, her eyes flooded with tears. She started crying without thinking to invite me in. I leant down to kiss her, with the accumulated longing of the years I had not seen her, with the longing imparted by her son, with longing for my own mother, to whose loss I was still not reconciled after two-and-a-half years.

'How are you, *Amma* Zahra?'

Her sobbing rose as she hugged me and asked in turn, 'How are you, my son?'

Was she crying with joy to see me, or with sadness at my state, at my amputated arm, which she was seeing for the first time? Was she crying because she expected to see her son, but saw me? Or just because someone had knocked at the door and brought joy and a little news to a house that a man had not entered for months?

'You're safe. Come in, my son, come in.' She spoke as she finally made it through the door and wiped her tears. Before I spoke she repeated, 'Come in. Come in,' in a loud voice like a signal to your mother, who came running when she heard the words. I only saw the back of her robe as she walked in front of me and then disappeared behind a door quickly closed.

I loved that house with its trellised vines climbing the walls of the small garden and hanging over it so that the rich red

79

grapes dangled in the middle of the courtyard. The jasmine tree that spread and peered from the outside wall, like an inquisitive woman fed up with the confines of her house who goes to see what's happening outside and seduces passers-by to pick her flowers or gather those fallen to the ground. The reassuring smell of food and a vague warmth that made a person reluctant to leave.

Amma Zahra went before me into a room overlooking the courtyard, repeating all the while, 'Sit down, my son. Sit down.' She took the box of sweets and put it on the round copper tray on a wooden table.

As soon as I sat down on the woollen cushion on the floor, you appeared in the corner of the room, as tiny as a doll. You crawled quickly over to the white box and tried to pull it to the ground to open. Before I could intervene, *Amma* Zahra took the box away and put it in another spot, saying, 'Thank you, my dear. You shouldn't have gone to the trouble, Khaled, my son. Seeing your face is enough for us.'

Then she told you off as you headed towards the domed wooden rack on top of the stove, where your tiny white clothes were hanging to dry. You gestured towards me, your small hands held out, asking for my help. Right then, as I stretched out my single arm in an effort to lift you, I felt the horror of what had happened to me. With my one uncertain hand I was unable to pick you up, put you in my lap and dandle you without you slipping away.

Wasn't it amazing that my first meeting with you should also be my first test and my first difficulty? That I should be defeated by you in the hardest test I had faced since becoming a one-armed man – no more than ten days before?

Amma Zahra came back with a tray of coffee and a plate of

tammina. 'Tell me Khaled, my son, I beg you, how's Taher?' She said this before she sat down. There was a taste of tears in her question. The question whose answer was feared stuck in her throat. I reassured her, telling her I was under his command and that he was at the border. His health was good, but he couldn't visit for the time being due to the situation and his many responsibilities.

I didn't tell her that the battles were intensifying every day, that the enemy had decided to surround the mountains and burn the forests so that their planes could observe our movements. That they had arrested Mostafa Ben Boulaïd together with a group of commanders and fighters, thirty of whom had been sentenced to death. That I had come for treatment with a group of wounded and crippled men, two of whom had died before they arrived.

My appearance told her more than a woman of her age could bear, so I changed the course of the conversation. I gave her the money *Si* Taher had sent with me, and asked her, as he had requested, to buy you a present. I promised that I would come back soon to register you in the name he had chosen for you. *Amma* Zahra repeated it with difficulty, somewhat surprised, but without passing comment. For her, what *Si* Taher said had a sacred quality.

As if you had suddenly noticed that the conversation concerned you, with childish spontaneity you took hold of my trouser leg and pulled. Helping you on to my lap, I couldn't stop myself hugging you with my one arm. I drew you to me, as if embracing the dream for which I had lost my other arm. It was as though I were afraid it might escape along with the dreams of the man who was yet to throw his arms around you in joy.

Caught between tears, joy and pain, I kissed you for *Si* Taher and for comrades who hadn't seen their children since joining the FLN. And for others who died dreaming of a simple moment like this when they would hug not rifles, but their children who had been born and grown up out of sight.

I forgot that day to kiss you for me, to cry before you for me, for the man you would make me a quarter-century later. Alongside your name I forgot to register my name in advance, to request in advance your memory and years to come, to reserve your life. I should have stopped the toll of the years racing with me towards twenty-seven as you entered your seventh month. I forgot to keep you in my lap for ever, playing and toying, saying things neither you nor I understood.

I told the story with deliberate brevity and kept the incidental details to myself. You didn't interrupt once and only seemed to pause at the date, 15 September 1957, when I officially registered your actual name. Even though nobody had told you the story before, you didn't ask a single explanatory question and didn't utter a word of comment. Perhaps no one had found it worth telling.

Stunned, you listened in alarming silence. A haze of stubbornness obscured your gaze, and you, who in the same place had laughed so much, wept in front of me for the first time. Did we realise at the time that we laughed to evade the painful truth, to evade something we were looking for and putting off at the same time?

I looked at you through the fog of your tears. Right then I longed to enfold you with my one arm like I'd never held a woman, or a dream. But I stayed where I was, and you stayed where you were, facing each other. Two stubborn mountains with a secret bridge of compassion and longing between them, and many rainless clouds.

The word 'bridge' caught my mind, and I recalled the painting – as if I had remembered the most important chapter in a story. I was telling it to you, but perhaps, also to myself so that I could believe how strange it was. I stood up and said, 'Come on, I'll show you something.' You followed me without question. I stopped in front of the painting. Bewildered, you waited for me to speak. 'You know, that first day when I saw you standing in front of this picture, a shiver went through me. I sensed that there was a definite, if unknown, link between you and the picture. That's why I came and said hello to you – perhaps to learn whether my intuition was wrong or right.'

You said in surprise, 'And was your intuition correct?'

'Haven't you noticed the date on the picture?'

Looking for it at the bottom, you said, 'No.'

'It's close to your official birthday. You're only two weeks older than this painting. Your twin, if you like!'

'Wow, that's incredible!' you said.

You looked at the picture as if searching for yourself and said, 'Isn't that the mountain suspension bridge?'

I answered, 'It's more than a bridge. It's Constantine, which is the other kinship you have with this picture. The day you entered this exhibition hall, you brought Constantine with you. She came in your figure, in the way you walk, in your accent and in the bracelet you were wearing.'

You thought a while, then said, 'Ah, you mean the *miqyas*. I sometimes wear it on special occasions, but it's heavy and hurts my wrist.'

'Memory is always heavy,' I said. 'Mother wore one for many years and never complained about the weight. She died with it on her wrist. It's just a question of getting used to it!' I wasn't telling you off, there was sadness in my voice. But what

I was saying meant nothing to you. You were from a generation that finds everything too heavy. That's why traditional
Arab clothes have been cut down to one or two contemporary
pieces. Old bracelets and jewellery have been reduced to
baubles taken on and off in an instant. History and memory
have been reduced to a couple of pages in textbooks, and
Arabic poetry to one or two names.

I didn't blame you. We belong to countries that don memory
only on special occasions; between one news broadcast and
another. As soon as the lights go out and the cameras leave, they
take it off again, like a woman removing her finery.

As if apologising for an unintentional mistake, you said, 'If
you want me to, I'll wear that bracelet for you. Would that make
you happy?'

What you said surprised me. The situation was a bit sad,
despite its spontaneity. Perhaps it was sadly funny: I was offering
you my paternal feelings while you were offering your maternal
ones. A girl who might have been my daughter was, without
realising, turning into my mother!

I could have answered you then with one word that encapsu-
lated all the contradictions of that scene and all the intense – and
shy – feelings I had for you. But I said something else. 'That
would make me happy, but I'd also be happy if you wear it for
your own sake.

'You have to be aware that you'll understand nothing of the
past you're seeking, nor the memory of a father you didn't know,
if you fail to internalise Constantine and her customs. We don't
uncover our memories by looking at a postcard, or a beautiful
painting like this one, but when we wear them and live them.

'That bracelet, for example. I instantly had an emotional relationship with it. Without my knowing it, it symbolised motherhood

for me. A fact I only discovered the day I saw you wearing it. If you hadn't, all the feelings it aroused would still be lying dormant in the labyrinth of forgetting. Do you get it now? Sometimes memory needs waking up.'

What a fool I was. Without realising, I was waking up a genie that had been sleeping for years. In febrile madness I was turning you from a young woman into a city. You listened with the wonder of a pupil, accepting my words as if in a hypnotic trance.

That day, I discovered my power to tame you and control your burning fire.

I decided that I would turn you into a city, towering, proud, authentic, deep, unassailable by dwarfs or pirates.

I sentenced you to be Constantine.

I sentenced myself to madness.

We spent more time together that day. We parted reeling psychologically, drained by the extreme emotions resulting from four hours of non-stop talking. Accompanied at times by stubborn tears or disturbing silence, we had said a lot.

Perhaps seeing you cry for the first time had made me happy. I despised people who didn't cry. I felt they were either tyrants or hypocrites, and in either case didn't deserve respect.

You were the woman I wanted to laugh and cry with. That was the most wonderful thing I discovered that day.

I remembered that our first date started with unplanned laughter. That day, I remembered the saying, 'The quickest way to win a woman is to make her laugh.' I've won her without trying, I thought. Now I've realised the stupidity of that saying. It encourages quick victory and behaviour where it doesn't matter if the woman you made laugh to begin with cries afterwards.

I didn't win you after a fit of laughter, but when you cried in front of me as you listened to your story that was also mine. At the moment you looked at that painting, clearly affected. Perhaps you were about to kiss me on the cheek or hug me in a moment of sudden tenderness. But you didn't. We parted as usual with a handshake, as though fearful that a peck on the cheek might ignite the dormant volcano.

We understood each other in complicit silence. Your presence awoke my masculinity. Your perfume drove me wild and lured me towards madness. Your eyes, even when dripping sadness, disarmed me. Your voice. Ah, your voice that I loved so much. Where did you get it? What was your language? What your music?

You were my constant wonder and my certain defeat. Could you have possibly been my girl, when logically you could only be a daughter to me?

I resisted you with imaginary barriers I put between us every time, like hurdles on a racetrack. But you were a stallion bred for the challenge and to win the bet. You jumped all of them at one go with a single glance.

Your gaze would linger on me, pausing here and there, before halting at my eyes or the open neck of my shirt.

Once as you looked especially hard, you said, 'There's something of Zorba about you – his stature, his tan, his trimmed, unruly hair. Perhaps you're more handsome than him, though.'

'You could add,' I replied, 'his age, his craziness, his extremes, and that my heart feels something like his loneliness, his sadness, and his victories that always end in defeat.'

Surprised, you said, 'You know all that about him! Do you like him?'

'Perhaps.'

'You know, he's the man who's had the most influence on me.'

Your admission shocked me. I thought that either you didn't know many men or didn't read many books. Before I could reply, you went on passionately, 'I like his madness and his unexpected behaviour. His strange relationship with that woman. His philosophy of love and marriage, of war and religion. Even more, I like the way he links his feelings with their opposite. I remember the story of the cherries – he used to love them and decided that to be cured of his craving he would eat loads of them, enough to make him sick. Afterwards he treated them like an ordinary fruit. That was his way to put an end to things that he felt were enslaving him.'

I said, 'I don't remember that story.'

'Do you remember,' you asked, 'his dance in the midst of what he called "beautiful destruction"? It's amazing that someone's disappointment and tragedy can make him dance. He stood out in his defeats as well. Not all defeats are available to all. You have to have extraordinary dreams, joys and ambitions for those feelings to become their opposite in that way.'

I listened in wonder and pleasure. Instead of the 'beautiful destruction' that you were ardently describing rousing fears of any sado-masochistic tendencies you might have, I was taken in by the beauty of your idea. Without much thought, I said, 'True. What you're saying is beautiful. I didn't know you loved Zorba so much!'

Laughing, you said, 'I'll make a confession. The story really disturbed me. When I read it, I felt an estatic sadness. I wanted to love a man like that, or write a novel like that, but that was impossible. So that story will haunt me until I can overcome it in one way or another.'

I said sarcastically, 'I'd be happy, then, if you find some

similarity between me and him. You might fulfil both wishes at the same time.'

You looked at me with adorable mischief and said, 'I only want to fulfil one of them with you.' Before I could ask which, you continued, 'I won't write anything about you.'

'Oh, why not?'

'Because I don't want to kill you. You make me happy. We write novels to kill the people whose existence has become a burden to us. We write to get rid of them.'

I spent a long time that day discussing your 'criminal' view of literature. As we parted I said, 'Do I finally get to see your first novel, or your first "crime"?'

You laughed and replied, 'Of course, provided you don't become a detective or party to the case!'

Perhaps you were foretelling what awaited me; you knew in advance that I wouldn't be an impartial reader from then on.

The following day you brought me the novel. As you were handing it over, you said, 'I hope you find something enjoyable in it.'

Playfully, I said, 'I hope the number of your victims won't spoil my enjoyment!'

In the same tone, you replied, 'No, rest assured, I hate mass graves!'

How did I forget that last sentence?

When I recall everything now, I'm convinced that your new story, the one being promoted in the papers and magazines, will be a grave for one character, who might be Ziyad or might be me. Which one of us has the luck to die like that? Only your book can answer that question and all the others haunting me.

But why does everything you write fill me with questions?

Why do I feel I'm an element in all your realist fantasies? Even the one you wrote prior to me.

Perhaps because I imagine I have a historic right over you, or because, when you gave me that first book, you didn't write a dedication to me. You just made a comment I'll never forget. 'We only write dedications to strangers. Those we love do not belong on the blank first page, but in the pages of the book,' you said.

I devoured the book in two nights. I raced from page to page, breathless, as if looking for something other than the words. Something you had written to me in advance, before even meeting me, something that might connect us through a story that wasn't ours.

I knew that was crazy. But aren't there so many coincidences in life? Like the picture I painted in September 1957 and that waited a quarter of a century for you without me realising it was yours. That it was you.

That was pure fantasy.

The only things you secreted in that book for me were bitterness, pain and stupid jealousy – whose fire I tasted for the first time. Insane jealousy towards a man on paper, who might have passed through your life or might have been a fictional creature that you used just to fill empty days and blank pages.

Where was the line dividing fantasy and reality? You never once gave me an answer to that question. You simply increased my confusion with ambiguous answers, like, 'Only what we write matters. The writing alone is literature and will endure. Those we write about are incidental, just people we paused before one day for some reason or another, before continuing on our way with or without them.'

'But the writer's relationship with his muse can't be so simple,'

I said. 'The writer is nothing without his inspiration. He owes it something.'

You interrupted, 'Owes what? What Aragon wrote about Elsa's eyes is more beautiful than eyes that will grow old and dim. What Nizar Qabbani wrote about Bilqis' plaits is surely more beautiful than her thick hair destined to go grey and fall out. The Mona Lisa's smile painted by Leonardo attains its value not as a woman's naive smile but as the sign of the artist's incredible ability to convey contradictory emotions in a vague smile that combines melancholy and joy. Who is in debt to whom, then?'

Our conversation was taking a different course, perhaps one you desired in an effort to escape the truth. I put the question to you again more directly. 'Did that man pass through your life, or not?'

You laughed and said, 'Amazing! Agatha Christie's novels contain more than sixty murders. The works of other women writers contain even more. Yet not once has a reader raised his voice in judgement or demanded their imprisonment. But if a woman writes a single love story, every finger points in accusation, and forensic investigators find plenty of evidence to prove it's her story. I think critics really ought to resolve this once and for all. Either they admit that women have more imagination than men, or they put us all on trial!'

I laughed at your surprising but unconvincing reasoning. 'While we wait for the critics to resolve the matter,' I said, 'allow me to repeat the question you haven't answered. Was that man really part of your life?'

You said, winding me up, 'What matters is that following the book he died.'

'I see. Because you can kill the past just like that, with the stroke of a pen?'

You continued to be evasive and said, 'What past? We might also write to bury our dreams, no?'

I had a feeling deep down that the story was your story. That that man had entered your life, and perhaps your body. Between the lines I could almost smell the scent of his tobacco, almost sense his things strewn on the pages. There was something of him in every paragraph, his tan, the taste of his kiss, his laugh and his breaths. There was also your shameless desire for him.

Perhaps he loved you creatively, or was your description of him creative? Maybe he was a purely feminine invention that your language covered in manliness and dreams and for which it fashioned a beautiful, made-to-measure tomb afterwards. What logic made me read this book as a lover disguised in the uniform of the morality police? I delved between the words, I investigated the chapters in the chance of catching you red-handed in a kiss here or the first few letters of his name there.

My thoughts roaming widely, I remembered you had been in Paris for four years and that you had been living with your uncle since his posting to Paris – only two years earlier. I wondered what you were up to before that, for all the time you were on your own.

That book of yours exhausted me. It was enjoyable and tiring, like you. Subsequently, I admitted to you that my relationship with you changed after I read you and I doubted that I would be able to endure. I wasn't prepared for words as weapons.

As if it did not at all concern you, you said, 'You shouldn't have read me, then!'

Stupidly, I replied, 'But I like reading you. Besides, I don't have another way to understand you.'

You answered, 'Wrong. You won't understand anything that

way. A writer, despite living on the edge of truth, isn't necessarily a professional in it. That's the preserve of historians. In fact, he's a professional dreamer, or a kind of refined liar. A successful novelist is someone who lies with shocking truth, or a liar who speaks truth.'

After a little thought, you added, 'I think that's more correct!'

Oh, you little liar! Your lies were the sweetest and most painful. I decided that day not to delve into your memory any more. You wouldn't confess anything. Perhaps because you were a woman who specialised in evasion, or was there nothing to confess?

You just wanted to make me imagine that you were no longer the child I knew. In fact, you were empty and your lies filled the emptiness. What else would explain your attachment to me? Why did you pursue my memory with questions and why did you induce me to speak about everything? Why such greed for knowledge, such a desire to share my memory and everything I loved and hated? Was memory your complex?

My exhibition had to come to an end for us to realise that we had only known each other for two weeks, not the months it felt like. How did we spill our memories in a matter of days? How in the few hours we spent together did we learn to be sad and happy and dream all at once?

How did we become versions of each other? How could we leave this place that had become part of our memory? For a few days inside a large silent hall hung with art we were transported beyond time and space into a quarter-century's worth of suffering and madness.

We were a painting among other paintings. A mutable poly-chrome painting started by chance and finished by the hand of fate. I relished my new situation as I turned from the artist into one of his paintings on display.

I had never felt this sad taking an exhibition down before. I packed the paintings one by one in their cases. The hall would be left empty for another painter who would come with his pictures, with his sadness and joy, with other stories unlike mine.

I felt I was packing up my days with you.

My hand suddenly stopped as it was about to take down the picture I had left till last. I contemplated it again and felt it lacked something. On its surface there was only a bridge crossing from one side to the other, suspended from above by cables at both ends like a swing of sadness. Beneath this iron swing was a rocky gorge of great depth that expressed its blunt contradiction with the pure mood of an annoyingly calm and blue sky. Before that moment, I had not felt that this painting needed new details to break the contradiction and cover the nakedness of the two colours that were unique to it.

In truth, *Nostalgia* wasn't a painting. It was an *aide memoire*, the draft of dreams that had been overtaken by fifteen years of nostalgia and bewilderment, not just a quarter-century of time.

I carried it under my arm, as if marking it out from the others. Suddenly I was in a hurry. After all these years, I wanted to sit in front of it with a brush and a new palette and imbue it with life and energy. I would finally move the stones of the suspension bridge, one by one. But right then my mind was distracted by an overpowering obsession. How could we meet again from now on? And where?

Your break from university ended more or less at the same time as the exhibition. We were now confined by the practicalities of when and where. Our secret might be stolen out in the open by people we didn't know but who knew us. What madness

93

my destiny with you! Why did my disability give only me away? Why all this caution? And why you, in particular? But the mere possibility of meeting *Si* Sharif some day when I was with you made me give up the idea and realise the awkwardness of the situation and how my embarrassment would betray me.

We agreed that you'd call me on the phone and that we'd come up with a new plan. That was the only solution. I couldn't visit you in the university quarter – your cousin was studying at the same university. Could we have found a more complicated set of circumstances?

I spent the longest weekend waiting for you to call on Monday morning.

On Sunday the phone rang. I rushed over, betting it was you. Perhaps you had managed to steal a few brief minutes to talk to me. Catherine was on the line. I hid my disappointment and listened to her chattering away about her everyday preoccupations and her planned trip to London. Then she asked me about the exhibition and, skipping from one subject to another, said, 'I read a good article about your exhibition in a weekly magazine. No doubt you've seen it. It's by Roger Naqqash, who seems to know you, or he knows your paintings very well.'

I didn't have any desire to talk and said curtly, 'Yes, he's an old friend.' I politely got rid of her. I had no desire to meet that day. Perhaps my need to paint was stronger than my other physical needs. Perhaps I was just too full of you.

With heavy steps I went back to my studio. I had started preparing a palette to add some touches to the picture. Yet I was bewildered and, in front of it, I reverted to the beginner I had been twenty-five years before. Did its new kinship with you add this tinge of confusion? Or was I confused because I was standing before the past, no less? To retouch memory, not the painting.

I felt I was about to do something stupid. I knew, despite my illogical desire, that one should never toy with the past, that any attempt to beautify it would only end in disfigurement. I knew that, but the painting suddenly annoyed me. Everything about it was simplistic to the point of naivety. So why not continue painting it, then? Why not just treat it aesthetically?

Didn't Chagall spend fifteen years painting one of his pictures? He would go back to it again and again in between works to add some new feature or face after he decided to include all he had loved since childhood. Wasn't it also my right to go back to this painting and mark the steps of those crossing? At the side, I might scatter some houses hanging above the rocks. Beneath the bridge I might leave some trace of the river – at times scanty, at times glistening and foaming – that divided the city. Was it no longer necessary to mark the traces of my original memory, those I had been unable to include before, when I was only a beginner?

I thought about Roger Naqqash, a friend from childhood and in exile. I recalled his infatuation with Constantine, his attachment to her memory, even though he had never returned since leaving in 1959 with his family and the bulk of the Jewish community who wanted to build a secure future in another country.

Every time I visited him at home, he insisted that I listen to a tape by the Jewish singer Simone Tamar. With her marvellous voice and rendition, she would sing the *maalouf* or *muwashshah* of Constantine. She was pictured on the box wearing the luxurious Constantine robe she had been given on her first visit back.

One day Roger told me that Simone's husband had killed her

in a jealous rage after accusing her of being in love with an Arab man. I asked him if the accusation was true. He said, 'I don't know.' Then he added somewhat bitterly, 'I know she loved Constantine.' Roger also loved Constantine. His secret dream was to go back, even if only once. Or for someone to bring him even a single fig from the tree that shaded the window of his room and had been in the garden of his house for generations.

I felt a mix of happiness and shame listening to him tell me in his beloved Constantine accent, whose tones hadn't faded at all, how much he loved that deadly city. My shame was compounded by all that Roger had done to help me over the years since I had come to settle in Paris. He had friends and connections that could (without my asking) make many of the problems faced by someone in my situation much easier.

Once I asked him, 'Why haven't you gone back to visit Constantine? I don't understand what you're afraid of. People still know your family in the neighbourhood and remember them fondly.'

I remember he then said, 'It's not that I'm afraid that people won't know me, but that I won't know the city, its alleys and a house that hasn't been mine for decades.' He continued, 'Let me imagine that that tree is still there bearing figs every year. That that window still looks out on the people I loved. That the narrow alley still leads to places I knew. You know, the hardest thing is for memory to confront a reality that contradicts it.' There was the glint of a tear in his eye that day. Somewhat playfully, he added, 'If I should change my mind, I'll go back with you. I'm afraid to confront my memory alone.'

His words came back to me that day, even though he never mentioned the subject to me again. Did he really manage to deceive his memory? What if he was right? We would have to preserve the original look and feel of our memories and avoid confronting them with reality, which would cause everything inside us to shatter like glass. What matters in such cases is to save memory.

I was convinced by the reasoning. Catherine's phone call had indirectly saved me from making a stupid mistake. The painting would have no historical value if I added or removed something. It would become the rootless painting of a falsified memory. Would it matter then if it was more beautiful?

I looked at the palette of colours in my hand. I still felt I had to use them and the paintbrush that, like me, was nervously awaiting the decisive moment of creation. A simple and logical solution suddenly occurred to me. I replaced the painting on the easel with a new blank canvas. Without thinking, I started painting another bridge over another valley under another sky, adding houses and people.

This time, I paused over all the details of the picture, studying every aspect of them as though in close-up. I surprised myself by rushing to start with these details, as though the bridge no longer concerned me in the end as much as the stones and rocks it stood upon, the plants scattered beneath in the dampness, or dankness, of the depths and the secret paths worn by feet between its rock. Since the days of Maxentius, the old bridge had been oblivious to all this, in its towering nobility unable to see what was happening 700 metres below.

Isn't circumventing bridges the first and timeless goal of mankind that is born between troughs and peaks? This random idea stunned me, and these details stunned me more. They were forcing themselves upon me that day, but hadn't caught my attention a quarter of a century earlier, when I first painted that picture. Was that because in my initial effort I was controlled by the broad outlines of objects, like any beginner, and my ambition then was no greater than a desire to amaze the doctor, or amaze myself, and take on the challenge with one hand?

That day, after a lifetime, I was no longer worried about proving anything to anyone. I just wanted to live my secret dreams and spend the time I had left posing questions that would have been self-indulgent to answer in the past. They weren't questions that could be grasped by a young man, nor by the wounded fighter I was.

Perhaps it hadn't been a time for details. It had been a collective time that we lived as a whole and spent as a whole. It was a time for grand causes, grand slogans and grand sacrifices. Nobody wanted to discuss peripheral matters or think too much about small details. Perhaps it was the foolishness of youth, or of revolutions.

The painting took all of Sunday evening and a large part of the night to complete. But I was happy painting, as though hearing the voice of Dr Kapucki return after a lifetime to say, 'Draw the thing you love most.' Now I was obeying him and painting the same picture in the same confusion.

But what I painted this time wasn't an exercise in painting; it was an exercise in love.

I felt I was painting nothing less than you. You, with all your contradictions. I painted another, more mature version of you. More sinuous. A copy of another painting that grew up with you. I painted that picture with an incredible urge to paint, perhaps even with hunger and a hidden desire. Had desire for you started to infiltrate my brush without my knowledge?

The next day, your voice surprised me at exactly nine o'clock in the morning. A cascade of joy as jasmine blossoms landed on my pillow. I lay in bed, tired out after the night's work. I felt your voice on the phone come in through the window and give me a morning kiss.

'Did I wake you up?'

'No. You didn't wake me up. You kept me up all night, that's all!'

In a half-serious, half-funny Algerian accent you said, 'Why? Everything's OK, I hope.'

I said, 'Because I was painting until really late.'

'That's not my fault.'

'You're only fault is to be my inspiration, O muse!'

As usual when you lost your patience, you suddenly cried out in French, '*Ah, non!*' Then you added, 'I hope you weren't painting me. What a nightmare you are!'

'Where's the nightmare in painting you?'

You continued in irritation, 'Are you mad? You want to turn me into a picture to tour from city to city for everyone I know to see?'

I felt a morning desire to quarrel – perhaps because I was so happy, perhaps because I really was insane and didn't know how to be happy like other people.

I said, 'Didn't you say that we draw inspiration from people we once stopped and stared at, chance encounters? That I paint you only means that I once bumped into you on the street.'

You shouted, 'Are you an idiot? Do you want to convince my uncle and other people that you painted me after bumping into me on the street, waiting at a red light, for example. We only paint what excites us or what we love. Everyone knows that!'

Perhaps that was the confession you were luring me into making and circling around. Or you were foolish enough to believe my claim that I didn't know that. That morning, on the line that separated and joined us at the same time, I had the chance to be honest.

I said, 'Let's suppose, in that case, that I love you.'

I waited for the words to take effect and anticipated a range of responses. After a moment's silence you replied, 'Let's suppose, in that case, that I didn't hear.'

I didn't understand whether you found my admission more or less than you expected, or whether as usual you were playing delightfully with words while knowing that you were playing with my nerves. You jumped from one question to another.

'Where shall we meet?'

That was the more important question, and we decided to take it seriously. We took time discussing where would be a safe place to drink coffee or have lunch. But Paris closed in on us. You only knew student places, and I only went to cafés in my neighbourhood. In the end, we decided to meet in a café near my house.

That was one of my biggest mistakes. I didn't realise at the time that I'd given my memory an address right next to my house and, in consequence, the right to haunt me.

I no longer remember how our madness took up permanent residence in that café. Over the course of two months of stolen happiness, the café, responsive to our changeable moods, gradually came to resemble us. It always presented us with a new corner, and we would meet at various hours, according to your timetable and my work schedule.

You got used to calling me on your way to university every morning at nine o'clock. We would agree on the day's programme, although in the end there was no programme but us.

With each day I was slipping further towards the precipice of your love. As if against stones and rocks, I smashed into the impossibility of it all. But as I loved you, I disregarded the scars on my feet and on my conscience that, prior to you, had been pristine. I kept descending at breakneck speed towards the ultimate insane love.

I felt no guilt about loving you. Well, at least while I was content with your love, once I had convinced myself that I wasn't harming anyone. I dared not dream of more. I was content that overwhelming emotion was passing through me for the first time, from extremes of happiness to extremes of sadness. I was content with love.

When did my mania for you begin? I ask myself whether it was the day I saw you for the first time, or when I was alone with you for the first time, or when I read you for the first time. Or perhaps when I stopped after a lifetime of exile to paint Constantine, like the first time. Perhaps the day you laughed or the day you cried; when you spoke or when you remained silent; when you became my daughter, or when I imagined you were my mother.

Which of the women in you made me fall in love?

I was always surprised by yet another woman inside you. You were like those nested Russian dolls. After a few days you had acquired the features of all women. Whether you were there or not, I was surrounded by women taking turns with me, and I fell in love with them all.

Could I possibly have loved you just one way?

You weren't a woman. You were a metropolis. A metropolis of contradictory women of various ages and features, wearing different perfumes and clothes, more or less modest or forward. Women from before my mother's generation up to your own time. Women, all of whom were you. I learned that too late, after you had swallowed me as a forbidden city swallows its children.

I witnessed your gradual transformation into a city that had for ever lived within me. I witnessed you change unexpectedly day by day as you took on the features of Constantine. You put on her contours, dwelt in her caves, her memories and her secret grottos. You visited her saints and perfumed yourself with her incense. You dressed in a wine-red velvet *kandoura* – the same colour as Mother's – and went back and forth on her bridges. I could almost hear the ring of the heavy gold anklets in the caverns of memory. I could almost see the traces of henna decorating the soles of your feet for a feast.

I reverted to my old accent with you. I pronounced 't' as 'ts' in the Constantine fashion. Flirting, I would call you '*yalla*' – something the men in Constantine no longer do. In tenderness, I would call you 'Omayma', a nickname that Constantine alone inherited from the tribe of Quraysh ages ago. When desire for you robbed me of my last weapon, I would admit defeat in the manner of Constantine lovers: 'I want you. Damn your beauty!' Words that have lost their original meaning over the years and just become words of affection.

Constantine was a hypocrite city that neither admitted to longing nor permitted desire. Like all ancient cities, she took everything by stealth to preserve her reputation. She might have been blessed with her holy saints, but she also had her adulterers and thieves.

I wasn't a thief, a saint or an old man claiming to work miracles that Constantine might bless. I was just a lover who loved you with the obsession, passion and folly of an artist. I created you like the pre-Islamic Arabs created their gods as idols to worship and offer sacrifices to. Perhaps that was what you loved most about my love.

One day you said to me, 'I used to dream that a painter would fall in love with me. I've read incredible stories about them. They're the craziest creative type of all. Their insanity is extreme, sudden and scary – nothing like what they say about poets or musicians. I've read the biographies of Van Gogh, Delacroix, Gauguin, Dalí, Cézanne, Picasso and lots more who are less famous. I never get bored of reading the lives of artists.

'It's not so much their fame that interests me, as their volatility and extremeness. I'm interested in the line between creativity and insanity: the moment that out of the blue they declare that they have transcended and rejected logic. Only that moment deserves consideration, esteem even. They act out of defiance and leave us overawed with the canvas of their life.

'Some artists are happy to distil their genius into their work, but others insist on signing their lives with genius. They leave us a life that cannot be replicated or forged.

'I think that only painters are capable of such madness. A poet couldn't match Van Gogh's despair and contempt for the world that led him to cut off his ear as a gift to a prostitute. Or that little-known artist – I forget his name – who spent his days painting the woman he loved, then hung her portrait and hanged himself from the ceiling of his room. They were united, and he had signed his painting and his life in one swoop.'

'What you find fascinating in the end,' I said, 'is painters' superior ability to torture or mutilate themselves, no?'

You replied, 'No. Painters are specially cursed. They're subject to their own particular correlation: the greater their suffering, hunger and derangement, the higher the price of their paintings. Then they die, and their works go through the roof.

It's as if they have to disappear, and the paintings take their place.'

I didn't discuss your view. I listened to you repeating familiar material, which was surprising, nevertheless, coming from you. I didn't ask myself at the time whether you loved me for my potential madness or for some other reason. Or whether you intended, unconsciously, to turn me into a valuable painting whose price I would pay with my ruin.

Would suffering really increase the value of anything I painted – no matter its quality – when hungry or temporarily insane?

I was content to ask myself about the origins of art and of the sadistic tendency in others. For I believed that the correlation had nothing to do with creativity or art, but with human nature. We are inherently sadistic and take pleasure in hearing about the suffering of others. We believe, out of selfishness, that the artist is a new messiah to be crucified for us. His suffering both grieves us and makes us happy. His story might make us cry, but won't stop us sleeping at night, or make us feed another artist who is dying of hunger or oppression before our eyes. For the same reason, in fact, we find it natural for others' hurt to be turned into poetry or a treasured (or sellable) painting.

Was mania really the exclusive preserve of painters? Wasn't it the shared fate of all creative people, all those haunted with an unhealthy desire to create? By the very logic of creativity, those who create could not be ordinary beings of ordinary character, subject to ordinary sadness and joy, with ordinary standards of gain and loss, of happiness and misery. They were turbulent and mercurial, not understood and with inexplicable behaviour.

That was the first time I talked to you about Ziyad.

'I knew a Palestinian poet who was studying in Algeria,' I said. 'He was happy to be sad and lonely, and content with his modest income as a teacher of Arabic literature, his small dorm room and his two poetry collections. Then his fortunes improved and he moved into a flat. He was going to get married to a student of his with whom he was madly in love, and whose family had finally agreed to the match. Suddenly, he decided to give all of that up and go back to Beirut and join the freedom fighters.

'I tried in vain to get him to stay. I didn't understand his stupid insistence on leaving when finally about to fulfil his dreams. He responded sarcastically, "What dreams? I don't want to kill the homeless Palestinian inside. If I do, all I have left will be valueless."

'Slowly blowing out smoke as if it were a screen to hide behind while he confessed a secret, he added, "Besides, I don't want to belong to a woman. Or, if you like, I don't want to settle down in her. I'm scared of happiness when it turns into house arrest. Some prisons weren't built for poets."

'The girl who loved him came to see me in the hope that I'd convince him that he was crazy to head off to certain death. But it was useless; nothing could persuade him to stay. He was suddenly so far gone that my arguments only further encouraged him to leave.

'I remember he once said to me with a touch of sarcasm, as if enlightening me, "There's a certain greatness in leaving somewhere at the peak of our success. That's the difference between ordinary people and exceptional men!"'

I asked you if you thought that a poet like that was any less demented than a painter who cut off his ear. He swapped ease for hardship and life for death without being forced to. He wanted to go proudly to death, not defeated or compelled. That was his way of overcoming its invincibility.

You asked me avidly, 'Did he die?'

'No. He hasn't died. Or at least he was still alive on the date of his last card. That was about six months ago, at New Year.'

A moment's silence fell between us, as though we were both thinking of him.

I said, 'You know he was an indirect cause of my leaving Algeria? I learnt from him that we can't reconcile all the personalities within us. We have to sacrifice some for others to live. Because we are instinctively drawn towards what matters to us, we only discover our true self when faced with such a choice.'

You interrupted, 'Right, I forgot to ask you why you came to Paris.'

As if revealing feelings couched in disappointment, I sighed and answered, 'My reasons might not convince you, but like that friend, I hate sitting on high awaiting a fall. In particular, I can't bear my position turning me into someone who doesn't resemble me.

'After independence, I shunned the political posts that were offered to me and that everyone else was chasing after. I dreamed of something low-profile where I could make some difference without much fuss or getting tired. So when I was made responsible for publishing in Algeria, I felt I was the man for the job. I had spent the years in Tunisia perfecting my Arabic and had overcome my old complex as an Algerian fluent only in French. In a matter of years, I became bi-cultural. I didn't go to sleep until I had read my fill in one of those languages.

'My life revolved around books. At one point, I almost abandoned painting for writing, especially because in those days some considered painting deviant, a sign of artistic decadence unconnected to the liberation struggle.

'When I came back to Algeria, I was overflowing with words. And because words aren't neutral, I was also full of ideals and values. I wanted mindsets and values to change. This meant a revolution in the Algerian mind, still untouched despite the historical upheavals. But it wasn't the right time for my great dream, which I don't want to call the "cultural revolution". Those two words, together or separately, no longer signify anything to us.

'Major mistakes were being made in good faith. Change had begun in the factories, peasant villages, construction and infra-structure. People, however, were left till last. How could a wretched, empty person, drowning in the mundane problems of daily existence and with a mindset decades behind the rest of the world, build a nation or undertake an industrial, agricultural or any other revolution? All the world's industrial revolutions began with the people themselves. That's how Japan and Europe became what they are.

'Only the Arabs erect buildings and call the walls a revolution. They take land from one person to give to another and call that a revolution. When we don't have to import our own food, that'll be a revolution. When citizens are as advanced as the machinery they operate, that'll be a revolution.'

All of a sudden my voice had a new tone, full of the bitterness and disappointment that had accumulated over the years. You looked at me in some astonishment and perhaps silent admira-tion as I told you for the first time about my political sorrows.

You asked me, 'Is that why you came to France, then?'

'Not exactly,' I said, 'but probably because of the results of mistakes like those. One day I decided to leave behind medioc-rity and the naive books that I had to read and publish in the name of literature and culture to be consumed by a people hungry for knowledge.

'I felt I was selling something off, past its use-by date. I felt somehow responsible for dumbing down the population. I was spoon-feeding them lies and had turned from an intellectual into a contemptible policeman. It was my job to spy on the alphabet and excise the occasional word. What others wrote was my sole responsibility. I felt ashamed inviting a writer to my office to persuade them to remove an idea or opinion that I shared.

'One day, Ziyad – the Palestinian poet I told you about – came to see me. That was the first time we met. I had called and asked him to cut or change some text in his poetry that seemed to me overly critical of certain regimes and Arab leaders. He made clear allusions to them and called them everything under the sun.

'I'll never forget the look he gave me that day. His eyes stopped at my amputated arm for a moment, then he gave me a withering look and said, "Sir, my poems do not undergo amputation. Give me back my book. I'll publish it in Beirut."

'I felt my Algerian blood stir in my veins and was about to get up and slap him. But I calmed down and tried to ignore his provocative looks and words.

'What intervened for him at that moment? Perhaps his Palestinian identity, or the courage that no other writer had shown before. Perhaps his poetic genius – his collection was far and away the best I read in that dismal period. Plus, I felt in my heart that poets, like prophets, were always right.

'His words brought me back to reality with a shaming slap. This poet was right. How had I failed to realise that for years I had only turned the works before me into dismembered and defaced versions of themselves, just like me?

'I cast an absent-minded glance at the cover of the manuscript and said defiantly, "I'll publish it word for word." There was some machismo in my stance, a bravado that no civil servant, whatever his rank, could flourish without putting his job on the line. After all, civil servants have traded their manhood for the job!

'When his collection came out it caused me some headaches. Yet I felt there was something phoney I could no longer put up with. What stopped me allowing vile, bloody regimes to be discredited? We were still keeping silent over their crimes in the name of steadfastness and unity. Why was it OK to criticise some regimes and not others, all depending on the way the wind was blowing for the captain of our ship?

'My despair slowly grew bitter. Should I change my job, swapping one set of problems for another, and become a player in a different game? What to do with all the dreams I had collected over my years of exile and struggle? What to do with forty years, one amputated arm and one good one? What to do with the proud, stubborn man inside me who refused to haggle over his freedom, and that other man who had survived by learning to go against his principles and adapt to every job?

'I had to kill one of them for the other to survive. I made the choice.

'Meeting Ziyad was a turning point in my life. I discovered subsequently that stories of close friendship – like violent love stories – often begin with confrontation, provocation and a trial of strength. Two highly intelligent and sensitive men with strong personalities, men who had taken up arms and grown used to the language of violence and confrontation, cannot meet without a clash. Out of mutual defiance, that first clash was inevitable. We needed it to understand we were made of the same stuff.

'Afterwards, Ziyad slowly became the one friend I felt really at ease with. We would meet several times a week, stay up late drinking, talk at length about politics and art, curse everyone and part happy. It was 1973. He was thirty and two poetry collections old: some sixty poems, as many as his scattered dreams. My life consisted of a few paintings, little joy, much disappointment, two or three posts I'd moved between since independence, with vague prestige – a driver, a car, a vague bitter taste in my mouth.

'Ziyad left two or three months after the October 1973 war. He went back to Beirut to join up with the PFLP, which he had been involved with since before coming to Algeria. He left me all his favourite books that had accompanied him from country to country. He also bequeathed me his philosophy of life, some memories and that girlfriend who came to see me every now and again to ask after him. He refused to write to her; she refused to forget him.'

Emerging from a long silence, you said, 'Why didn't he write to her?'

'Perhaps because he didn't like to disturb the past. He wanted her to forget him and get married quickly. He wished her a fate different from his.'

'And did she get married?'

'I don't know. I haven't heard from her for a few years. Probably, yes. She was very beautiful. But I don't believe she's forgotten him. It would be hard for a woman to forget a man like Ziyad.'

At that moment I felt your thoughts drift away. Did you start dreaming about him? Did I begin a succession of stupid mistakes that day as I answered your many questions about him in a way that roused your curiosity both as a woman and a writer?

I told you a lot about his poems. In his last collection he wrote poems like someone firing in the air at a wedding or funeral, saying goodbye to a lover or relative. He was bidding farewell to his old friend poetry, swearing he would only write with his gun from then on. That man wasn't really writing, he was just emptying a machine gun loaded with anger and revolution into the words. Once he no longer trusted anything, he fired bullets at everything. Ah, Ziyad was incredible!

I must admit again today that he really was incredible, and that I was a fool. I shouldn't have talked to you about him under the illusion that mountains don't meet. Why did I talk about him with such enthusiasm, with such lyricism? Did I want to use him to get closer to you and grow in your eyes by convincing you that I had old links with writers and poets? Or did I describe him in glowing terms because until that day I believed I was like him and was describing nothing less than myself to you?

Perhaps all of that was true, but I also wanted you to discover Arabism in men so exceptional it seemed they could not be of this nation. Men born in different Arab cities, belonging to different generations and political trends, but who all had a certain kinship with your father and his loyalty, nobility, pride and Arab identity. All of them had or would die for the sake of this nation.

I didn't want you to shrink into the shell of the lesser nation and turn into an archaeologist of memories within one city. Every Arab city could be called Constantine. Every Arab who gave up everything and went to die for a cause could be called Taher. And you could be a relative of his.

I wanted you to fill your novels with other, more lifelike heroes. Heroes who would take you out of your political and emotional adolescence. Didn't I, foolishly, say to you once, 'If you knew a man like Ziyad, you would no longer love Zorba or need to create fictional heroes. This nation already has heroes beyond the imagination of writers.'

I didn't, then, anticipate all that would happen. I would be the one to turn into an archaeologist, digging between your lines for traces of Ziyad and asking which one of us you loved more. For whom did you build your last tomb and your last novel? For him or for me?

That day, as we were about to get up and leave, you suddenly kissed me on the cheek. You said in your Algerian accent, 'Khaled, I love you.' At that instant everything around me came to a standstill. My life came to a halt on your lips. I could have embraced you right then, or kissed you, or responded with a thousand I-love-yous and then a thousand more. I just sat down in amazement and ordered another coffee from the waiter. I said the first thing that came to mind. 'Why today in particular?'

You answered in a lowered voice, 'Because I respect you more today. It's the first time in months that you've talked about yourself. I discovered incredible things today. I didn't think you'd come to Paris for those reasons. Artists usually come here seeking fame or fortune. I didn't expect you'd given up everything there to start from scratch here.'

I interrupted you to correct what you were saying. 'I didn't start from scratch. We never start from scratch when we start a new direction. We just start from ourselves. I started from my convictions.'

I felt that day that we were entering a new stage of our relationship, that you were suddenly malleable to my convictions, into the shape of my hopes and dreams to come.

I remembered something I had read in a book of art criticism: 'In a painting, the artist does not present us with a personal portrait. He only gives us a rough sketch of himself, the outlines of his features to come.' You were my sketch to come. You were my features to come, my city to come. I wanted you more beautiful, more wonderful. I wanted you to have another face, not mine exactly, and another heart, not mine, other fingerprints unconnected to the blue marks time had left on my body and soul.

That day, after some hesitation, I suggested you come and visit me one day in my studio so I could show you what I had been working on. I was happy that you accepted my offer without hesitation or fear. I was careful for you not to think badly of me, and had decided to dismiss the idea if you were uncomfortable. But you surprised me as you laughed, as happy as a child who has been invited to the circus. 'Wow! I'd be really happy to come and see it!'

The next day you called me to say you had two hours free in the afternoon when you could come round. I put down the receiver and started daydreaming, leaping ahead of the intervening hours and of time. Would you really be in my house? Would you really ring the doorbell, sit down on this sofa, walk in front of me here? You, at last?

At last I would sit next to you, not opposite you. At last no waiter would bother us. The eyes of patrons and passing strangers would not bother us. At last we could talk and be sad and happy, our moods unobserved.

Out of joy I went and opened the door in advance, not realising I was opening my heart to a maelstrom. How crazy to bring you here. To open up my other secret world and turn you into part of this house. This house, which, as I waited, became my Eden and might become my hell after you. Was I aware of all this at the time? Or was I a happy fool of a lover, seeing no further than the next date? I asked myself subsequently whether it was really only my latest painting and my secret garden of obsession that I wanted to show you.

I remembered Catherine and her painting. It was my apology for having been unable to paint anything but her face that day in the College of Fine Arts. Others competed to depict the inspiration of her nudity. When I suggested that she come round and see the painting, I didn't expect its innocence would give rise to a less-than-innocent relationship that had lasted for two years.

Did inviting you to my studio lack sense or contain a secret wish to set a train of events in motion? Perhaps I did it with Catherine's words as she surrendered herself to me in mind. In that studio, amidst the chaos of blank canvases and unfinished paintings leaning against the walls, she said, with deliberate intent, 'This place incites love.'

I answered her matter-of-factly, 'I didn't know that before now.'

Was it my studio that incited love? Or does every creative space induce madness? Still, I knew you weren't Catherine, and never would be. There were barriers between us that no obsession could break down.

Today, six years since that visit, I go over that day as if reliving all its psychological shocks. You came in wearing a white dress (why white?), your perfume beating you to the tenth floor, my racing heart taking the lift before you. Halting words of welcome in French (why French?). I almost kissed your cheek, but shook your hand (why a handshake?). I asked if you found the house easily. The words came out in French (why French again?). Perhaps that language, essentially foreign to my traditions and psychological barriers, might have given me the freedom and courage to speak.

You sat down on the sofa. As you looked over the room, you said, 'I didn't imagine your house would be like this. It's great, really tastefully done!'

I asked, 'How did you imagine it?'

'Messy and full of things.'

Laughing, I said, 'I don't need to live in a dusty garret strewn with junk to be an artist. That's another misconception about painters. I might be a mess, but I don't have to be messy. It's the only way for me to create some order inside.

'I chose this high-rise flat because it's filled with light, which is all a painter needs. A painting isn't a space filled with chaos, but with light and the play of shadow and colour.'

I opened the large window and invited you on to the balcony. I said, 'See this window? It's the bridge between me and this city. From my balcony I deal with Paris's changeable sky. Every morning, Paris reveals its latest mood to me, and I sit on the balcony watching it change from one state to another. I often paint in front of this window or sit outside watching the Seine as it turns into a vessel for the tears of a city expert at weeping. I like to sit here at the edge of the rain, close to it but sheltered at the same time. Seeing the rain induces extreme feelings. As Malek Haddad wrote, "Man feels young again when it rains."'

You looked at the sky as if praying for it to rain and said in Arabic, 'The rain makes me want to write. What about you?'

I almost answered, 'Me, it makes me want to make love.'

I looked at the sky for a long time. It was the clear blue of June. The blue suddenly annoyed me. Perhaps I was used to it being grey. Perhaps because I secretly hoped it would rain right then, conspiring to throw you into my arms like a drenched sparrow. I said nothing of all that.

I shifted my gaze from the sky into your eyes. It was the first time I had seen them in the light of day. I felt I was becoming acquainted with them. I was confused, like the first time I had seen them. They were lighter than usual, more beautiful perhaps.

They held a certain depth and calm, a certain innocence and a lover's collusion. Maybe I stared for a long time. You asked me, as if you already knew the answer, 'Why are you looking at me like that?' Your voice in Arabic was a unique musical rendition.

I found my answer in the opening lines of a poem. 'Your eyes are two palm-tree forests in early light/Or two balconies in receding moonlight.'

You asked me in disbelief, 'Do you also know Al-Sayyab's poetry? Wow!'

I gave an answer with a double meaning, 'I know "The Hymn of the Rain".'

I felt that perhaps you loved me more at that moment, as if I had become Al-Sayyab to you as well.

Like every time I surprised you with a line of poetry or an Arabic saying, you asked me, 'When did you read that?'

This time I replied, 'I've done nothing but read, my dear. Other people's wealth may be reckoned in banknotes, mine is in the titles of books. I'm a rich man, as you can see. I read every-thing I could get my hands on, just as they stole everything they could get their hands on!'

Staring at the grey stone bridge over the Seine, ultramarine in summer, you said, 'You're lucky to have this view. It's lovely to have a balcony overlooking the Seine. What's the bridge called?'

'It's Pont Mirabeau. I recently discovered that Apollinaire immortalised it in some poems, which I came across in one of his collections. It seems he was infatuated with it. Poets, like paint-ers, have an irresistible habit of immortalising any place they lived in or passed through and loved. They might give immortal-ity to an unknown farm or a café they once wrote in or a city they passed through by chance but which they fell in love with for ever.'

You asked, 'Have you painted this bridge?'

With a sigh, I answered, 'No, because we don't necessarily paint what we see, but what we once saw and fear we'll never see again. That's why Delacroix spent his life painting Moroccan cities that he only spent a few days in, and Atlan spent his life painting one city – Constantine.

'I wasn't aware of this until two months ago when I stood here opposite the window to paint my latest picture. I was feeling unusually anxious. My eyes were seeing the Pont Mirabeau and the Seine, but my hands were painting another bridge in another valley in another city. When I had finished, I had painted nothing less than the viaduct of Sidi Rachid and the Wadi Rummal. I realised that in the end we don't paint where we live, but what lives in us.'

You asked avidly, 'Can I see that painting?'

Leading you to my studio, I said, 'Of course.'

You stopped in the spacious room filled with paintings. You looked at the walls and at the paintings stacked on the floor with the amazement of a child in an enchanted city. With the same sense of wonder, you said, 'Wow, this is incredible. You know, I've never visited an artist's studio before.'

I wanted to say, 'No woman before you has visited it.' But Catherine's portrait leaning against the wall reminded me that another woman had passed through. My thoughts turned to her for a moment, and you suddenly said, 'Where's the painting you were talking about?'

I took you over to the other side of the room. The picture was still on the easel, as if from its superior position it were erasing all the other paintings scattered around.

There is an erotic relationship of sorts between a painter and his most recent picture. A silent emotional complicity only broken by the appearance of another, virgin, painting in the spotlight. The painter, like the writer, is unable to resist the painful siren call of the colour white. A white space always tempts him towards the mania of creativity. How then, after two months, could I still resist the challenge of the colour white and the seduction of all the canvases that flaunted their whiteness in my face?

Why had I refused to paint anything after that picture, preferring to leave it on the easel to attest that it was my mistress, and mistress of all the paintings around me? It was as if I had refused to move it into a corner or on to a wall like a passing lover. Was it possible for a painting to intoxicate me more than a woman? Perhaps, because I had never before made love to the homeland in paint!

Looking at the painting, you said, 'It's similar to your first painting, *Nostalgia*, but lots of the details are different. Especially the crude earth colours you've used. They give it maturity and more life.'

Turning my gaze from the picture to you, I said, 'You filled it with life. It's of you.'

'Me?'

'Do you remember the day I told you on the phone that I had stayed up very late the previous night painting you? You accused me of being crazy and were scared I'd expose your features. Don't be scared. I'll never paint you, and no one will know that you passed through my life. The brush has honour, too.

'You are a city, not a woman. Whenever I paint Constantine, I paint you. Only you will know that.'

Suddenly, as your eyes flicked towards the portrait of Catherine, you said, 'And her?' In your question there was the defiant selfishness of a child, and the defiant jealousy of a woman.

Picking the painting off the floor I said, 'Does this picture really annoy you?'

Plainly lying, you said, 'No.'

I felt that I was capable of anything at that moment and continued, 'If you want, I'll destroy it in front of you.'

You shouted, 'No! Are you insane?'

'I'm not insane,' I said calmly. 'This painting means nothing to me. A passing woman in a passing city.'

Looking at me with an unsettling smile, you said, 'She's your other city, no?'

Where did that last shot at the painting come from?

My admission held a clear hint. 'No. She isn't my city. She's my other pillow or, if you like, just my other bed!'

I sensed a slight reddening of your cheeks. Conflicting emotions and sensations had run through you, instantly changing your expression. You mumbled quietly as if talking to yourself, 'It doesn't matter.'

Taking you by the arm, I said, 'Don't be jealous of this picture. There's only one woman in this house you should be jealous of. It's her . . .'

You looked over at where I was pointing. There was a life-size statue of a woman standing on the floor.

'Her?' you asked, 'Why her?'

'Because, up to now, she's the only woman I have felt comfortable with. She has shared most of my years of exile. I used to have a scale model of her. Then two years ago I decided to give myself a bigger version. That was a bout of insanity. But I don't regret buying her. She's a lot like me. I've got one arm and she lacks both. We lost our limbs at different times for different reasons, but we endure together. Our disability won't deny us immortality.'

You made no comment; it seemed you didn't believe me. Wasn't it insane for a man to live with a woman's statue? Even if the man was an artist and the statue none other than Venus!

Your problem was that you were captivated by half-crazed genius, but were too rational to realise. So whenever I wanted to give you proof of my madness, you didn't fully believe me.

With a woman's silliness, you just stole glances at Catherine's portrait, as if it alone interested you. I tried to understand you. What annoyed you about that painting? Did it silently come between us, reminding you that another woman had passed through my life? Or was it the woman's blondeness, the seductive pout of her lips and her eyes concealed behind locks of wild hair?

Were you jealous of the picture or the person? Why did you have the right to reproach me for one picture I had painted of a woman, when I had no right to make you answer for everything you had written prior to me, for that real or imaginary man you tortured me with?

Your gaze returned to the last painting. You studied it for a while then said, 'So, that's me!'

'Perhaps it wasn't you,' I said, 'but the way I see you. You have something of the contours of that city, the curvature of her bridges, her pride, dangers, caves and valleys, the foaming river that splits her body, her femininity and secret seductiveness, her vertigo.'

You interrupted, smiling, 'You're dreaming. How can you find an affinity between me and that bridge? How did the idea occur to you? Don't you know I only like the small wooden bridges of Christmas cards, covered in snow and glitter and crossed by sleighs? Constantine's iron bridges suspended in space are frightening. Sad. I don't recall ever walking over one or looking down without feeling panic and vertigo.'

'But desire is vertigo,' I said. 'It's standing on the edge of an irresistible drop. It's viewing the world from the summit of fear. It's a mass of conflicting emotions and sensations that draw you to the depths and the heights at the same time. Falling is always easier than standing on shaky legs. To paint you as a proud bridge like this means admitting you are my vertigo – something no man has said to you before.

'I don't understand how you can love Constantine and hate bridges. How you can seek to create, but fear vertigo. Without the bridges there would be no city; without the gasp of vertigo, no one would love or create.'

You were listening to me as though discovering something basic you hadn't realised before. Yet you said, 'Perhaps in the end you're right. But I would have preferred it if you'd painted me and not this bridge. Any woman who gets to know a painter dreams in secret that he will immortalise her, paint her – not a city. Equally, any man who gets to know a woman writer hopes she will write something about him, not about something else unconnected to him. It's narcissism, or pride or something unexplainable.'

Your admission surprised me. I felt a little disappointed.

Had I painted a fake representation of you? Was there really no communion between you and the bridge? Was the painting an authentic copy of my memory, while, ultimately, you dreamt of becoming a copy of Catherine, turned into an ordinary portrait in a compromising pose and with a heavily made-up face like hers?

Hadn't we been cured of that complex?

With a note of despair, I said to you, 'If that's what you want, I'll paint you.'

You answered in a voice tinged with shame. 'I confess that from the beginning I've been desperate for you to paint me. I would keep the picture as a memento, provided, if possible, you didn't sign it.'

As I grasped the amazing logic, I felt the urge to laugh or, more accurately, to grieve. I had the right to sign abstract paintings that bore no resemblance to you. But I couldn't sign myself at the bottom of your image. My name would never be joined with the only woman I had loved, even if only once and at the bottom of a painting. Some only bought my signature, not my paintings. But you wanted an unsigned painting.

I was a stubborn man who rejected this new logic of things, and refused in the name of love to turn you into a stray painting that could be claimed by any brush and any artist.

My silence threw you. In a semblance of apology you said, 'Would it upset you to paint me?'

Sarcastically I said, 'No. I've just realised again that you are an authentic copy of a nation whose features I once defined, only for others to sign my achievements. There are always signatures ready for such occasions. Since time immemorial there have been those who write history and those who sign it. That's why I hate paintings that are easy to forge.'

I wonder if you understood all I said to you then. I suddenly began to have doubts about your political awareness. In the end, all you cared about was the question of your picture.

As you were leaving the studio, you said, 'You know, we won't see each other for two months. I'm going to Algeria next week.'

I stopped you in the corridor and exclaimed, 'Is what you're saying true?'

'Of course,' you said. 'I always spend my summer holidays with my mother in Algeria. I have to go back next week with my uncle and his family. There won't be anyone left in Paris.'

I stood stunned in the passageway. I gripped your arm as if to stop you leaving and asked you sadly, 'And me?'

'You? I'll miss you a lot. I think it'll be a bit painful for us – it's our first separation. But we'll trick time into passing fast.' Then, as if you wished to solve a problem, or make it disappear quickly, you continued, 'Don't be sad. You can write, or call me on the phone. We'll stay in touch.'

I was on the verge of tears, like a child whose mother has told him she will be going away without him. You were breaking this to me with a degree of sadism that shocked me, as if my suffering was attractive to you.

Should I have grabbed the hem of your dress like a child and burst into tears? Should I have spent hours talking to you, persuading you that I wouldn't be able to live without you? That after you, time wouldn't be counted in hours or days? That I was addicted to you?

How to persuade you that I had become a slave to your voice over the phone? A slave to your laughter, your figure, your delectable feminine presence, your impulsive inconsistency in everything, at all times. Slave to a city and memory that you had become, to all that you ever touched or passed.

Sadness suddenly surged over me as I stood in the corridor looking at you in the shock of disbelief.

You were so close we were touching in a way that hadn't happened before. I searched your face for something that revealed your feelings. But I understood nothing.

Did your perfume, which permeated my senses and paralysed my mind, make me unable to look deeply? I was only aware that in a few minutes you would be far away, just as then you were close.

You lifted your face towards me.

I wanted to say something I've now forgotten. But before I said a word, my lips went ahead and devoured your lips in a sudden passionate kiss. My one arm was around you like a belt and in one swoop turned you into a piece of me.

You squirmed a little in my arms like a fish out of water and then surrendered.

Your long black hair suddenly came loose over your shoulders like a black gypsy shawl. An old desire to pull you by your hair in a frenzy of forbidden passion awoke. My lips were still searching for a way to leave my signature on your lips outlined in advance for love.

This had to happen.

You were the one who had shadowed your eyes and made your red lips feverish. Could I have held out for long against your femininity? My fifty years were devouring your lips and the fever was spreading to me. I finally melted into a kiss with the taste of Constantine and the confusion of Algeria.

There was nothing more beautiful than your fire. The kisses of exile had been cold, if only you knew. Overly red lips lacking warmth had chilled me. The bed with no memory had been cold. Let me stock up for the icy years. Let me bury my head in your neck. Like a sad child, let me hide in your arms.

Let me steal from fleeting life one moment and dream that all these flaming spaces are mine.

Set me aflame, Constantine.

Your lips were delicious, like two slowly ripened mulberries. Your body was fragrant, like a jasmine tree opening in haste.

My hunger for you was a lifetime of thirst and waiting. A lifetime of complexes, obstacles and contradictions. A lifetime of desire and shame, of inherited values, of suppressed desires. A lifetime of confusion and hypocrisy.

On your lips I gathered my life's dispersion.

In one kiss from you I resolved all my opposites and contradictions. The man I killed long ago in obedience to another man came back to life. The man who was once a comrade of your father's. A man who almost was your father.

On your lips I was born and died at the same instant. I killed one man and brought another to life.

Did time stop at that moment?

Were we at last the same age? Was memory wiped away for a time?

I don't know.

All I knew was that you were mine and that I wanted to scream right then one of Goethe's Faust's screams, 'Stop, time. You are so beautiful!'

But time didn't stop. It was lying in wait for me as usual. Plotting against me as usual. After a few moments you were looking at your watch in an effort to hide your confusion and remind me of your need to go back to university.

I suggested we have a cup of coffee in a final attempt to make you stay.

You were in front of the mirror, tidying up your appearance and gathering up your hair. You said, 'I'd prefer something cold, if that's possible.'

I left you in the living room and went to the kitchen. Deliberately I didn't hurry back, as if I'd become ashamed of the traces of my kiss on your lips.

When I came back, you were studying the titles of the books on the bookshelf and picking some of them up. You pulled a slim volume off the shelf. As you looked at the cover, you asked me, 'Isn't this the collection by your friend the poet you were telling me about?'

I answered happily, having finally found a way out of my confusion. 'Yes. There's another collection of his on the same shelf.'

'Is he called Ziyad al-Khalil?' you asked. 'I've heard that name before.'

You handled the book. I saw you look for a long time at his picture on the back. You read a few lines, then said, 'Can I borrow these two collections? I'd prefer to read them at leisure over the summer, and I've got nothing else to read.'

I answered, eagerly or stupidly, 'Of course. It's a good idea. I'm certain those two books will leave their mark on your writing. You'll find some excellent pieces, especially in the latest one, *Plans for a Love to Come*. It's the best thing Ziyad has written.'

Delighted, you buried the books in your handbag. It was the delight of a child going home with a toy she loved.

Of course, then, I hadn't been aware that later on I would be your other plaything, and that those two books would also leave their mark on the course of our story.

Gradually you restored your usual face and normal expression, as if the whirlwind of my love hadn't touched you. Was that an act or was it real?

I tried to forget my frustration with you in front of the painting that had been the primary reason for your visit. I also tried to ease your frustration. I said, 'I will paint you. Your picture will be my leisure this summer.' Without any particular intention, I continued, 'You have to come and see me one more time and sit for me so I can paint you. Or give me a photograph to copy.'

You said, as if the answer was prepared, 'I don't have enough time to come and see you again, and I don't have a photograph with me. You can make do with the photo on the back of my book until I come back.'

I admit that, then, I also didn't understand whether your response hinted that you would never come back to my house, or you were just replying with automatic innocence.

Hadn't you insisted that I paint you? So why did you turn that picture into a personal issue only I was interested in?

I didn't discuss it with you. Whatever the case, I knew I would paint you. Perhaps because I didn't know how to turn down a request from you, or perhaps because I didn't know how I would spend the summer without making you present, even as a painting.

You left after kissing my cheeks and promising me we'd meet soon. After our kiss it was no longer possible to shake hands.

I was aware that something in our relationship had changed. After that day it would no longer be possible for the genie that had suddenly emerged from deep inside us to go back into the bottle where we had sealed it.

I was aware that in a few moments I had moved with you from love to desire. From innocent emotion to hunger, and that it would be hard from then on to forget the taste of your kiss and the heat of your body pressed against mine for a few minutes.

How long did our kiss last? Two minutes? Three? Five?

Could those few minutes have caused all that happened to me afterwards?

How come I felt no regret or shame regarding my memory of *Si* Taher? That day, I committed my first moral betrayal.

No. There was only love in my heart.

I was filled with desire, lust, obsession. Finally, I was happy. Why ruin my happiness with regrets, with questions that would lead me to misery?

I don't remember who said, 'Regret is the second mistake we make.' There was no room in my heart, not even a tiny space, for anything but love to well from.

Wasn't the whole thing crazy?

How did I allow myself to be so happy when I knew I had had nothing of you in the end except a few minutes of stolen happiness, and that before me was a lifetime of torture?

Chapter Four

YOUR DEPARTURE HAD THE same taste as my first tragedy. In a matter of days loneliness reduced me to the level of an orphaned painting on the wall. The opening line from a novel by Malek Haddad that I had once loved came to mind: 'How great is God! As great as my loneliness. I see the Creator and he seems a painting.'

In my isolation and loneliness I was both the creator and the painting. I was hanging from the wall of a vast and cold universe, waiting for you.

After you left I entered a downward spiral of mental and emotional disappointment. I was living with the inexplicable anxiety that always came before and after an exhibition, when I would spontaneously run through my joys and disappointments.

So my exhibition was over. As usual, only the specialist French press and some émigré Arab magazines had shown any interest. Yet I could say it had received sufficient media coverage, and there was a consensus that Paris had witnessed an Arab artistic event.

Only the Algerian press ignored it, out of simple neglect, as usual. One newspaper and a weekly magazine mentioned it in passing, as if they lacked newsprint, not news. Abdel-Qadir, the journalist friend who had promised me he would be in Paris for personal reasons and interview me at length didn't show up.

Although I didn't love the limelight or sitting for hours with a journalist to talk about myself, I had hoped the interview would take place so that I could finally address at length the only person who really concerned me – the Algerian reader.

Abdel-Qadir called to tell me that he had to stay in Algeria to cover one of the festivals that were on the rise in those days, for reasons only God, and a few others, knew. I didn't blame him. There was no comparison between an organised, official festival or gathering, paid for in hard currency, and an exhibition, no matter whose and no matter the years spent on the paintings.

In the end, I couldn't even really blame the Algerian press. What enjoyment or entertainment could an exhibition of arty paintings offer to Algerian citizens about to explode, or commit suicide even, and with no time for contemplation or taste. They preferred a Rai music festival, where they could dance and shout and sing until dawn. On those suspect pop songs, they might spend the few dinars stuffed in their pockets and the sexual energy accumulated in their bodies. That was the only real 'wealth' our youth possessed. And just like our currency, they could only spend it on the black market in despair. Some had realised this before others.

In 1969, at the height of the desperate cultural vacuum being endured by the nation, someone, over a few days, came up with the idea for the biggest festival ever seen in Algeria or Africa. It was called the Pan-African Festival, and the whole African continent and its tribes were invited to spend a week singing and dancing (at times naked) in the streets of Algiers in honour of the Revolution.

How many millions were spent on this first and last festival of joy? Its most important achievement was to cover up the trial of a historic leader. During the festival, his men were interrogated and tortured in closed sessions in the name of that Revolution. The leader was also called Taher, and though we weren't friends, I didn't have any particular hostility towards him. He had once also been a fighter and a commander. I started to be aware of the game and greed of power and became wary of regimes that held many festivals and conferences. They were always hiding something!

Was it a coincidence that my problems began back then, and I started to have a bitter taste in my mouth?

I met that friend a few months later. He apologised sincerely and promised not to miss my next exhibition. I patted him on the shoulder and said, laughing, 'Don't worry. In a few days' time the name of the festival will be forgotten, but history will definitely remember my name, even if after a hundred years!'

Joking, but with a hint of seriousness, he said, 'Do you know you're arrogant?'

'I'm arrogant,' I replied, 'so as not to be despised. We have no choice, my friend. We belong to a people that doesn't respect its creative artists. If we lost our arrogance and pride, we'd be trampled by the illiterate and ignorant!'

Later I asked myself if I really was arrogant. After a little thought, I understood that I was only arrogant when I stood, brush in hand, before a blank canvas. How arrogant did I have to be, then, to conquer its blankness and take its virginity as I circumvented my embarrassment with an outpouring of manhood and the virility of my brush?

But as soon as I had finished and wiped all the colours off my hand, I would fling myself on to the nearby sofa and look at the painting in amazement, to discover that I alone had sweated and bled in front of it. They were Arab females, greeting my revolution with fearsome, inherited indifference.

When I would collapse in disappointment, I would rip up a picture that annoyed me and throw it in the wastepaper basket. Some paintings were so naive and cold that they gave me a sexual as well as a creative block. Even so, no one would ever know, or perhaps even anticipate, my weakness and secret defeats. Others would only see my triumphs, hanging on the wall in elegant frames. The wastepaper basket would always be in a corner of my studio and my heart, out of sight.

To sit before an expanse ripe for creation meant being a god or else finding another vocation. Could I have been a god? Me, whom your love turned into a ruined Greek city of tall, weathered columns?

Was my arrogance of any use while every day your love was causing me to crumble from the inside? Two months and nothing but an impossible phone number and parting words that had dried up my brushes.

Silence had become my favourite colour.

I understood the opposition between painting and your form of writing. You emptied yourself of things when you wrote about them, as though killing them with words. When I painted I became fuller, as though investigating life through forgotten details. I would grow more attached to them and re-hang them on the walls of memory.

After I'd settled you in my heart, wouldn't painting you mean installing you in the rooms of my house, too? That was a mistake I decided from the outset not to make. But night after night I discovered the futility of my decision.

Why was night my undoing? Because whenever I was alone

with myself, I was alone with you? Or because art has secret rituals of longing, born mostly at timeless, lawless night?

Teetering on the edge of reason and madness, on the divide between the possible and the impossible that is blacked out by darkness, I committed the sin of you.

With my lips I drew the boundaries of your body.

With my manhood I drew the boundaries of your femininity.

With my fingers I drew where the brush could not reach.

With one arm I embraced you. I planted you and harvested. I stripped you naked and clothed you. I changed the contours of your body to meet my ideals.

Woman in the guise of nation, give me another chance at heroism. Let my one arm change your ideals of manhood, love and pleasure. How many arms have embraced you without warmth? How many hands have run over you, leaving scratches on your neck and a signature beneath your wounds? They loved you and they hurt you, but it was wrong.

Thieves, pirates and bandits loved you. But their hands were not cut off. Only those who loved you selflessly became handicapped. They had it all; I had only you.

That night, like every night, you were mine. Who would take your vision away from me, ban your body from my bed, steal your perfume from my senses, prevent me restoring you with my other hand? You were my secret pleasure, my secret obsession, my secret attempt to overthrow logic.

Every night your fortresses fell into my hand and your guards surrendered. You came in your nightdress and stretched out next to me. I ran my hand through your long black hair flowing over my pillow. You trembled like a bird drenched by the rain, and your sleeping body responded.

How did this happen? What led me to lose my mind? Perhaps

it was your voice that I grew addicted to, that cascaded love and music and sprinkled droplets of pleasure over me.

Your love was a caller asking, '*Washik?*' A phone that wrapped me at night in a blanket of kisses, that left its eyes as a lamp of passion next to me when the lights went out. It was afraid for me from the dark. It was afraid for me from my loneliness and old age. It took me back to my childhood without consulting me. It told me bedtime stories believed by children, and sang me lullabies. Was it lying? Would a mother lie? No child would ever believe that!

What brought me to the brink of derangement? Perhaps the impossible kiss I stole from you. But could kisses have caused all of that?

I remembered reading about kisses that changed lives, but I never believed it.

How could Nietzsche, the philosopher of power, who spent years investigating might and superiority, be bowled over by a single kiss? A kiss stolen by chance on an outing to a temple in the company of Lou, the woman he loved more than any other writer or poet of the time. These included Apollinaire, who long courted her and wept over her on this very Pont Mirabeau. Because her name sounded like *loup* – 'wolf' in French – this was, to him, decisive proof of his fate with her.

Nietzsche said, 'When you visit a woman, do not forget to bring a stick.' But before Lou he was a crushed, weak man, lacking will. His mother even said, 'That woman only left my son three choices: marry her, kill himself or go mad!'

Such was Nietzsche's fate when he loved. Should I have been ashamed of my weakness before you, when I wasn't the philosopher of power or Samson, who lost his hair and his legendary strength because of a kiss?

Was I ashamed of your kiss? Did I regret it? Me, whose life began on your lips?

I don't know how Nietzsche got over the woman he didn't marry. Did he commit suicide or go mad? All I know was that I spent two months in mental turmoil, during which I almost touched the point of insanity – the kind of insanity that seduced you and that you often praised, as you believed it was the only proof of an artist's genius.

So be it. After all these years, I will confess to you that I did reach the fearsome limits of irrationality.

Was it simply passion, or an unconscious wish to give you the plaything you had yet to acquire: the madman you dreamed of?

At that time I often went over my story with you, chapter by chapter. Each time I reached opposite conclusions. Sometimes your love seemed to be a myth too big for you and me. Something predestined perhaps centuries before, at a time when Constantine was called Cirta.

At times I would ask myself whether I was a man whose memory had struck you and whose madness had seduced you to start a story. Or whether I was just the victim of a literary crime you dreamed of committing in a future book. Then your childhood would suddenly outweigh the 'criminal' in you. I would remember that I was also a copy of your father, and that because of a foolish kiss I had for ever blown up the secret bridge between us.

I decided to apologise to you. I would wake up and go into my studio. I would sit for ages in front of your blank portrait and ask myself where I would start you.

I would contemplate your photograph for a long time – the one on the back of your novel, which you gave me without a dedication. Your face seemed to have no connection with the photo. How would I fix an age for your face, both old and new together? How to make a copy of you without betraying you?

In the midst of my confusion I remembered Leonardo da Vinci, who could draw equally skilfully with both his right and left hand. Which hand did he use to paint and immortalise the Mona Lisa? With which hand would I have to paint you?

What if you were a woman who could only be drawn with the left hand, my missing one?

It once occurred to me to paint you upside down and then sit and look at you in the hope of finally uncovering your secret. Perhaps that would be the only way to understand you. I even considered the possibility of exhibiting that painting upside down. It would be called *You*. Many people would stop in front of it. They might think it impressive without completely knowing you. Wasn't that what you wanted, in the end?

More than a week, and several weather reports, passed before your voice came without introduction one morning.

'How are you?'

My heart, not expecting such a morning gift, got a shock. Speech tangled. 'Where are you?'

Your voice sounded close, or so I imagined. But you answered with a diversionary laugh. 'Try and guess!'

Like one dreaming, I answered, 'Have you come back to Paris?'

You laughed and said, 'What do you mean, Paris! I'm in Constantine. I arrived a week ago for a relative's wedding. I thought I must call you from here. Tell me what you're doing with the summer. Haven't you gone anywhere?'

I abbreviated my suffering with a few words. 'I'm tired,' I said, 'really tired. Why didn't you call before?'

As if you were a doctor writing a prescription, or a sheikh who's been asked to write an amulet or magic spell, you said, 'I'll write to you. I swear I'll write soon. You have to forgive me. You don't know how annoying and difficult life is here. You never have a moment to yourself in this city. Even talking on the phone is a detective story.'

'What are you doing?'

'Nothing. I go from one house to another, from one invitation to another. I don't even wander round the city on foot. I've just seen it from a car.' As if you'd remembered something important you added, 'You know what? You're right. The most beautiful thing in Constantine is its bridges. I remembered you as I went over them.'

At that moment I wanted to ask you if you loved me, but stupidly I asked, 'Do you love them?'

After a brief silence, as if I'd put a question that merited some thought, you answered, 'Perhaps I've started to love them.'

'Thank you.'

You laughed, and to end the conversation you said, 'You idiot! You'll never change.'

'You open your window to look outside. You open your eyes to look inwards. Looking is only the scaling of the wall separating you from freedom,' wrote Malek Haddad.

That morning I lit an early cigarette, which wasn't my habit. I sat on the balcony with a cup of coffee contemplating the Seine flowing slowly beneath Pont Mirabeau. Its beautiful summer blue annoyed me that morning, for no reason. It suddenly reminded me of blue eyes, which I didn't like. Perhaps its not being a river in Constantine made me hostile. I stood up without finishing my cigarette. I was suddenly in a hurry.

So be it. Forgive me, river of civilisation. Forgive me, bridge of history. Forgive me, Apollinaire, my friend. I'm going to paint a different bridge this time, too.

I was bursting with you and your voice coming from over there to rouse that city within me. I hadn't picked up a brush for three months. All the conflicting emotions and sensations I had experienced before and after you left had built up into an internal time bomb, in one way or another about to explode.

I had to paint to relax at last.

I painted with my whole hand, with all my fingers, with the hand that was there and with the one that was missing. I painted with all my turmoil and contradiction, with my reason, my memory and my oblivion, so as not to die – that summer in a city empty except for tourists and pigeons – a despairing death.

That morning I began to paint a new bridge, the viaduct of Sidi Rachid.

When I started, I didn't anticipate that I was embarking on my strangest ever experience of painting. It would be the beginning of ten other paintings, done in six weeks without a break except for a few snatched hours of sleep. Even then, I would mostly wake up seized with a crazed desire to paint.

The colours suddenly acquired the tones of my memory, and became an unstoppable flow. No sooner had I finished one painting than another was conceived. No sooner had I finished with one neighbourhood than another awoke. I had barely finished one bridge when another would rise inside.

I wanted to satisfy Constantine, stone by stone, bridge by bridge, neighbourhood by neighbourhood, as a lover satisfies the body of a woman no longer his. I went over her, backwards and forwards, with my brush, as if with my lips. I kissed her soil, her stones, her trees and her valleys. I spread my desire over her in coloured kisses. I splashed her with longing and love till the sweat flowed.

I was happy when my shirt stuck to me after hours being fused to her. Sweat is the body's tears. When we make love, like when we paint, we don't make our bodies cry for any old woman, or for any old painting. The body chooses for whom to sweat.

I was happy that Constantine should be the painting for which my body wept.

In that last month of summer, I was still waiting for a letter from you. It would restore part of the strength and enthusiasm I had lost in the two months you had been away. A letter from Ziyad took me by surprise.

His letters from Beirut always amazed me, even before I opened them. Each time I asked myself how it had managed to arrive. Under which collapsed roof in which camp or at which front had he written it? Which postbox had he mailed it from, and how many postmen had handled it before it reached my mailbox here in the sixteenth *arrondissement?*

I always treated them with particular love. They reminded me of the war of liberation, when letters to our families would be smuggled under clothes. Many letters didn't arrive, but died with their writers. Many letters arrived too late. Stories good enough for novels.

Ziyad would write for no particular reason. Long letters at times, short at others, which he called 'life notices'. I laughed at the name. He just meant he was telling me he was still alive. Then I became frightened at his long silences and his letters' stopping. To me this meant the chance of another kind of notice.

In Ziyad's latest letter he wanted to let me know he would be in Paris at the beginning of September. He was expecting a quick reply from me to make sure I would be there. His letter surprised, delighted and threw me.

My thoughts turned to you and I said, 'This man has a charmed life. I just mentioned him to you and here he is.' Then I wondered whether you had read his poems, and whether you had liked them. What would your reaction be if I told you he was coming to Paris? After all, you had feared he was dead and expressed interest in his story.

Summer was gradually receding, and I was gradually restoring my equilibrium.

The paintings had saved me from a breakdown. I had to paint them to get away from the jolts of madness you had caused.

I had lost a lot of weight. But that didn't matter to me, or perhaps at the time I hadn't noticed. I only looked at the paintings and forgot to look at myself in the mirror. I believed that the weight I lost I would gain in eternal glory. For this reason I found it gratifying to contemplate the haemorrhaging of my madness hanging before me – eleven paintings, too many for the walls of my flat.

Perhaps I was also attached to them because I knew as I added the final brushstroke that a few months might pass before I once again had a desire to paint. In one go I had emptied my memory. I relaxed.

September was approaching and I was happy, or in a state anticipating happiness. You would return at last. I awaited autumn as I never had before. Winter clothes in shop windows and school supplies filling stationers' shelves announced your return. The wind, the orange sky, the changeable weather all carried your suitcases. You were coming back. With autumnal gales, reddening leaves and pencil cases. You were coming back. With children returning to school, with traffic, strikes and Paris's return to its bustle. With vague sadness, with rain. With the onset of winter, with the ending of insanity. You would come back to me, my winter coat, my confidence for a tired life, my firewood for frozen nights.

Was I dreaming? How could I forget that wonderful remark of André Gide: 'Don't prepare your joys!' How could I forget such advice?

In reality, you were a tempest of a woman who came and went in storm and destruction. You were another's overcoat and my cold. You were the firewood that burned me instead of keeping me warm. You were you.

I waited for September then, for your return so we could finally say the absolute truth. What exactly did you want from me? Who would I be for you? What would we call our story?

I was wrong again. It wasn't time for questions and answers. It was time for a different lunacy. I was waiting for security, and you came. One tempest colliding with another called Ziyad.

And then there were hurricanes.

Ziyad hadn't changed since the last time I'd seen him, in Paris five years before. Perhaps he had filled out a little, become a little more masculine compared with the tall, slim young man with fewer worries who had first visited my office in Algeria in 1972.

His hair was still a polite mess. His shirt, tieless and unbuttoned at the collar, was still that of a rebel. His distinctive voice still had the same warmth and sadness. It made one imagine he was reciting poetry even when saying mundane things. He seemed like a poet who had lost his way and had found himself where he was by mistake.

In every city that I met him, I felt he had yet to reach his final destination. He was always on the point of departure. Even when sitting on a chair, he seemed to be sitting on a suitcase. He was never relaxed where he was, as though the cities he lived in were stations where he was waiting for a train whose time of arrival was unknown.

He was as I had left him, surrounded by his few things and laden with memories, wearing the same pair of jeans, as though they were his other identity.

Ziyad resembled the cities he passed through. There was something of Gaza, Amman, Beirut and Moscow about him, of Algiers and Athens. He resembled all those he had loved, and had something of Pushkin, Al-Sayyab, Hallaj, Mishima, Ghassan Kanafani, Lorca and Theodorakis.

Because I often shared Ziyad's memories, it meant that I loved everything and everyone he loved without realising.

I needed him those days. When I welcomed him, I realised that I had missed him all those years without knowing it, that I had never met someone else to call a friend.

Time and geography had taken him far away. But our old convictions kept us close. That's why he had not faded from my heart or lost my respect over all those years. Wasn't that a rare thing?

Ziyad arrived, and the apartment that for two months had been shut to others – even Catherine – came to life. He filled it with his presence, his stuff and his mess, and his raucous laugh sometimes. His vaguely furtive presence was a constant. I almost thanked him simply for opening the windows and taking one of the rooms, perhaps the whole house, even.

We spontaneously reverted to the routine of his first visit to me in Paris five years before. We went to virtually the same restaurants. We sat and talked about virtually the same subjects, for nothing had changed. Not one Arab regime that Ziyad was counting on falling since I met him had fallen. No political earth-quake here or there had changed the nation's map.

Only Lebanon had become a homeland for earthquakes and shifting sands. But who would be swallowed up in the end? That outcome we tried variously to predict. The discussion would always flow into the question of Palestine: factional splits, battles between partisans in Lebanon, assassinations and their toll of Palestinian figures abroad.

Ziyad usually ended up cursing the regimes that acquired glory with Palestinian blood under euphemisms like rejection-ism, steadfastness or confrontation. In his fury he would describe them using the full gamut of crude oriental epithets. I would laugh when I heard one of them for the first time.

I also discovered that all revolutionaries have their own special vocabulary, refined by their revolution and life. Nostalgically, I would recollect other words from another time and revolution.

Perhaps that week was the most beautiful time I spent with Ziyad. For several years afterwards I tried to remember no other so as not to feel sad about all I experienced after, rightly or wrongly. All the pain I went through, the jealousy and shocks after putting the pair of them together face to face without any introductions or special explanations.

I just said to him, 'We're going to have lunch tomorrow with a writer friend of mine. I really should introduce her to you.'

He didn't seem especially interested in what I was saying. He started reading the newspaper again but added, in his particular style, 'I hate women when they try to have literature instead of having something else. I do hope your friend isn't a spinster, or menopausal. I have no patience for such types!'

I didn't answer. I delved deep in his thoughts and smiled.

143

On the phone, I told you, 'Come and have lunch tomorrow in the usual place. I'll bring you a surprise you won't believe.'

You said, 'It's a painting, isn't it?'

After some hesitation I replied, 'No, it's a poet!'

So you two met.

I could say on this occasion, too, that those who say mountains never meet are wrong. Those who build bridges between them, so they might greet each other without stooping or diminishing their pride, know nothing of the laws of nature. Mountains meet in massive earthquakes. And even then they don't shake hands, but turn into dust.

So you two met. You were both volcanoes. It's hardly surprising that I was the victim this time, too.

I still remember that day. You arrived a little late. Ziyad and I had ordered a drink while waiting. You came in. Ziyad was talking about something when he suddenly went quiet. His eyes lit on you as you came through the door. I turned and saw you coming over in a green dress; elegant, seductive, as you'd never been before. Ziyad stood up to greet you as you approached. In my bewilderment I remained seated. It was obvious he hadn't expected you to be like that. There you were at last.

I felt that something was pinning me to my seat, as though the exhaustion of the past weeks, the agony since you had left, suddenly hit me and stopped my legs working.

There you were at last. Was it really you?

Before thinking to introduce you, you had introduced yourself to Ziyad. He in turn was about to introduce himself to you, when you interrupted him. 'Let me guess. Aren't you Ziyad al-Khalil?'

Ziyad stood amazed, then asked you, 'How did you know?'

At that point you turned to me, as if noticing my presence,

kissed me on both cheeks and said, directing the words at him, 'You've got quite an advocate in this guy.'

Checking my expression, you asked me, 'You've changed a bit. What happened to you over the holidays?'

Ziyad intervened to say sarcastically, 'He painted eleven pictures in six weeks. He hasn't done anything else. He even forgot to eat and sleep. I think that if I hadn't come to Paris, the man in front of you would have died of hunger and exhaustion among his paintings. That's not the way artists die any more!'

Rather than asking me, you asked Ziyad, in a touch of panic, as if you were afraid I might have painted eleven portraits of you, 'What did he paint?'

With a smile aimed at me, Ziyad replied, 'He painted Constantine. Nothing but Constantine. And lots of bridges.'

Pulling out a chair to sit down, you exclaimed, 'Please no! I beg you, don't talk any more about Constantine. I've just come back from there. An unbearable city, the perfect recipe for suicide or insanity!'

Then you spoke to me. 'When are you going to be cured of that city?'

If we had been alone, I could have said to you, 'When I am cured of you!'

But Ziyad answered, perhaps for me. 'We are never cured of our memory, *mademoiselle*. That's why we paint and why we write. That's why some of us die.'

Ziyad was incredible, poetic in everything. He spouted poetry without effort, loved and hated without effort, seduced without trying. I watched him as he asked you, 'You're Algerian, then?' I didn't hear what you said to him. It seemed that the conversation was just between the two of you and that I hadn't uttered a word since your arrival. I was just a third party at this strange meeting with fate.

I looked at you, seeking an explanation of what was happening to me in your smallest details. I asked you one day, 'What's the most beautiful thing about you?' You gave a vaguely beckoning smile and didn't reply. You weren't the most beautiful. You were the most delectable. Was there an explanation for desire? Perhaps Ziyad was like you, too.

I discovered that gradually as I watched you talking to each other in front of me. There was something ambiguously charming about him, something attractive that had nothing to do with beauty. The idea that you were alike or made for each other annoyed me. Perhaps it annoyed me from the very first, when you drew my attention to my poor health and pallor as I watched both of you in front of me glowing with enviable health.

Did jealousy start worming its way in from the instant I realised I was just a ghost between you, a face stuck by mistake into your double portrait?

You didn't notice that day that I had reached such a state because of you. So you didn't apologise to me; even worse, you didn't talk much with me, but lots with him. You said to him, 'I loved your last collection, *Plans for a Love to Come*. It helped me bear this miserable holiday. There are sections I've learned by heart, I've read them so often.' To Ziyad's astonishment, you started reciting:

Sadness has ambushed me. Don't abandon me to evening
    sadness
Lady, I will leave
I will knock on your door today before crying
See, these places of exile beguile me to stay

146

These airports are a waiting whore
Enticing me to the final journey.

That was the first time I heard you recite poetry. Your voice
was a musical instrument as yet uncreated. I came to know it for
the first time in the sadness of your tone, originally created for
joy. Here it was playing in another key.

Ziyad listened, quite amazed, as if all of a sudden he was sitting
outside time and memory. As if he had finally decided to sit on
something other than his suitcases and listen to you. When you
fell silent, he recited the rest of the poem as if reciting his fortune:

I have no nation but you
No memento of the soil, a bullet of desire the colour of shroud
I have nothing but you
Plans for love, in a short life!

At that moment, I felt an electric bolt of sadness, and perhaps
love too, had surged through the three of us.

I loved Ziyad. I was in awe of him. I felt he was stealing my
words of sadness and the nation, and of love too.

Ziyad was my voice. I was his hand, as he liked to say.

At that moment I felt that you had become the heart of us all.

I should have expected everything that happened.

Could I have stopped you two being swept away? I was like
the scientist who creates a monster and then loses control of it. I
discovered that I had foolishly authored your story with my own
hand. A model of stupidity, I had written it chapter by chapter
and allowed my characters to slip out of my control.

How could I sit before you, and then try and compare myself

with a man twelve years younger, more striking and more attractive than me?

How could I undo the complicit link of words between you to prevent a writer from loving a poet whose verse she had learned by heart?

How could I have convinced him – who might still not have got over his previous Algerian love – not to love you who came and roused memory and opened forgotten windows?

How did this happen? How did I bring you together with your destiny, which was also my destiny?

That evening, he said to me, 'That girl is great. I don't remember if I've read anything by her. She started writing after I'd left Algeria, it seems. But I know that name. I've read it before somewhere. It sounds familiar.'

At the time I said, 'You haven't read the name. You've just heard it. There's a street in Algiers named after her father, Taher Abdelmoula, who died in the Revolution.'

Ziyad put his newspaper aside and looked at me in silence. I felt he was lost in thought. Perhaps he had also begun to discover the exciting hidden dimension to your meeting, all the incredible details he would be unable to treat with coolness.

I felt a desire to talk more about you.

I was on the verge of telling him about *Si* Taher. I almost told him you were the daughter of my commander and friend. I even almost told him my incredible story with you. You, who could once have been my daughter, suddenly becoming my beloved a quarter of a century later.

I almost told him the story of my first painting, *Nostalgia*, and how it coincided with your birth. And the story of my most recent paintings: their connection with you, and the reason for my declining health and recent obsession.

I almost explained the secret of Constantine.

Did I keep silent to keep your secret to myself, like a big secret we take pleasure in bearing alone? Did your love carry the hint of clandestine operations and their deadly pleasure?

Without knowing all your feelings towards me, perhaps I was ashamed to confess to him, even though I'd never felt ashamed by him and had shared everything with him.

Did I decide from the outset that you would be only one of ours, because your love was not created for sharing?

Was it out of friendship, or idiocy, that I wanted to give him, perhaps as a last chance at love, the chance to love you? A few days of happiness stolen from the likelihood of death, which stalked him at all times and in every city?

What had Ziyad come to do in Paris? Clearly, it wasn't sightseeing. Maybe to make clandestine contacts, meet certain parties, give or receive orders. I didn't know which. But he was rather nervous, avoided making appointments over the phone and rarely went out alone.

I didn't ask him his reason for visiting Paris. The residue of the period of struggle in my life made me respect others' secrets when they were connected to a cause. I respected his secret. He respected my silence. So our secret and our silence took us to our shared story with you.

With his superlative intuition did he anticipate something between you and me? Faced with my show of indifference, perhaps he didn't expect such a burning passion inside me. How could he have figured it out when I was gradually withdrawing on tiptoe to leave him more space? Instead of doing it myself, I let him answer the phone, talk to you and invite you over.

You would come round, and I would try not to ask myself for whom, and for whom you had made yourself beautiful.

Perhaps the most painful day was when you came round for the first time. Ziyad had to point out my paintings for you to take note of them. You moved from room to room as though going through the rooms in your own house. The corridor didn't make you pause. The memory of a kiss that turned my life upside down.

Was that the most hurtful moment, or when I opened (by mistake?) a door and told you in explanation, 'This is Ziyad's room.' You stood in front of the half-open door for what seemed to me longer than all the time that you'd spent in front of my paintings.

On the way back to the living room you said, 'I don't understand why you painted so many bridges. It's mad. One or two would have been enough.' You sat down on the same sofa.

Did Ziyad volunteer to answer for me out of conviction or politeness when he noticed the impact of your words on me? I was so crushed I had lost my voice.

'You haven't studied those pictures, but judged them at first glance. In painting, pictures are not the same, even if they look alike. There's a key that cracks the code and solves the riddle of every painting. You have to find it in order to grasp the message the painter wishes to convey.

'If you walked by *The Card Players* in the same rush, you'd only take note of two card players sitting at a table. You wouldn't spot that the cards they are holding and shielding from each other are blank. That what Cézanne wished to convey wasn't a card game, but a scene of fraud, agreed upon or perhaps inherited, since one of the players is older than the other.'

Before Ziyad could continue, you interrupted, 'How do you know all that? Are you an art expert as well? Or have you caught Khaled's illness?'

Ziyad laughed and moved slightly closer to you. 'It's not my area of expertise at all,' he said. 'That would be a luxury not available to a man like me. My ignorance of art would surprise you. I only know a few artists, and I came across their works by chance, mostly in books. But I love some modernist schools that pose questions in their work.

'I'm not convinced by art for art's sake. And the esteemed *Mona Lisa* doesn't move me. I like art that challenges me existentially. That's why I thought Khaled's last paintings were great. It's the first time he's really impressed me.

'Painting after painting, he's become one with this bridge – in joy, then sadness grading into darkness, as if he had lived a day or a lifetime to its time.

'In the last painting only a distant shadow of the bridge remains visible under a pencil of light. Everything around it has disappeared in the mist, and the bridge shines like a question mark suspended in the sky. There are no supports extending below, nothing demarcates it to the left or the right, as though it has lost its original purpose as a bridge!

'Do you think it's early morning or dusk? Is it a moment of demise, or birth with the thread of dawn? This question remains hanging like a bridge in picture after picture, each haunted by the continuous play of light and shadow, of death and rebirth, because anything suspended between heaven and earth contains the seeds of its own death.'

I listened to Ziyad in amazement. Perhaps I had discovered something that hadn't occurred to me when I was painting the pictures.

Was it true what he was saying? Ziyad was certainly talking about my pictures better than I could. He was like any critic who gives an astonishing interpretation of works of art that the artist produced naively, without any philosophical reflection. The critic makes the artist laugh if he is genuine and straightforward, uninterested in symbols or convoluted theories of art. Alternatively, the critic may fill the artist with arrogance and rage if he's like many who take themselves seriously and start to theorise and evangelise for a new artistic school.

Ziyad's critique contained an important truth that I hadn't perceived before and that stunned me. When painting the bridges, I believed I was painting you. In fact I was only painting myself. The bridge was an expression of my suspended situation, now and always. Without realising, I used it to project my anxiety, my fears and my vertigo.

Perhaps that's why the first thing I painted when I lost my arm was a bridge. Do all these bridges mean that no part of my life has changed since then? That might have been accurate, but not the whole story. Ziyad could have philosophised about the symbolism of the bridge in other ways. But it was certain that he wouldn't go beyond familiar symbols – the symbolic dimension is created by our lives, and in the end, Ziyad didn't know all the folds of my memory. He hadn't visited the only city that knows the secret of bridges!

I remembered a contemporary Japanese artist who, I had read, spent a number of years painting nothing but grass. When he was asked why, he said, 'One day I painted grass and understood the field. When I understood the field I grasped the secret of the world.' He was right. Everyone has a key that opens the riddle of the world – his world.

Hemingway understood the world when he understood the sea. Alberto Moravia when he understood desire, Hallaj when he understood God, Henry Miller when he understood sex, Baudelaire when he understood sin and damnation.

Perhaps Van Gogh understood the baseness and sadism of the world when he sat febrile at his window with his head bandaged. He saw only vast fields of sunflowers and, exhausted, could only paint the same scene over and over. His febrile hand was only capable of painting those naive, simple flowers. But he kept painting. This wasn't to make money from his pictures, but to get revenge for them, even if a century later. Didn't he predict to his brother that a day would come when his paintings would be more valuable than his life? *Sunflowers* once broke all records for the price of a painting.

That idea prompted me to wonder whether painters were also prophets. Then I linked that idea with Ziyad's comment that 'anything suspended between heaven and earth contains the seeds of its own death'. I asked myself what prophecy was contained in each of the pictures I had painted in an advanced stage of madness and unconsciousness. Was it the death or rebirth of that city? Was it the endurance of her bridges that had hung for centuries in the face of crosswinds and so many changes of weather? Or their total and sudden collapse at that moment when only a pale thread of indifference divides night and day – the indifference of history?

I was under the influence of that shocking vision when your voice shook me out of my nightmare. 'You know, Khaled, you've been lucky not to visit Constantine for a few years, otherwise she wouldn't have inspired you to paint such beautiful things. When you wish to get over her, just visit and the dream will be over!'

At the time of course, I didn't know that one day you would personally take on the task of killing that dream and would force me to the threshold of Constantine.

Ziyad intervened, once again to say things before their time, like prophecy. In polite reproach he said, 'Why are you so determined to kill this man's dream? There are dreams that kill us. Allow him to be happy, even with a fantasy.'

You made no comment, as though my dreams no longer interested you to any great degree. You just asked him, 'And you? What's your dream?'

'Maybe a city as well,' he said.

'Is it called Khalil?'[1]

He said, smiling, 'No. We don't always carry the name of our dreams. Nor do we belong to them. My name is Khalil and my city is Gaza.'

'When did you last visit?'

'Before the 1967 war. More than fifteen years ago.' He then added, 'What's happening to Khaled today makes me laugh. In the past, when we were in Algeria, he tried to convince me to get married and stay there for ever. He didn't understand that Gaza haunted me so much it made me leave every city. Now he's reached the same conclusion of his own accord, and is also haunted by a city.

'What's amazing is that he never talked about it to me. It's as though he attached no importance to it before. We don't pay attention to things like happiness until we've lost them!'

Perhaps that was what happened to me. I gradually became aware that I had been happy with you before that summer holiday, before Ziyad came and our love turned from a couple's violent passion into a love triangle with equal sides. From a two-player game of chess, where love filled the black squares and the white squares and whose only rule was love's ebb and flow, into a three-handed card game where we sat around a table, revealing our cards and our sadness. We shared a heartbeat and memory, laid traps for each other and created new rules for love.

---

1 Hebron in Arabic.

We forged our hands, all of which were identical. We cheated the logic of things, not for one of us to win the game, but to stop one of us losing and so make our ending less painful than the beginning.

It was clear that Ziyad sensed that I loved you in some fashion. But he was unaware of the roots or extent of that love. So he drifted into loving you without thought or guilt.

We all lacked the sense to realise that desire only has enough room for two. Once we were three, it swallowed us up like the Bermuda Triangle swallows ships.

How did we get there? What winds blew us to those alien shores? What fate scattered us, then reunited our disparate, contradictory fates, with our different ages and histories, with our separate battles and dreams, for us to end up there, unconsciously battling between ourselves?

Months later, I read in Ziyad's papers an idea very close to those feelings. He wrote:

Our desire is another defeat in an age of losing battles. Which defeats hurt most, then?

All that happened was destined.

We were two people for one land.

Two prophets to one city.

Here we are two hearts for one woman.

Everything was ready for pain. (Was the world big enough for us?)

We share our pride like an Arab loaf, circular like our wound, a round-tipped bullet fired at a red square where fate is trained to shoot black circles that dizzily telescope until the centre of death

Where the bullet doesn't miss

Where the bullet shows no mercy
Where one of our hearts shall be.

During those wintery evenings Ziyad sometimes stayed up late writing in his room. I took this as an unmistakeable sign. He had to be in love to return to writing with such passion when he hadn't written anything for some years.

Sometimes I smiled as the sound of low music came from his room until late at night. It was as if Ziyad wanted to fill his lungs with life, or as if he didn't trust life completely and feared it would steal something from him while he slept. He always listened to the same tapes; I don't know where he got them from. Classical music: Vivaldi, Theodorakis. I wasn't particularly fond of them.

I might spend the whole evening alone in front of the television and would say to myself, 'He's also living his obsession. There is summer fever and winter fever. Mine has ended and his begun!'

But how could I know the degree of his madness? Where to get a seismograph to find out what was happening deep inside him? How to do that when his bouts were secret jottings only revealed on paper? My madness was eleven paintings hanging on the walls, testifying against me and shaming me.

Was my obsession really over? No. It just became internalised and without relation to creativity. Sick feelings I squandered uselessly in jealousy and despair. When Ziyad changed his suit, I felt he was expecting you to come by. When he sat writing, he was writing to you. When he left the house it was on a date with you. In the crush of my jealousy, I even forgot the reasons why Ziyad had come to Paris, his meetings and other fixations.

Then came the trip that I have almost forgotten. Perhaps that was the most painful experience of all. I had to leave the two of you together in one city for ten whole days, and given the difficulty of your meeting elsewhere, probably in my house.

I left trying to convince myself that it was an opportunity for all of us to sort out our relationship. One of us had to be absent for the ambiguity between us to be resolved. Of course, deep down I wasn't convinced by this logic, or at least by this perverse fate that made the lot fall upon me.

It was clear that fate was a partisan for you two. That hurt me a lot. But what was the most painful thing? Knowing that you were with another man, or that he was none other than Ziyad, or that the betrayal would take place in a room in my house where I had not enjoyed you?

How far would you go with him? How far would he go with you? Would our shared memories and values stop him?

I spoke to you a lot about Ziyad, but didn't tell you what really mattered. Ziyad had been my secret cell, my secret ticket of belonging. He had been my defeats and triumphs, my proofs and convictions. He was the secret life of another lifetime. Would Ziyad betray me?

I started to blame, and perhaps to despise him in advance.

In my mad jealousy I forgot that I had done nothing different with you. I had disavowed *Si* Taher, a man who had once been my commander and my friend. A man who had entrusted me with you as a last wish and died a martyr.

Which one of us was the bigger traitor? He, the one who put his dreams and desires into effect, or me, the one who didn't, because he failed to find an opportunity? Me, who had been sleeping and waking up with you for months, taking you in my sleep, or him, whom you would willingly give yourself to?

* * *

157

There are cities like women. Their names defeat you in advance. They seduce and bewilder you, fill you up and drain you. Their remembrance strips you of all your plans; your whole project becomes love.

There are cities that weren't created to be visited and explored alone, for you to sleep and wake up in, and then have breakfast alone.

Cities as beautiful as memory, as close as a tear, as painful as loss. Cities so like you!

Could I have forgotten you in a city called Granada? Your love came with the low white houses and their red-tiled roofs, with the trellises of vines, with the flowering jasmine trees, with the streams that traversed the city. With the water, the sun and the reminiscence of the Arabs.

Your love came with the perfumes, the voices, the faces. The brown skin and deep black hair of the Andalucian women. With wedding dresses, with guitars as passionate as your body, with the poems of Lorca, whom you loved. With the sadness of Abu Firas al-Hamdani, whom I loved.

I felt you were a part of that city, too. Were all Arab cities you? And all Arab memory?

Time flowed on, and you remained like the waters of Granada, glistening with longing, and with a superior taste, unlike water from pipes and taps.

Time flowed on, and your voice echoed like the magical fountains in the ruined castles of Arab memory, when evening suddenly falls over Granada and Granada surprises herself as the lover of an Arab king who has just deserted her.

He was Abu Abdullah, the last Arab lover to kiss her!

Maybe I was that king who did not know how to keep his throne. Maybe I had lost you with the same foolishness, and would weep for you one day as he did.

When Granada fell, and he was oblivious, his mother told him, 'Cry like a woman over a lost kingdom, for you have not protected it like a man.'

Did I really not protect you? Whom should I have declared war against, I ask you? Against whom, when you two were my memory and my dearest ones? Against whom, when you were my city and citadel?

Why should I be ashamed? Has there been one Arab king or ruler since Abu Abdullah who hasn't wept for some city?

Fall then, Constantine, this was a time of easy conquest!

Did she really fall that day? That I would never know.

I only knew the date of your last fall, your final fall, which I witnessed thereafter.

What madness to increase the expanse of your love and let you assume the features of that city, too. Like a lunatic, I sat every night writing you letters born out of my wonder, longing and jealousy for you. I would tell you the details of my day and my impressions of a city incredibly like you.

One day I wrote to you:

I want to make love to you here. In a house like your body, painted in Andalucian style.

I want to escape with you from tin-can cities and give your love a home that has the same features as your Arab femininity. A house where my original memory is concealed behind its arches, carved inscriptions and meanderings. A house with a garden shaded by a large lemon tree like those planted by the Arabs in the gardens of their houses in Andalucia.

I want to sit by your side, like I'm sitting here by a pool filled with goldfish, and look upon you in awe.

159

I inhale your body, like I inhale the scent of the unripe green lemons.

Forbidden fruit, by every tree I pass, I hunger for you.

Many letters I wrote to you – could a writer resist words?

I wanted to garland you with words, to bring you back with them, to join you two in the circle of words closed in my face for being a mere painter. So for your sake I composed letters never before written to woman. Letters that exploded in my mind after fifty years of silence.

Without realising, maybe I started writing this book that day. My passion for you had shifted into the language of those letters, a language I was writing for the first time. I had written to women before you, those who passed through my life in my youth and adolescence. But I didn't exert myself then looking for the right words. The French language, with its freedom, naturally induced me to speak openly and without complexes or shame. I discovered Arabic afresh with you. I learned to get around its gravity, to submit to its secret seduction, its contours, its allusions.

I was biased towards the letters that resembled you. The feminine ending, the *ha* from the throat and the *he* from the breath, the proud-standing *alif*, the dots strewn over their empty, brown bodies.

Was language also feminine? A woman we inclined towards above others and learned to cry, laugh and love the way she did? If she left us we would feel cold and orphaned without her.

I wonder whether you read those letters. Did you sense my fear of being an orphan and of ice-cold seasons? Did they startle you or did they come at an inopportune moment? I should have written them to you before Ziyad crept under your skin and became your language.

Would love letters have been of any use when they came too late for love?

Salvador Dalí and Paul Eluard loved the same woman, and in vain Eluard wrote the most beautiful letters and poetry to win her back from Dalí, who had snatched her from him. But she preferred the then-unknown Dalí's madness to Eluard's rhymes. She remained enamoured of Dalí's brush until her death. He married her several times in several ceremonies, and painted no other woman all his life.

Actually, love does not always repeat itself. Painters do not always defeat poets, even when they try to take up the guise of words.

When I returned to Paris, I had a permanent lump in my throat. This had spoiled the success of my exhibition and the pleasant or useful meetings that went along with it. Something inside me was bleeding profusely – a new emotion of jealousy and vague spite that never left me and constantly reminded me that something was going on.

Ziyad greeted me warmly – was he really happy at my return? He handed me the post that had arrived and a list of the people who had called while I was away. I took it without looking. I knew I wouldn't find your name. Then he asked me about the exhibition, about the journey and my news. He told me the latest political developments anxiously, which I put down to embarrassment on some account.

I listened to him while checking out the house with my senses like the fairytale giant who, whenever he returned to his lair, would sniff the air for the trace of any man who had crept in during his absence.

I had a strange feeling you had passed through the apartment, although I could find no proof to confirm my suspicions. Did proof matter? Could ten days have passed without you two meeting? And where could you have met, if not here? And when you had met, would talk have been enough?

You were a source of brimstone and Ziyad a Zoroastrian lover who worshipped fire! Could he have held out for long before you, a woman in whose fire men dreamed of being consumed, even if only in fantasy?

I searched Ziyad's face for signs of happiness, for definite proof that you were his. But he revealed nothing but anxiety. He suddenly spoke about you. 'I've asked her to come round tomorrow for our last meal.'

I cried out in some surprise, 'Why the last?'

He said, 'Because I'm leaving on Sunday.'

'Why Sunday?' I said this feeling a mix of sadness and joy.

Ziyad replied, 'Because I have to go back. I was just waiting for you to come back before leaving. I was only supposed to stay for two weeks, but it's been a whole month and I have to go.' Jokingly he added, 'Before I get used to Parisian life.' Maybe you were the Parisian life he was afraid of getting used to. Maybe he was running away from love again, or his mission had finished and he had nothing left to do but leave.

Saturday was taken up with the business of my return and Ziyad's preparations to leave. That evening, I tried to avoid sitting down with him. But Sunday lay in wait for us and finally set the three of us face to face at a fateful last meal.

You greeted me with unexpected warmth. For my part, I interpreted this as guilt – or gratitude, perhaps. Hadn't I presented you with love on a platter of poetry laid on the table of my apartment? Then you thanked me for my letters, expressing admiration at my style, as though you were a teacher marking a pupil's essay. Your openly expressed thanks annoyed me. I felt you had talked to Ziyad about them and perhaps had shown them to him, too.

I was about to say something when you resumed, 'I wish I could have been there with you. Is Granada really so beautiful? Did you really go to Lorca's house in Fuente Vaqueros – isn't that the name of his village, like you said? Tell me about it.'

I found something quite incredible in your way of broaching the conversation with me from the margins, something thought-provoking, too. Was that all you could find to say after all the storms we'd been through? After ten days of hell that I had experienced alone?

A scene from a film about Lorca came to mind.

I said to you, 'Do you know how Lorca died?'

'He was executed,' you said.

'No. They took him to the open country and told him to walk. He started walking and they shot him in the back. He dropped down dead without really knowing what had happened. That's the saddest part. Lorca did not fear death; he expected it and headed towards it as though going to meet a friend. He would have hated the bullets coming from behind!'

At the time, I felt that Ziyad took my words as a bullet to the chest. He lifted his eyes towards me and I felt he was about to say something, but he remained silent. We understood each other with few words. Later on, I regretted my deliberate attempt to hurt him. Hurting him cost me more than the pain you caused. Still, it was the least I could say to him after all the suffering I had gone through because of him. Perhaps it also was the most I could say.

Our dinner suddenly turned into embarrassing silence

occasionally punctuated by forced conversation, initiated by you in a woman's way to lighten the atmosphere. Or perhaps evade it. But it was useless. Something pure as crystal had shattered. There was no hope of putting it together again.

'Will you take Ziyad to the airport with me?' I asked later.

'No. I can't go to the airport,' you said. 'I might meet my uncle there. He goes by the Air Algeria office sometimes. Besides, I hate airports and farewell ceremonies. We never really leave the ones we love, so we don't say goodbye to them. Goodbyes were made for strangers.'

That was one of your marvellous outbursts, like when you had said before, 'We only write dedications to strangers. Those we love do not belong on the blank first page, but in the pages of the book.'

Why goodbye?

Was there a need for another farewell?

Over lunch I watched your gaze consume him. You ate nothing else. Your eyes were saying goodbye to his body piece by piece. They lingered over every part of him, as though you were recording images for a future when images of him would be all you had.

He avoided your gaze, perhaps out of consideration for me or because my hurtful words had made him lose the desire to love – and the desire to eat – and made him turn his sad looks inwards and to the future after his journey.

I was no less sad than you two. But my sadness was unique and individual, like my disappointment. It had multiple, obscure reasons, including my belief in your wild affair. Perhaps your refusal to come with me to the airport made the lunch more tense. My great hope was that on the way back I would finally be alone with you. Then, with a few questions, I would know whether you could erase those days from your memory and return to me unharmed.

I knew that your heart favoured him. Perhaps your body, too. But I trusted in the logic of time and believed that in the end you would come back to me, because there would only be me. I was your first memory, your primal longing for a father figure.

I backed logic and waited.

Ziyad had left.

I gradually got my apartment, and my old habits, back.

I was happy, but with a vague bitterness. I had grown used to him being around, and suddenly felt lonely when he abandoned me to face winter on my own with its grey days and long startling nights.

Ziyad had left. The apartment was all at once as empty of him as it had been full. Only a suitcase remained behind to attest that he had been there. He left it at the bottom of the wardrobe after packing away his papers and other things. I saw in it the prospect of his return, perhaps on your account.

Still, I have to admit I was more happy than sad. I felt that getting the apartment back without him meant getting you back. I felt that, in one way or another, the house would finally be filled with you. That when I was alone, I would be alone with you.

I would gradually bring you back. Hadn't you readily admitted that you loved the apartment, how it was arranged, its light, the view of the Seine below? Or perhaps you had only loved Ziyad's presence that saturated everything and made things better!

To begin with, I anticipated your call. I held on for it to rescue me. But your voice gradually receded. You called every week, then every fortnight, then calls came sparingly, like drops of medicine. At times I felt you only bothered out of politeness, or boredom, or from an unspoken desire for news of Ziyad. Then the calls stopped completely.

I wondered whether he wrote to you at home so you had no need to ask after him. Or, as usual for him, he had told you in advance that he wouldn't write and that like him you had to learn to forget. But you went and imposed that punishment on me, too.

Ziyad hated half-solutions. Like any man who has carried a gun, he was an extremist. So he also hated what he used to call 'half-pleasures' or 'half-measures'. He was a man of fateful choices: either he loved and renounced everything else for that love, or he left for something more important. In either case, there was no reason to make himself suffer with longings or memory.

For a long time afterwards I wondered what he had chosen. Perhaps he had done the same as he had years before in Algeria with that girl he nearly married. Or had he changed this time? By virtue of age, or just because of you? After all, what happened between you two was no ordinary story of ordinary people.

Sometimes I tried to coax you to talk about him. I might end up understanding the new rules of the game and accommodating them. As usual, you were evasive. It was obvious that you loved it when I talked about him. But you gave nothing away. You contradicted yourself all the time. You mixed the funny and the serious, truth and lies in an effort to evade something.

Your words were white lies that I coloured with a paintbrush to match what I knew about you. I became used to applying anxious mauves, blues or greys to what you were saying. I turned its gist into an illustrated scenario, a series of drawings.

I could add touches belonging to another conversation we had not had.

It was then that I might have started to fathom the mysterious link forming in my memory between you and the colour white. It wasn't just that your words were a white lie. You were a woman with a special ability to evoke that colour in all its antonymic forms. Or it was then that I may have started, without realising it and by blind intuition, to remove that colour from my paintings entirely. I tried to do without it in a deranged effort to obliterate you.

It was a colour in league with you. The day I saw you as a baby crawling towards your white clothes drying on slats over the stove, fate gave a forewarning that, rather than drying clothes, it was cooking me and you together over a low flame. Like you, white was an ingredient of all tones and objects. I would have to destroy so many things before I could be rid of it. I would have to blank so many paintings if I stopped using it.

In every way (and colour) I was trying to finish with you. But in truth I just became more caught up in loving you. In a moment of despair, I admitted over the phone, 'You know that your love is a desert of shifting sands and I no longer know where I stand.'

With hurtful irony you replied, 'Stand still. What matters is not to move. Any attempt to extract yourself will make the sand drag you down further. That's the advice desert people give. How could you not know that?'

I should have been sad that day. But I laughed. Perhaps because I loved your clever irony even when it hurt. It is rare to meet a woman who makes us suffer with her intelligence. Perhaps you were offering me the possibility of a death that I saw was as beautiful as it was final.

I recalled a wonderful proverb that I had not paid attention to before: 'The free bird has no ruler, but if caught it will not flap its wings!' At the time, I felt that I was that proud bird descended from eagles and falcons that cannot easily be hunted but, once caught, whose nobility lies in a superior surrender without the resistance or struggle of a small bird trapped in a net. I answered you that day with that proverb, and you marvelled, 'How wonderful. I've never heard it before!'

With a sigh I replied, 'That's because you don't know men. These aren't the times of eagles and falcons. It's the time of tame birds waiting in the park.'

Six years have passed since that conversation. I'm remembering it now by chance and recall your final advice: 'Stand still. What matters is not to move.'

How did I believe that tempests and shifting sands made you afraid for me? You who stopped me here for a few years at the mercy of my wound, stirred up storms around me, shifted the sands under my feet, and incited fate against me.

I have not moved. I have remained stupidly standing at the threshold of your heart for years. I didn't know that you were swallowing me up in silence, removing the ground from under my feet as I slid down to the depths. I didn't know that your tempests would keep coming, even years later, to kill me.

Today amidst the recent storms, along comes your book to provoke a whirlwind of extreme and contradictory feelings inside me. *The Curve of Forgetting*.

Where will forgetting come from, I ask you?

I still remember that February day when *Si* Sharif's voice came over the phone and invited me to dinner at his house. I was surprised by the invitation, and didn't ask what the occasion was.

I simply understood that he had invited other people to dinner, that I wouldn't be on my own.

I admit I was delighted, and embarrassed by my delight. I was ashamed of myself because I had only called him once since our last meeting – at Eid – despite his insistence that I come and have coffee at his office, even if only once.

Suddenly I made a decision that might have been foolish. I decided to take him one of my paintings as a present. Wasn't he making me unexpectedly happy? Wordlessly, I would prove to him that my paintings were only traded for the currency of the heart, not suspect banknotes. Later on, I realised the idea also had a bonus. I would become a fixture in the house you lived in, even if hanging on the wall.

The next day I took the painting and went to dinner. My heart was racing with me, getting ahead of me in the search for the building in that high-class district. I don't remember whether my eyes or my heart led me to it. When I entered, your fragrance waylaid me at the entrance and in the lift. Your perfume was leading the way.

Si Sharif greeted me at the door with a warm embrace. His warmth increased when he saw the bulky painting I was lugging. It seemed he didn't quite believe it was a present for him. He hesitated before taking it, but I stopped him to say, 'This is a painting of mine. It's a present for you.'

All of a sudden I saw rare pleasure and delight on his face. He tore off the wrapping with the curiosity of someone who's won the tombola. He saw the bridge hanging in a foggy sky and yelled, 'That's the suspension bridge!'

Before I said anything, he hugged me and patted my shoulder while saying, 'Thank you! Live long, my friend!'

I couldn't restrain myself from kissing him with the same

passion. After all, he had given me a gift whose value to me he might not have been aware of.

Si Sharif accompanied me to the living room, holding my arm in one hand and the painting in the other. He guided me over to introduce me to his guests. It seemed he wanted the group to witness his gratitude or, perhaps, our relationship and firm friendship which, in those vulgar times, I was reputed to share with only a few.

He uttered a number of names to go with a number of faces. I shook hands with them, mostly wondering who they were. I only knew one or two of them. As for the rest, they were what I called 'parasitic growth', like the weeds that spring up from nowhere in every flowerbed. They spread their roots and are suddenly full of branches and leaves, until they alone end up covering the ground.

I don't know why I've always had a powerful sense for such creatures, wherever they were. Despite any differences in kind, appearance or status, they possessed shared features that gave them away. Those were pretence and extreme hypocrisy, the telltale signs of newly and rapidly acquired wealth and status, and a shared vocabulary that made a person believe they were more important than he thought.

A quick glance and a few words were enough to work out the nature of this 'high-class' party that comprised the elite of émigré society, who specialised in public slogans and secret deals. It was clear I was from another world.

Si Sharif showed off the painting to his friends with a mixture of pride and affection. He turned to me and said, 'You know what, Khaled? Today you've made one of my dearest dreams come true. I've always wanted something of yours as a memento in my house. Don't forget you're a childhood friend and a neighbour from Koshat al-Ziyyat. Do you remember that neighbourhood?'

I liked *Si* Sharif. He had some of Constantine's dignity and presence, something of Algeria's authenticity and memory, something of *Si* Taher in his voice and stature. There was something pure inside him, still untainted despite everything. But for how much longer? I felt he was surrounded by flies and the filth of the time. I was afraid that one day the rot would seep into his core. I was afraid for him and, perhaps, that the great name he had inherited from *Si* Taher would be tarnished. Were these feelings intuitive, or the logical conclusion to the painful reality of his environment?

Would *Si* Sharif escape infection? What would he choose? In which lake would he take a dip, which current would he go with and which against? Little isolated fish could not survive in murky, shark-infested waters. The answer was in front of me, but I didn't pay attention that evening. *Si* Sharif had chosen his polluted waters and the matter was over.

The smartly dressed person next to me said from behind his Cuban cigar, 'I've always been an admirer of your paintings. I requested that you be contacted to participate in some of our projects. But I don't recollect seeing any of your work in our possession.'

At the time, I didn't know who he was or anything about the projects he was talking about. That he referred to himself in the plural was enough for me to understand that he wasn't an ordinary person.

As if *Si* Sharif had noticed that I didn't know who it was I was talking to, he interjected by way of clarification, '*Si* — — loves art. He looks after big projects that will change the cultural face of Algeria.' As if noting something, he added, 'But you haven't visited Algeria for a few years. So you won't have seen these new cultural and commercial structures yet. You must get to know them.'

I didn't respond. I watched him slide down the scale of values, whether out of stupidity or complicity I didn't know. What I had heard about those 'facilities' and all the accompanying national monuments built brick by brick on a foundation of kickbacks and deals, I kept to myself. Greater and lesser thieves taking turns before the eyes of the martyrs whose misfortune meant their tombs had to stand alongside this betrayal.

So that was *Si* — —. He would have appeared a decent and quite simple man were it not for his very sharp suit and his incessant talk about current and future plans, all of which passed through Paris and involved suspect foreign names that seemed shameful on the lips of a former officer.

So that was him. Perhaps he was the manifestation of culture in the world of the junta, or the manifestation of the junta in the world of culture. Or was this unnatural marriage now natural since becoming official among Arab chiefs-of-staff?

Everyone fawned and flattered him. Perhaps they were licking at the honeyed river of hard currency flowing from his arms in an age of privation and drought.

The whole evening I asked myself what I was doing at this strange party. I had expected a family event, or at least a rare encounter with the homeland where I would recall distant memories with *Si* Sharif. But that evening the nation was absent. Its still-open wounds and newly disfigured face stood in. It was a *soirée* in France where we spoke in French about projects to be carried out, in the main, by foreign agencies with Algerian funding. Had we really gained our independence?

The evening ended around midnight. *Si* — — was tired and

had commitments and meetings in the morning, and perhaps at night too. Ready money quickens our appetite for pleasure.

I might have been happy that evening. I had been the focus of interest for everyone, for reasons I didn't want to go into. Perhaps I was the co-star along with *Si* — — in whose honour the party had been held, as I understood. I had been invited because he liked the company of artists at parties as proof of his passion for creativity and his non-military taste.

Actually, he was nice and polite. He gave me his views on various artistic fields and explained his love for particular Algerian painters. As a joke, he even said he envied *Si* Sharif for the painting, and if I always had a painting with me, he would invite me to his house in Algeria.

I laughed at the joke. But I was sufficiently sad afterwards to be on the verge of tears when I was alone in bed. I asked what idiocy had made me go to that house. A house that I had expected to be yours. But I had been and gone without even seeing the hem of your dress crossing the passage that divided me from your world.

The next morning, the phone rang. I expected it to be you, but it was Catherine. She said, 'Morning kisses and most beauti-ful wishes for you.' Before I could ask what the occasion was, she said, 'It's St Valentine's Day. The patron saint of lovers. I thought I'd call rather than send a card. What would you like to wish for on the holiday for love?' Met by my shock, or my hesitation, she added in the sarcastic tone I loved, 'Ask, you idiot! All requests are met today!'

I laughed. I almost told her that I only wanted a little forget-fulness. But I said something along these lines: 'I want to go into emotional retirement. Can you let your saint know my request?'

'You madman,' she said. 'I hope he doesn't hear you and

173

deprive you of his blessings for ever. Was our last date so exhausting?'

I laughed that day with Catherine. Then I put down the receiver to cry with you.

I discovered the pain of that day I had not even heard about before.

You didn't even call to thank me for the painting or the visit, that supposed date that I had gone on and that you had given a miss. It was Valentine's Day, then.

You, my celebration and my misfortune, my love and my hate, my forgetting and my memory. May you be all of that with every return of the day.

So love has its day. Lovers and mistresses celebrate it. They exchange cards and longings. Where is the day for oblivion, madam? Every day of the year is a saint's day, and among these 365 saints isn't there one to mark forgetting? Separation is the flipside of love, just as disappointment is the flipside of desire. So why isn't there a forgetting day when the postmen go on strike and the phone lines go dead? A day when they don't broadcast romantic songs and we stop writing love poetry!

Nearly two centuries ago, Victor Hugo wrote to his mistress Juliette Drouet saying, 'How sterile is love. It never stops repeating those three words, "I love you." But ever fertile, too, since there are a thousand ways to say those very words.'

Let me amaze you on Valentine's Day and try a thousand ways to say the same words of love. Let me tread the thousand divergent pathways to you and love you with a thousand contradictory emotions, forget you and remember you with the extremes of memory and oblivion. Let me be your enslaved subject and at liberty in the contradiction of desire and hatred. On love's day let me hate you with love.

I wonder if I started to hate you that day. When exactly was that feeling born within me, growing astonishingly fast to rival love in its intensity? Following my repeated disappointments with you, after all our anniversaries passed unmarked, or because of the vague anxiety that possessed me, that permanent hunger for you that made me desire no other woman?

I wanted you and no other, and in vain tried to deceive my body by offering it to another woman. But you were its only hunger, its only desire.

Perhaps the most painful thing when making love was that I stroked Catherine's hair and was brought up by her short, blonde tufts. I suddenly lost my desire as I remembered your long, dark, gypsy hair that could have covered my bed by itself.

Her skinniness reminded me of your full figure. The angular lines and flat planes of her body reminded me of the curves and recesses of yours.

In its absence, your perfume assailed my senses and masked her perfume. Like a child first exploring his senses, I was reminded that this perfume wasn't the secret scent of my mother.

You crept into my body every morning and forced her from my bed. Your secret pain woke me up. The body's accumulated desire for you was a time bomb, a delayed nocturnal longing day after day. Do men wake up with erections or does desire not sleep? Answer me, woman who sleeps deeply every night. Are only men insomniacs?

Why does the body become confused? I almost broke down on someone else's chest and admitted to her that I was another woman's lover. That I was impotent with her because my manhood was no longer mine but only took orders from you!

When did I start to hate you? Perhaps the day Catherine put her clothes back on, claiming out of politeness that she had an

175

appointment, and left me on my own in a bed that no longer satisfied her. That day I discovered, when shedding a proud male tear, that manhood can also fly at half-mast and refuse to perform out of politeness or masculine pride. That in the end we are not the masters of our bodies as we believe.

That day, I asked myself in bitter irony whether Saint Valentine had answered my request so quickly and really turned me into a lover in retirement.

I remember I cursed you and resented you at the time. I felt the bitterness that goes with tears. I, who didn't cry even when they amputated my arm, could have cried when you stole the last thing I possessed.

You stole my manhood.

One day I asked you, 'Do you love me?'

You said, 'I don't know. Your love rises and falls like faith!'

I can say today that my resentment at you also rose and fell like your faith. But that day I said, with a lover's naivety, 'Are you a believer?'

'Of course,' you exclaimed. 'I practise all the rites and commandments of Islam.'

'Do you fast?'

'Of course I fast. It's my way of defying this city, of reaching out to the homeland and memory.'

I don't know why I didn't expect you to be like that. There was something about the way you looked that suggested you were liberated from vestigial things. When I expressed my surprise you said, 'How can you call religion a vestige? It's a conviction, and like all our convictions, something that only concerns us individually.

'Never trust in outward appearance in such matters. Faith,

like love, is a secret emotion that we experience on our own in a permanent retreat into the self. It is our secret confidence and shield. Our secret escape to the depths to recharge our batteries when we need to. Those who seem overly religious are mostly those who've emptied themselves inside and make an outward display of their faith, for reasons unrelated to God.'

Such beautiful words from you that day. They came and turned the folds of memory inside out and awoke the sound of Constantine's minarets at dawn within me. Your words came bearing prayers, the chanting of the Qur'an, the voices of the monitors at the old religious schools of Constantine. I went back in the same childhood confusion to the mat where I had sat and repeated verses with other boys. We didn't yet under-stand them, but still copied them on to our slates and memorised them, fearful of the rod, the long cane lying ready to bloody our feet at the first slip.

Your words came and reconciled me with God. Me, who hadn't fasted for years. They reconciled me with the homeland and incited me against this city that, every day, stole a small space of faith and memory from me.

That day you were the woman who awoke my angels and my demons at the same time. Then you watched after turning me into a battleground where good and evil struggle ruthlessly.

That year, victory went to the angels.

I decided to fast, maybe as a result of what you said, but also to escape you through God. Didn't you say, 'Worship is our secret shield?' So I decided to deflect your arrows with faith. I tried to forget you, your dumping me, your very presence in the same city.

I spent days between dread and awe, religiously comatose. By conditioning my body to hunger I tried to condition myself to being deprived of you. I wanted to restore control over the senses that you had infiltrated and that only took orders from you. I wanted to restore to my former self the prestige, sanctity and principles I had before you. All the values you declared war on.

I admit I had some success in that. But you, I completely failed to forget. I fell into another trap of your love: I was living to your schedule. I fasted and sat down to break my fast with you. I ate the night meal and refrained from food with you. I had the same Ramadan dishes with none other than you. Without realising, I became one with you in everything.

In the end you were like the homeland. All things led to you, then. Love for you, like love for the homeland, remained present in faith and thought even when it stopped and went silent.

Was worship also a form of reaching out?

June was a month that provided plenty of reasons for pessimism.

In addition to June 1967 there were other painful recollections linked to that month. The most recent was June 1971, part of which I had spent in prison under investigation and as punishment along with others who had not learned to hold their tongues. The first painful memory went back to Kidya prison in Constantine, which I had entered with hundreds of others following the demonstrations of May 1945. Our military trial finished at the beginning of June.

Which June was the most unjust and which experience the most painful? I started to avoid posing those questions the day my answers led me to pack my bags and leave Algeria.

Algeria, the homeland that had become a prison with no official name, whose cells had no fixed location and whose inmates faced no clear charges. I was led in at dawn, blindfolded and flanked by two unknown figures taking me to an unknown destination. An honour not even bestowed on our biggest criminals.

As a youth full of enthusiasm and energy, and with soaring dreams, had I anticipated that, astonishingly, a quarter of a century later a fellow Algerian would remove my clothing, and even my watch and possessions, and fling me into a cell (solitary this time)? A cell I entered this time in the name of the Revolution. The Revolution that had already removed my arm!

More than one reason and memory made me take flight from the month that had chewed up so much of my happiness over the years.

Perhaps I harassed fate more that year, and it answered my pessimism with all the shocking tragedies that befell me in one month. Or perhaps it was just in the nature of disasters to come all at once: good things come led by a hair but leave in chains.

That was the absurdity of life. A coincidence as slender as a strand of hair was enough to bring unexpected happiness, love and good fortune. But once the strand was cut, all the chains attached to it broke even though they were thought too strong to break like a hair.

I hadn't noticed beforehand that meeting you that day, after a quarter of a century of forgetting, was a slender coincidence bringing with it all the happiness in the world. When it left, it severed the chain of dreams and pulled the carpet of security from under me.

Years after that summer of 1982 that strand of hair has come back today to knock down the last pillar in my house, bringing the roof down on top of me. Even though I believed back then that there was nothing left in my life to collapse, and that I had paid enough for fate to forget me at times.

At the time I did not know rule number one of the law of life.

'Man's destiny is but the end of a chain of folly,' Malek Haddad wrote.

Summer 1982, which combined personal and national failures, had a bitter taste of deadly despair.

I was living between two news items: your continuing silence and Arab catastrophes. This time, however, fate struck from another direction. Israel launched a surprise attack on Beirut that summer and for several weeks took up residence in an Arab capital. This was visible to more than one ruler and more than one million Arabs and took me several rungs down the ladder of despair.

I remember a minor incident struck me at the time and over-shadowed other news. To protest the Israeli incursion in the south, Lebanese poet Khalil Hawi committed suicide by shooting himself. The south was his alone and he refused to share its air with Israel. The death of this man, whom I had not heard of before, had a uniquely bitter pain. When a poet's only means of protest was his death, and his only writing paper his body, then we have also been shot.

All the time my heart went out to Ziyad. He used to say, 'Poets are butterflies who die in summer.' At the time he was mad about the Japanese novelist Mishima, who also killed himself – in another way and protesting at another failure. Perhaps he was inspired to say it by one of Mishima's titles, *Death in Summer*, or it was an old idea he still upheld by reciting a list of the names of poets who had chosen that season to die.

I would listen to him then and try to confront his pessimistic view of the summer with humour, fearful that the condition would spread to me. I would joke to him, 'But I can also give you a list of dozens of poets who didn't die in the summer!' He would laugh and reply, 'Of course, there are those who die between summers.' I could only respond, 'Poets! Stubborn fools.'

Ziyad came to mind and I suddenly wondered where he might be. In which city, at which front line, in which street when all the streets were surrounded and all the cities were graveyards prepared for death?

Since he had left, I had only received one brief letter, where he thanked me for my hospitality. That was eight months ago. What had become of him since then?

I hadn't been anxious about him until now. He had always lived in the midst of battles, ambushes and random bombardment. He was a man whom death feared or respected, whom death did not want to take cheaply. Even so, a vague feeling aroused my fears. I took it as a bad omen when I recalled his words on summer, and the suicide of that poet.

What if poets imitate each other in death too? What if they are not just butterflies, but like the giant baleen whales who prefer to die together at the same seasons on the same beaches?

Hemingway also committed suicide in the summer of 1961. He left behind the draft of his last novel, *The Dangerous Summer*. What was the link between the summer and all these novelists and poets who had not met? I shouldn't have thought too deeply about this, as though I were baiting or challenging fate that summer to give me the blow I haven't recovered from yet, even years later.

Ziyad died.

By chance, his obituary, a small square of newspaper, struck the eye and then the heart. Time stopped. The news formed a lump in my throat. I didn't shout or cry. I was paralysed by shock, stung by the tragedy.

How had it happened? Why didn't I expect his death when his last looks towards me held more than one farewell?

His suitcase was still in the wardrobe in his room. It would give me a start several times a day when I was looking for something. He went back without possessions. Did he know that he didn't need much to keep him going on his final journey or, as my jealousy made me imagine, was he contemplating coming back to settle down and live close to you?

I hadn't asked him the day he left. There had been silence between us for a few days. I avoided sitting with him, as if afraid he would confess to a thing I feared or a decision I expected. He left carrying a small bag and revealed nothing. He just apologised, 'You don't mind if I leave this suitcase with you? You know what it's like at airports these days, and I don't want to lug my things from one airport to another yet again.' He went on with something like sarcasm, 'Especially as nothing awaits me at the final destination!' His intuition hadn't been wrong. There was only the fatal bullet to come.

I still remember he once said, 'In every homeland we have a grave. We die at the hands of all in the name of all revolutions and all books.' His convictions didn't kill him this time. Just his identity.

That evening I got drunk toasting his laugh, toasting his distinctive tone unlike any other voice, toasting his proud, unequalled sadness, toasting his beautiful death, his final departure.

I wept for him that evening, obdurate painful tears that we secretly steal from our manhood. I wondered which man in him I cried for most, and what I was crying for.

He had died just as he wanted, as a poet, in summer and in battle. Even in death he defeated me.

At the time I remembered the wonderful words of Jean Cocteau. He made a film of his death in advance, where he turns to Picasso and his few friends standing in mourning and says to them with the painful irony of which he was a master, 'Don't cry so. Just pretend to cry. Poets do not die, they just pretend to die!'

Perhaps Ziyad just pretended to die and did it out of stubbornness to convince me that poets really die in summer and come back to life at every season.

And you? Did you know? Had you heard news of his death? Or would it reach you some other time in the middle of another story with other actors?

What would you do that day? Would you cry for him or would you sit and construct a mausoleum of words and bury him between the covers of a book, in haste, as was your custom for all those you loved and decided one day to kill?

He hated eulogies as much as he hated smart suits and ties, so in what language would you lament him? Ziyad defeated you just as he defeated me. He made you see the difference between death as a game and death itself. Not all heroes can die on paper. Some choose their own death and we cannot kill them just by writing a novel.

He told lies, like a hero ready for a novel. He would obstinately claim that Palestine alone was his mother. Sometimes, but only after a few drinks, he would admit that his mother had no grave of her own but lay in a mass grave from an earlier massacre, Tel al-Zaatar. They had taken souvenir pictures and raised victory signs, stood on corpses in their boots. Her corpse could have been among them.

Only at that moment did it seem he was crying. Why tears, Ziyad? You had a corpse in every battle, an unmarked grave at every massacre. Now your death continued the same logic.

Nothing awaited you except the train of death. Some rode the train of Tel al-Zaatar, some took the train of Beirut 1982 or of Sabra and Shatila. Here or there, in a camp or in the ruins of a house, or even in some Arab country, some were still waiting for their final journey.

Between one train and the next comes a train.

Between one death and the next comes death.

Happy are those who took the first train, my friend. They are so happy and we so miserable at every news broadcast. After them the 'travel agencies' multiplied along with the 'mass departures'. It became an Arab phenomenon, with each regime specialising in its own way. After them the homeland became a mere railway station. Inside each one of us was a railway line waiting for a train that we were sad to take and sad to see leave without us.

Ziyad had died.

His black suitcase, forgotten in a corner of his wardrobe, suddenly overshadowed all the furniture in the house. It became the only piece of furniture and I could see nothing else. When I returned home, I felt it was waiting for me and that I had an appointment with him. When I left the house, I felt I was running away from it, and that its riddle was weighing on me without my knowing. But how to run away from it when it lay in wait for me every evening? I would switch off the television and sit alone smoking a cigarette before going to bed, and the torture would begin.

I returned to the same question: what was inside the suitcase and what to do with it?

I tried to remember what people usually did with the possessions of the dead – their clothes, for example, and personal effects. Mother came to mind and with her the painful days around her death. I remembered her clothes and her things. I remembered her burgundy *kandoura*. It wasn't her most beautiful item of clothing but the one I loved most. She wore it for every special occasion. It was the robe that was most redolent of her distinctive perfume, amber mixed with her sweat and something like jasmine blossom. A mix of simple, natural perfumes with which I breathed in motherhood.

I asked about the *kandoura* some days after she died. I was told in some surprise that it had been given, along with other things, to the poor women who had come to cook that day. I shouted, 'It's mine. I wanted it.' But my eldest aunt said, 'The things of the dead have to be taken out of the house before the dead person leaves. All except for a few very precious things that are kept as mementos or for luck.'

Mother's *miqyas*, the bracelet that never left her wrist, as if she had been born wearing it, what do you think they did with it? I wasn't bold enough to ask. My brother Hassan, who wasn't even ten years old, wasn't aware of anything happening around him except Mother's death and permanent absence. I was surrounded by crowds of women who were deciding everything, as though the house were suddenly theirs. Where was Mother's bracelet? Most likely it had become the share of one of her sisters, or perhaps my father had taken it along with the rest of her gold to give as a gift to his new bride.

Whenever I dwelt on the details of that memory, my relationship with that suitcase grew more complicated. Ordinary things left as a legacy sometimes had a value far beyond their worth to others. What should I do with a suitcase whose owner had left months before without instructions or explanation and then died?

If the things of the dead go to the poor, should I give it to charity? Or if we keep the precious objects, should I keep it as a memento of a friend?

Was it a burden or a pledge? If it was a burden, why did I accept it without any discussion? Why didn't I persuade him to take it with him, using the excuse that I might leave Paris, for example? If it was a pledge, hadn't its owner's death turned it into a last request? Would we give the requests of martyrs away as charity? Would we leave them at our door as a present for the first vagrant?

I spent days obsessed by the suitcase, but I knew I was exhausting myself in vain. Only its contents could determine its value and character and so determine what I might do with it. As a result, I was suddenly afraid of it, even though I had paid it no attention before.

Did Ziyad's death impart this confusing character to it? Or was I, in fact, afraid that it would reveal your secret to me, something about you I was afraid to know?

To shut the door on suspicion, I had to open the suitcase.

I took the decision on a Saturday night, a week after reading the report of Ziyad's death.

There was only one other, not entirely sensible, option: to take it to the offices of the PLO and give it to someone there to send to Ziyad's relatives in Lebanon or elsewhere.

But I rejected that naive idea when I remembered that Ziyad no longer had family in Lebanon. Who, then, would they send it to? With what kind of people would it end up?

Who would be its 'father'? There was more than one 'Abu' who thought he alone was the father of the Palestinian cause and the sole legitimate heir of the martyrs. To him the others were traitors.

How would I know who killed Ziyad? Was it at the hands of criminal 'comrades' or the criminal enemy? Didn't he say, 'They've turned the cause into "causes" so they can murder us without calling it a crime'?

Which bullet killed Ziyad when the prime of Palestinian youth was being killed by Palestinian or Arab bullets?

That evening my hand shook as I opened the catches on the suitcase. Something made me remember I only had one arm. The case wasn't locked with a key or padlocks. It was as though he intended to leave it to me half open like someone leaving a door ajar as a silent invitation to enter. I relaxed a little at this gesture, the prior or belated permission Ziyad had given me to enter his private world without feeling ashamed. Perhaps he had done so because he hated broken locks and doors forced open as much as he hated informers and jackboots.

Or because he had anticipated a day like this.

All these suppositions did not stop a shiver going through me and another thought crossing my mind. He had known in advance that he was going to die, and this suitcase was readied for me from the outset. I could have opened it months before. From the moment he left the apartment, it no longer existed for him. It was his way of severing the roots of memory, as usual.

I lifted up the top of the suitcase, after putting it on the edge of the bed, and took a first look at what was inside. Death and life assailed me equally as I saw his clothes and touched his grey woollen sweaters and the black leather jacket he always wore. I had proof of his presence, proof of his absence, proof of his death and proof of his life. The scent of life and of death breathed equally strongly from the corners of the suitcase.

Here I was before his remains, with him and without him.

An item of clothing, another. The external jacket of a human

187

book. A cloth front to a house of glass. The house broke and the front remained, memory folded into a suitcase. Why had he left me his exterior? Among the clothes was a sky-blue silk shirt still unopened in its clear glossy wrapper. I easily deduced this had been a present from you.

Then three cassette tapes, one of Theodorakis, the others excerpts of classical music. I put them to one side as I remembered that Ziyad, whenever he went, left me cassettes, books and clothes – and a love in suspension.

But this was the first time he had left things packed in a suitcase, favourite objects carefully arranged. It was as though he had packed it with all the things he loved in preparation for a journey. The things he might want wherever he was going: his favourite black jacket and the music of Theodorakis.

My hand came across your novel at the bottom of the case. I trembled, and my hand shook and paused some moments before picking up the book. I sat down on the edge of the bed before opening it. It was as though I were opening a letter bomb. I flicked through the book as though I didn't know it. Then I remembered something. I raced to the front page in search of a dedication. But there was only a blank page, not one word, no signature or inscription. I felt a wave of sadness that paralysed my hand and a vague urge to cry.

To which one of us did you dedicate your false version, when both of us had an unsigned copy? Which of us did you make imagine that he inhabited the book's inside pages – like your heart – and had no need for a dedication?

Had Ziyad believed you? Did he, too, believe you to the extent that he decided to take this novel with him to reread wherever he went? This blank page was enough to condemn you. Its unwritten words spoke more eloquently than anything you could have

188

written. Did it matter after this that I didn't find a letter to you in the suitcase?

You were a woman expert in invisible ink, and only I knew it.

Apart from your novel, I only found a medium-sized black diary, nestled at the bottom of the case like a secret. As soon as I picked it up, the *carte orange* Ziyad had used on the Métro fell out along with a newspaper cutting from October, the month he had left. I took a quick look at the ticket, but was only thinking about reading the diary. His photo stopped me, however. Photos of the dead are disturbing; photos of martyrs more so. Always a source of pain, martyrs suddenly become sadder and more mysterious in their photographs.

As enigmas, they become suddenly more beautiful while we become more horrified. We're suddenly afraid to stare at them. We're suddenly worried about our photographs to come!

My, he was handsome, that man. A concealed, ambiguous handsomeness. Even in a quick snapshot taken in less than three minutes for less than five francs he could appear special. Even after his death he could be attractive with that vague, ironic melancholy. It was though he was making fun in advance of a moment just like this.

I understood once again that you loved him. But I loved him before you in another way, the way we love a person we admire and wish to emulate for one reason or another. We meet them, go out with them and are seen with them as much as possible, as though, deep down, we believe that their beauty, mad passion and talent, all their brilliant features, might be transmitted to us by proximity.

What a ridiculous idea! I only discovered that it was the root of my disaster too late. That was when I read the wonderful words of a French writer (and painter): 'Do not seek beauty, because once you find it, you will have disfigured yourself!' I made exactly that stupid mistake.

I put his ticket and photograph back into the case and started turning over the diary.

I felt it contained something that would surprise me, that might disturb my mood and open the door to unseasonal gales. What, I wondered, did he write in it? I knew that truth was always born small and felt that the truth here was as small as this fearful pocketbook. I looked for a cigarette to light and lay down on the bed to leaf through the diary at leisure.

The pages came filled with stanzas of poetry scattered among the dates. There were notes in the margins and other, long poems that might take up two or three pages or brief jottings of a few lines always written in red in the middle of a page. It seemed he had wished to make these stand out from the rest of what he'd written. Perhaps because they weren't poetry, perhaps because they were more important than poetry.

Where should I have begun this diary? Where was the entrance to Ziyad's secret labyrinth, which I had always dreamed of sneaking into on the chance of finding you?

A title would stop me and I would start reading a poem. I would try and solve the clues and locate you, sometimes in the symbolism and sometimes in the most confessional details. But I couldn't wait, and rushed to another page in search of other proofs and further explanation, for words to tell me what had happened in black and white.

I was, in fact, so worked up and so full of extreme, clashing feelings that I could barely think. I was unable to distinguish between what I read and what I imagined I was reading.

At that moment, the vision of the suitcase open before me, its strewn contents and the small black diary that I was holding made me ashamed of myself. It was as if in opening it I were performing an autopsy on Ziyad's corpse, its remains strewn on my bed, in order to extract this notebook, which was nothing less than his heart.

Ziyad's heart, which had once throbbed for you and which that day, even after his death, continued to beat in my hands to the rhythm of words fraught with loss and fear, sadness and lust.

> Over my body run your lips
> They only ran blades over me
> Set me on fire, woman of flame
> Love will bring us close one day
> Death will part us one day
> A handful of dust will judge us
> Desire for the body will bring us close
> Then one day
> A wound the size of the body will part us
> I was one in you
> Woman of dust and marble
> I watered you, then I cried and said:
> Princess of my desire
> Princess of my death
>   Come near!

I read this passage so many times, with new feelings and new doubts every time. I asked myself with the impotence of an amateur poet, where did imagination end and reality begin? Where was the line between the symbolic and the real?

Each phrase cancelled out the one before. The woman's body so fused with the earth that it was impossible to separate or distinguish them.

Yet the reality of the words' blatant desire was unmistakeable. 'Over my body run your lips – Set me on fire, woman of flame – Desire for the body will bring us close – I was one in you.'

Was revolution nothing but a mess of words that Ziyad used to exonerate himself? He preferred defeat at the hands of death to defeat at the hands of a woman. It was a matter of pride and self-deception. 'Princess of my death/Come near.'

Death did come at last. Did you perhaps come that day?

Was he really alone with you? Did you run your lips over his body? Did you set him on fire? Was he one in you? Did . . .?

Most likely, it did happen. The date of that poem matched the date of my trip to Spain.

My heart started to overflow with a strange emotion, nothing to do with jealousy. We can't be jealous of the dead. Still, in cases like this we can't change the taste of bitterness.

My eyes were arrested by the colour red. Should I have stopped their tears when they read:

> Not much is left of life.
> You standing at the crossing of opposites.
> I know
> you will be my final sin.
> I ask you
> till when will I be your first sin.
> You have space for more than one beginning
> and all endings are short.
> Now I am ending in you.
> Who will give a life fit for multiple endings!

Some of the words made me stop in my tracks.
The red ink suddenly turned the colour of blood, a blush of

crimson sweeping over the page in the colour of 'your first sin'.

I quickly shut the diary, as if afraid that if I kept looking I might catch you in an unforeseen position.

Something that Ziyad had said long, long before came back. 'I have a great deal of respect for Adam,' he had said, 'because when he decided to taste the apple, a bite wasn't enough. He ate the whole thing. Perhaps he knew that there are no half-sins and half-pleasures. That's why there isn't a third place between heaven and hell. To avoid any miscalculation, we have to enter one of them on merit!'

At the time I admired Ziyad's philosophy of life. What was it that hurt me that day about the ideas we shared? Perhaps because he stole his apple from my secret garden or because he took a bite in front of me with the appetite of someone who, having made up his mind, had relaxed.

> Trees can also only
> make love standing up.
> Palm tree of my desire, stand up!
> I alone mourned the forests
> they burned down
> to force the trees to kneel.
> Trees die standing.
> Come and stand with me.
> In you, I want to send my manhood
> off to its final resting place.

I suddenly began to feel that opening the diary had been a stupid move, and started to regret it. My personal interpretations of every word had exhausted me. Despite everything, I didn't want to hate Ziyad, and couldn't. Death had given him immunity from my hatred and jealousy. I was insignificant compared to him and his death.

I had nothing to condemn him with except words open to interpretation. Why should I insist on the worst and stalk him with all these suspicions? I knew he was a poet who specialised in the violation of language, in revenge at a world not created to his specification, perhaps even created at his expense. Could I shoot him for words?

He had been born standing and shared the fate of trees. Should I blame him for the way he died – and the way he loved?

Now I remember that when I met him he had stood upright. I remember that day he came to my office for the first time, and I made some remarks about his poetry collection and asked him to cut some poems. I remember his silence, and his gaze lingering on my amputated arm. Then he said what went on to change the course of my life: 'Sir, my poems do not undergo amputation. Give me back my book. I'll publish it in Beirut.'

Why had I accepted his insult that day without responding? Why hadn't I slapped him with my other, unamputated hand and flung his manuscript at him? Was it because I respected his tree-like courage and individuality at a time when pens bent like wheat to any rustle of breeze?

I met Ziyad standing tall, and standing tall he left; a manuscript in front of me like the first time, but this time without comment. Since the beginning we had shared the complicity of the forest, and now its silence.

All of a sudden the traces of a previous profession stirred within me. I started turning the pages of the diary, counting and examining them with a publisher's eye. A sudden enthusiasm obscured my other feelings, and a crazy idea took hold. I would publish these writings in a poetry collection that I might call *Trees* or *Drafts from a Man who Loved You,* or some other title I might stumble across. What mattered was that Ziyad's last thoughts be published, that I grant them another life, without summer. Poets would always take their revenge on fate, which pursues them as summer pursues butterflies. They are transformed into poetry, and who can kill words?

Ziyad's diary rescued me from despair without my realising.

It gave me plans for days without plans. I spent hours copying out poems, hunting for another title or trying to arrange the chaos of these scattered thoughts and stanzas into a form suitable for publication.

I felt a mix of pleasure and bitterness. The pleasure of aligning with the butterflies and giving life to words that I alone had the right to bury alive in the diary or grant eternity in a book. The bitterness of delving into the papers of a dead poet, of exploring the blood in his veins, the beat of his heart, his sadness and his ecstasy, of entering his secret locked world without permission or licence from him, of selecting, adding and erasing on his behalf.

Did I really have such authority? Who could claim, for some reason, to have been given such a task? But would anyone dare to condemn the words of others to death and decide to appropriate them for himself?

Deep inside I knew that if the death of a poet or writer had an extra hint of sadness that distinguished it from the deaths of others, it might have been because when they died, they, like all creative people, left chapter headings, the headings for dreams and unfinished drafts on their desks. That was why their deaths shamed us as much as it grieved us. Ordinary people carried their dreams, worries and feelings on the surface. They put them on every day with their smiles and depression, their laughter and stories, and their secrets died with them.

To begin with, I was ashamed of Ziyad's secret, before it induced me to confess that his writings had created within me an irresistible desire to write. A desire that increased when I felt his words did not reach my depths and fell short of my pain. Perhaps this was because he had been ignorant of the other half of the story, the part only I knew.

When was the idea of this book born? Perhaps during the period I spent besieged by Ziyad's poetic testament, that unexpected reunion with literature and manuscripts, lost to me since I had lost my job in Algeria years before. Or was it during my other unexpected reunion, with a city? Belatedly, fate itself made that appointment.

Could I possibly find myself face to face with Constantine without advance warning, without floods of longing, madness and disappointment bursting inside me? The words swept me along to where I am!

Chapter Five

ISTILL REMEMBER THAT incredible Saturday when the telephone rang at evening-news time. *Si* Sharif was on the line. His warmth and excitement delighted me to begin with, breaking the monotony of my nightly silence and loneliness.

His voice itself signified a celebration: it was my only link with you after all avenues had been blocked. I took it as a good sign, always bearing the possibility of a chance meeting with you. But this time it brought more than that.

First, *Si* Sharif apologised for not being in touch since our last evening together. He had been very busy dealing with the non-stop flow of official visitors to Paris. He then added, 'All that time, though, I haven't forgotten you. I hung your painting in the living room and now I share the house with you. You know that your gesture has left a big impression on me and made people envy me. I keep having to explain that we've been friends since childhood.'

I was listening to him, but my heart foolishly raced ahead to you. Knowing that the conversation originated in the house where you were was sufficient to unleash all the emotions and folly of a new lover. His voice brought me back to reality when he asked, 'Do you know why I'm calling you tonight? I've decided to take you with me to Constantine. You gave me a painting of Constantine, and I shall give you a trip to her.'

I exclaimed, 'Constantine! Why Constantine?'

As if breaking good news, he said, 'To attend the wedding of my brother *Si* Taher's daughter.' After a little thought he added, 'Perhaps you remember her. She was at the opening of your exhibition with my daughter Nadia.'

I suddenly felt that my voice had separated from my body and was unable to utter a single word. Could words strike like lightning? At a word, could the body lose its ability to grip the telephone? At such moments I would suddenly remember that I had only one arm. I dragged a chair over with my foot and sat down.

Perhaps *Si* Sharif noticed my silence and that something had happened. He cut short my shock by saying, 'My brother, what are you worried about? Only a few days ago your name came up at a meeting with a few friends in the security service. They assured me that there were no instructions concerning you and that you could visit Algeria whenever you wanted. Things have changed a lot since you came here. You must go back to Algeria, even if only for a flying visit. I'll be responsible for making sure you come back. You'll travel with me and at my expense. What have you got to be so worried about?'

Looking for a way out of my anxiety, I answered, 'To be honest, I'm not mentally up to such a trip yet. I'd prefer it to be in other circumstances.'

'You'll never find better conditions than these for going back,' he said. 'I'm sure that if I don't take you in hand this time, it'll be years before you go back. Are you going to spend your life painting Constantine? Plus won't you be happy to attend the wedding of *Si* Taher's daughter? She's your daughter, too. You knew her as a child and you have to attend her wedding to give your blessings. Do it for her father's sake. You have to stand by me that day in *Si* Taher's place.'

Si Sharif knew that *Si* Taher was my weak point. He went and played on the loyalty I still owed to our shared past and memory. The situation was quite surreal, quite absurd. I was straddling the divide between reason and madness, between laughter and tears.

'You knew her as a child.' – No, my friend! I also knew her as a woman, that's the problem. 'She's your daughter, too.' – No, she wasn't my daughter, she only might have been, but she might have been my lover, too. She might have been my wife. She might have been mine.

I asked him, 'Whose will she be?'

'I've given her to *Si* —— —,' he said. 'You were at the party with him last time. I don't know what you think of him. But I think he's a good man despite what they say about him.'

His last sentence contained an answer in advance to the response he anticipated.

None less than *Si* —— —, then! 'A good man'. Was being good really his distinguishing feature? In that case, I knew more than one good man who could have become her husband. But *Si* —— — was more than that. He was the man of secret deals and front companies. A man of hard currency and hard missions. He was the junta's man, the man of the future. After that, did it matter if he was good or not?

More than one lump in my throat stopped me from really expressing my opinion about him, and from asking *Si* Sharif one question only: whether he thought a man without morals was capable of being good. Or maybe I shut up because I was no longer making any great distinction between him and his 'in-law'. I asked myself a different question: Could a person related by marriage to a corrupt man really be clean?

I suddenly lost the desire to talk. The successive shocks within one conversation had made me mute. I summed it all up in one sentence, open to interpretation. 'All things are blessed.'

Si Sharif gave the traditional response. 'God bless you.' Then he added in delight, as if he had passed an exam, 'So, we'll be seeing you. We're counting on you. We'll be travelling in about ten days' time and the wedding's on the fifteenth of July. Call me on the phone to fix the details.'

The conversation ended and a new phase of my life began. My other life began that day when it was made official that you would leave it. But had you truly left? I felt I was the only player at the board. All the squares were the same colour, and all the pieces had merged into one piece that I was holding – in one hand. Was I the sole winner or loser, and how could I tell? The board, along with room for hope and anticipation, had shrunk. Fate, the player we all stood in for from the beginning, was setting the rules.

Sometimes I did resent fate, but I often submitted without resistance. I took a strange pleasure in always wanting to know just how foolish fate could be. I was curious as to how unfair life could be. After all, life was a whore that only gave herself to those of suspect behaviour who got rich quick and took her in a hurry.

At the time, comparing myself with others' inadequacy was a rare pleasure. My personal defeats were proof of other triumphs that were not available to all. Perhaps in a moment of derangement like that I accepted the idea of attending your wedding. I would witness my own funeral and the depths to which some people would stoop without the slightest shame. Alternatively, perhaps like all creative people, I was a supreme masochist. Given the absence of absolute bliss, I would insist on living in absolute sadness. To get over you, I would take self-abuse to the point of branding my own heart.

I hated you that day with a fierceness I had not experienced before. My emotions flipped in an instant into something new, mixing bitterness, jealousy and revulsion, and perhaps resentment too.

How did you get to this place? Do women, like nations, really go weak before a man in uniform, even if faded? Even today I'm still asking how I agreed to go to Constantine for your wedding. I already knew that inviting me wasn't simply a pleasant gesture of affection and friendship on the part of a man I was close to in more ways than one.

Before everything else, it was exploitation of memory and misuse of one of the few pristine names left in an age of corruption. *Si* Sharif knew he was party to a dirty deal. In exchange for status and more deals, he was selling the name of his brother, one of the great *shahids*, in marriage. He was disposing of that name in a way *Si* Taher would never have accepted if he had been alive.

He needed me – friend and comrade in arms of *Si* Taher – and no one else, to give my blessings to your violation. I was the last disjointed skeleton from a bygone age still standing. He needed my blessings and presence to silence his conscience and be able to believe that *Si* Taher, whose name he had lived off for so long, would forgive him.

Why did I agree to play that game? Why did I agree, without argument, to hand you into their clutches? Is it because I knew that my blessings were for show? They wouldn't change anything.

If he didn't marry you off to *Si* — —, you would be the lot of another *Si* among the new masters. In the end, what did it matter which of the forty thieves' names you would carry?

Why did I agree to go? Was it because of all that, or did I submit to the seduction of Constantine? To its secret call that had pursued and haunted me for ages, like the song of the sirens haunted the sailors whose ships had been cursed by the gods. Perhaps I was simply incapable of resisting a date with you, even if the occasion was your marriage.

Some decisions are counterintuitive. How, today, can I explain an illogical decision? I was like a mad scientist who wanted to combine two explosive mixtures – you and Constantine. Two mixtures I created myself in a fit of longing, love and mad passion. I had calculated their destructive power individually but wanted to try them together, like testing an atom bomb in the desert. I wanted to experience them both together in one internal blast that would shake and destroy only me. I would then emerge from the firestorm and devastation as either a new man or the remnants of one.

Didn't you once say that all of us have a secret desire called 'the hunger for flames'? Afterwards I discovered for myself the symmetry between you and that city. Both of you possessed an unquenchable fire and a supernatural power to set things alight. But both of you pretended to declare war on fire-worshippers. That was the falsity of ancient, respectable cities and the hypocrisy of girls from good families, wasn't it?

Your voice came out of the blue on Monday. It held no special note of sadness or joy, no awkwardness or obvious embarrassment. You started talking to me as though resuming a conversation from the day before, even though your voice had not been on the line for more than six months. You had such a strange relationship with time, such a strange memory!

'Hi, Khaled. Have I woken you up?'

I could have said no, although it would have been more correct to say yes. But in the voice of someone coming out of an amorous coma, I said, 'You!?'

You laughed the childish laugh that had once captivated me and said, 'I believe I'm me. Have you forgotten my voice?' Faced with my silence you added, 'How are you?'

'Trying to keep going.'

'Keep going against whom?'

'Against time.'

After a silence, as though you were feeling guilty about something, you said, 'We're all trying to do that.' Then you added, 'Is it my news that has upset you?'

Your question was as incredible as your memory, as your relationship with those you loved!

I said, 'Your news is only part of the ups and downs of fate.'

In false innocence you replied, 'I was expecting you to take the news of my marriage differently. I heard my uncle on the phone with you yesterday and was amazed that you agreed to come to Constantine without any argument or hesitation. That made me really happy, and I decided to call you. I gathered you no longer blamed me. I want you come to the wedding. You must come.'

I didn't know why your words made me recall my earlier conversation with *Si* Sharif – the unbelievable situation of his persuading me that you were my daughter. Once again I felt I was straddling the divide between reason and madness, between laughter and tears.

'I wish I understood why you're all so insistent that I be there,' I said.

'My uncle's reasons for insisting don't interest me in the slightest. But I do know that I'll be miserable if you don't come.'

I replied sarcastically, 'Is being sadistic your latest hobby?'

In a tone that surprised me you said, 'I loved that city because of you.'

I adopted the words you had used when I admitted that I fell in love with you the day I read you. Then, you had said that I shouldn't have read you. Now I said, 'You shouldn't have loved the city, then.'

The response you gave stunned me fully awake and sent a jolt of electricity through me. 'But I loved you.'

Here were the words I had been awaiting in vain for a year. Should I thank you or cry? Or ask you why now and why all the suffering then? I just asked, 'And him?'

As if talking about something that didn't at all concern you, you answered, 'He's a ready-made fate.'

I interrupted, 'Everyone gets the fate they deserve. I expected a different fate for you. How did you agree to be joined with him?'

'I'm not joining with him,' you said. 'I'm running away with him from a memory unfit for habitation after I filled it with impossible dreams and successive failures.'

'But why him? How could you tarnish your father's name with garbage like that? You aren't just any woman – you are a homeland. Don't you care about the verdict of history?'

You replied, 'You're the only person who believes that history sits on our shoulders, like the good angel and the bad angel, to record our minor unknown victories or our sudden slips and downward descent. History no longer records anything. It only erases!'

I didn't ask you what you wanted erased, and I didn't raise your mistaken view of values.

I asked you, 'What exactly do you want from me?'

'I want you,' you said, like a child choosing a sweet.

It occurred to me at that moment that perhaps you were a woman incapable of loving one man, that you always needed two. In the past it had been me and Ziyad, and now it was me and that other.

Your voice returned, saying, 'Khaled, do you even know that I loved you? I wanted and desired you to the point of madness. Something about you once robbed me of my mind. But I decided to get over you. Our love affair was unhealthy. You yourself said that.'

I asked you, 'Why have you come back today, then?'

'I've come back to persuade you to come to Constantine. I want that city to give us her blessing, even if only once, even if falsely. She was complicit with us and led us to this madness of ours. I know that we won't meet there. We might not talk to each other. We might not shake hands. But I will be yours as long as you are there. We will defy them as she watches. Only she will know that I have given my first night to you. Does that make you happy?'

How many first nights could you have? How many imaginary first nights could you sign away like your first novel: two fake copies, for me and for Ziyad, unsigned.

After each imaginary night, who would have you? With whom did you first start lying? To whom did you dedicate your first booby-trapped gift?

When I recall your words now, I laugh as I compare myself to a starving Ethiopian who's being read a menu of delicious dishes he'll never taste and who's then asked what he thought of them and whether it made him happy. But at the time I didn't laugh. Perhaps I even cried as I answered you with the idiocy of a lover. 'It makes me happy.'

I didn't notice that you were giving me an imaginary night that I would have to give up straight away to that other man who would actually enjoy it. But did it matter as long as I was giving up something that, in any case, wasn't mine?

History and the past are always like that, my darling. We invite them to special occasions to take care of the crumbs on the table. We deceive memory, throwing it a bone to chew on, while setting the tables for others. Peoples are also like that. They're fed illusions, loads of bottled dreams and delayed gratification and they close their eyes to the banquets they will never be invited to.

But I was only conscious of all this once it was too late, once everyone had got up from the tables and gone home, leaving me alone with crumbs of memory.

I said, 'I want to see you.'

'No!' you cried. 'Meeting is no longer possible. Perhaps that's for the best. We have to find a less painful ending to our story. Let Constantine be our reunion and our parting. There's no need for more suffering.'

Like that, then, you decided to kill me decorously with one stab of the knife, in and out, one meeting and one separation. How compassionate you were with me, and how stupid I was!

More than one question that I didn't ask you that day has remained stuck in my throat. More than blame, more than reproach, more than desire.

Your call ended as it had begun, outside of time with me hovering between sleep and waking, stretched out in bewilderment on my bed.

I even asked myself afterwards: Did you really call me that morning or was it just a dream?

* * *

So we were like children, always rubbing away the chalk on the ground to draw the rules for a new game. We tricked everything to win everything. Dirtying our clothes and getting scratched as we hopped from one impossible square to another.

Each square was a trap set for us where we stood and let a few dreams slip to the ground. We ought to have admitted that we were too old for hopping and for skipping ropes, for living in imaginary chalk squares.

We got it wrong, my love. The homeland doesn't get drawn in chalk. Love doesn't get written in nail varnish. We got it wrong. History doesn't get written on a blackboard, chalk in one hand, duster in the other. Love doesn't seesaw between the possible and the impossible.

Let's stop playing games for a moment, stop running in every direction. In this game we have forgotten who was the cat and who the mouse, which one of us would eat the other. We forgot that we would be eaten together.

There's no longer space for lies. There's only this final descent. There is nothing beneath us but the abyss of destruction. Let's admit that we've disintegrated together. You are not my lover. You are my draft love for days to come, my draft story and joy to come, my draft other life.

In the meantime, love any man you wish and write any stories you wish. Only I know your story, which won't ever appear in print. Only I know the heroes you overlooked and those you made up. Only I know your perverse way of loving, the singular way you have of killing those you love, just to fill up your books. I am the one you killed for inscrutable reasons, and who loved you for other inscrutable reasons. I am the man who turned you from a woman into a city, and whom you turned from a precious stone into gravel. Don't offend my ruins too much.

The age of earthquakes has not ended, and in the depths of this homeland the volcanoes still have rocks to spew.

Let us stop playing games for a moment. You've told enough lies. I know you'll never be mine. Allow me, then, on the day of resurrection, to be resurrected with you wherever you are, that I might be your better half.

Allow me to reserve in advance a spot next to you, seeing as all the places around you here are taken and your diary is filled up to the end of your days.

Woman in the shape of homeland, does it matter any more if we stay together?

Just a small suitcase to meet the homeland. For your wedding reception, I only needed a black suit, two bottles of whiskey, some shirts and some razorblades. (There are nations that produce every justification for death but forget to produce razorblades!)

Tiptoeing around my wound, I returned to the homeland without personal effects, without excess baggage or an excessive bank balance. Memory alone had become too much to bear, but who would call me to account for the memory that I bear alone?

Walking on my latest wound, I returned in haste. Nearly ten years' absence followed by a sudden return. I expected a different reunion. I would have reserved myself a first-class seat, for example. Memory on such occasions might refuse to take the back seat.

It didn't matter in any case, my lady. All the front seats had been reserved in advance for those who had taken positions of power by order. So let me return as I left, on a sad seat to one side.

We leave the homeland with suitcases full of our lives and the papers from our drawers. We pack our photo albums, books we loved and gifts with sentimental value. We carry the faces of those we loved, the eyes of those who loved us, letters to us, and others we wrote. A final glance at an old neighbour whom we might not see again; a kiss on a young cheek that will grow up after we're gone; a tear for a homeland we might not return to.

We carry the homeland to furnish our exile. The homeland puts us out the door and shuts its heart in our face without so much as a glance at our suitcases. Our tears have no effect, and we forget to ask who will fill the homeland after us.

Then, when we come back, we return with suitcases of nostalgia and a handful of dreams. We return with rose-tinted dreams, not rose-patterned bags – dreams aren't imported from cheap shops. It's disgraceful that we buy and sell the dream of the homeland on the black market. There are worse insults to the martyrs than a thousand kinds of hard currency.

With a small holdall in nowhere land, suspended between heaven and earth, escaping from one memory to another, I took a second-class seat in forgetting.

I hovered over the contours of your love from a height that made it hard to see and hard to forget. I asked myself, even though it was too late, whether I was making the last stupid mistake of my life by running away from you into the arms of the homeland. I was trying to use it to get over you, having already failed with you to get over it.

The painting I brought as a wedding present for you occupied your empty seat next to me. Finally we were travelling together, you and me. We took the same plane for the first time, but we weren't on the same journey or going in the same direction.

There was Constantine. Just two hours for the heart to go back a lifetime.

A hostess opened the plane door, unaware that she was

opening the shutters of the heart. Who now would stop the bleeding of memory? Who would be able to shut the windows of nostalgia? Who would stand in the face of the headwind to lift the veil from the face of this city, and look into her eyes without crying?

There was Constantine.

I was carrying a holdall in my one hand and a painting making its final journey after twenty-five years of life together. It was *Nostalgia*, that incomplete copy of Constantine about to meet the original by night. Like me, it very nearly fell down the steps in tiredness and confusion. Narrow, cold glances flung orders at us. All those tight faces, all those faded grey walls.

Was this the homeland?

Constantine . . . How are you, Omayma? . . . *Washik?* . . . Open your door and embrace me . . . Exile is painful . . . Return is painful.

Your airport, which I no longer remembered, was cold. Your mountain night, which no longer remembered me, was cold.

Wrap me up, lady of warmth and coldness.

Hold back your chill a little. Hold back my disappointment a little. I am coming to you from frozen years of disappointment, from the cities of ice and loneliness. Don't leave me standing at the mercy of the hurt.

The signs in Arabic, some official pictures and all these similar brown faces assured me that I was finally standing face to face with the homeland. They made me feel a different kind of exile unique to Arab airports.

Only the appearance of Hassan's face filled me with sudden warmth and the ice melted between the airport and me.

He embraced me and took the weight from my hand and said, in a playful Algerian accent while taking the painting from me,

'What! You're still lugging *tableaux* about?' Then he added, 'This is a great day. Whoever thought we'd see you here!'

I felt that Constantine had suddenly assumed his features and had finally come to welcome me. Was Hassan anything other than the city herself, her stones, her tiles, her bridges and schools, her alleyways and her memory? He was born here, grew up and studied here. He became a teacher here. And only left rarely on brief trips to Tunis or Paris.

He came to visit me yearly to make sure I was OK and take the chance to buy a few things for his ever-growing family. It seemed that Hassan, after despairing of ever marrying me off, had resolved to stop the extinction of the family name single-handedly. After several unsuccessful attempts to tempt me, he realised that, apart from my paintings, I would have no children to carry my name. He always talked with a teacher's enthusiasm, certainty and repetition, as if addressing his students, not other adults. That day, I discovered that that very tall and clean-cut man was nothing less than my brother.

Had I been ignorant of that? No! But on that day of exceptional pain, disappointment − and joy! − I felt my brother represented the only solid ground in my upheaval and, were it not for my pride, the only shoulder I could cry on.

Over the course of nearly ten years, I had gone to wait for him at Orly airport. The roles were reversed then. He was the one arriving and I was waiting. Although I felt I was volunteering to perform a family duty, I was still particular about it. That was one of the few opportunities for me to play the role of older brother, with all its responsibilities and obligations. A role I did not always perform well, for in fact I was always quite distant with him. He had been orphaned at an early age, and his craving for tenderness and his attachment to me were obvious.

Perhaps also on account of that, he married early and hastily. He had lots of children so as finally to surround himself with the family he had been denied as a child. That was something I could not make up for with my transient presence and my absence between exiles.

Why did my meeting with Hassan that day overturn all the previous norms and make me feel, despite the difference in ages and his six children, that I was the younger brother, and at that moment he was seven years older than me, or more?

Perhaps because he was the one carrying my bag, walking in front and asking about my journey, or because the airport, which was an offence to my masculine pride, stripped me of the gravity of my years. So I left Hassan to handle it instead of me, as though his experience with the city and familiarity with her changeable nature made him seem older that day.

Perhaps at the first step on to the ground of Constantine, that mother of extreme emotions, love and hate, tenderness and abuse, I had turned into the confused, shy youth of thirty years before. I watched her from the car taking me home from the airport. I wondered whether she recognised me.

That city homeland allowed informers, the well-connected and dirty-handed to enter through gates of honour, while I entered with queues of strangers, street traders and the desperate. Did the woman who checked my passport but forgot to look at me recognise me?

A Bedouin woman was once asked, 'Which is your favourite child?' She answered, 'One who's absent, till he comes back; one who's unwell, till he's better; one who's young, till he grows up.'

I was her absent one who didn't come back, her unwell one who didn't get better, her little one who didn't grow up. But Constantine had not heard the words of this Arab woman and I couldn't reproach her. I just blamed what I'd read in books of Arab heritage.

I didn't sleep that night. Was the dinner – or feast – cooked by Hassan's wife, Atiqa, to blame? With an appetite verging on the historic, I had surrendered to its multiple dishes, most of which I had not tasted for years. Or was my anxiety down to the emotional shock of a reunion with the house where I had been born and raised? Its walls, stairs, windows, rooms and passages held many memories, of weddings, of funerals and of the religious holidays, of other ordinary days. Memories that had accumulated deep within me and suddenly came to the surface that day. Extraordinary memories that obliterated everything else.

When I was in that house, I was in my memory. How does one sleep on a pillow of memories?

The ghosts of the departed were still moving around the rooms. I could almost see the hem of Mother's deep red *kandoura* passing to and fro with its secret maternal presence. I could almost hear my father's voice asking for water to perform his ablutions, or shouting from the bottom of the stairs, 'Coming up, coming up,' to warn the women of the house that he was with a male companion and that they should clear the way and secrete themselves in the back rooms.

Beneath the new whitewash on the wall I could almost make out the traces of the nail where my father hung my primary school certificate forty years ago, and next to it, years after, another certificate.

And then nothing. He lost interest in me and started to take an interest in other things, other plans that culminated in Mother's death and a remarriage that had been waiting in the wings for some time.

I could almost see Mother's body leaving the narrow doorway

again, followed by a crowd of Qur'an reciters and professional female mourners. I could almost see another procession making its way in a few weeks later, that time with a young bride and professional female ululators and singers.

Then there was the night I kissed Hassan goodbye before I joined the FLN. He didn't ask me where I was going; at fifteen he was far ahead of his years. Like me, becoming an orphan had made him grow up fast. Having been humiliated taught him to keep quiet and keep his questions to himself.

He asked, 'And me?'

In the same panic, I answered him, 'You're still young, Hassan. Wait for me.'

As if suddenly taking on Mother's voice and her debilitating fear for me, he said, 'Take care of yourself, Khaled,' and burst into tears.

Here was the homeland that I had once let take the place of my mother. I believed that it alone could cure me of my child-hood complexes, my being an orphan and my humiliation.

Today, a lifetime of shocks and hurt later, I know that a person can be the homeland's orphan as well. There is the humiliation of homelands, their oppression and viciousness, their tyranny and selfishness.

There are homelands without maternal feeling. Homelands like fathers.

I didn't sleep that night until nearly daybreak.

My nocturnal reunion with the city had an aftertaste of bitter-ness. I had just fallen asleep when Hassan's youngest child woke me up. He started wailing for his mother's breast and breakfast. I envied his child's innocence and boldness, his ability to say what he wanted without words.

That morning, at my first encounter with the city, I lost my language.

I felt that Constantine had defeated me even before we met, that she had brought me here to convince me of that alone. I had no desire to resist my fate.

She defeated those who came before me, and as an example to others turned their obsession with her into tombs.

I was the last of her deranged lovers, another cripple who loved her, another Hunchback of Notre Dame, another Fool of Constantine. What led me to such madness? What made me stop at the gates to her heart for a lifetime?

She was like you. She had two names like you, and a number of birthdays. She emerged from history with two names, one familiar and one in memoriam. Once she was called Cirta. She was victorious like a feminine city.

Men with the arrogance of soldiers, Syphax, Masinissa and Jugurtha all passed through, and others before them. They left their memory in her caves, carved inscriptions of their love, fear and gods. They left their statues, their tools and coins, triumphal arches and Roman bridges, and departed.

Only one bridge and one name, given to her sixteen centuries ago by Constantine, have survived. I envied that arrogant Roman emperor who gave his name to a city that wasn't his greatest love. He was coupled with her for purely historical reasons. I alone have given you a name other than my own.

Perhaps because of this I flirted with the law of idiocy and called the city Cirta to restore its pristine legitimacy. Just as I had called you Hayat.

Like all invaders, Emperor Constantine was wrong. Cities are like women. We do not possess them simply by giving them our names. Cirta was a city devoted to love and war that seduced history. She waylaid every conqueror that she had smiled at from her rocky heights. Like her women, she beguiled with an illusion of conquest. But no one took the lesson from her graveyards!

There are the tombs of the Romans, the Vandals, the Byzantines, the Fatimids, the Hafsids, the Ottomans and the forty-one beys who succeeded each other until she fell to the French. Seven whole years the French army encamped at the gates of Constantine. France entered Algeria in 1830, but did not conquer the city on a rock until 1837, via a mountain path where it lost half its troops and Constantine lost her best men.

From that day, bridges have sprung up around the city and the paths leading to it have multiplied. But the mountain was always greater than the bridges because it knew that under the bridges there was only an abyss.

She was a city that accosted every conqueror, wrapping herself in her black shawl and hiding her secret from every visitor.

Her deep gorges and hidden caves guarded her on every side. Her holy saints, with their tombs scattered on the green slopes beneath the bridges, guarded her.

There was the viaduct, the closest bridge to my home and my memory. As though painting it, between puzzling vertigo and remembrance, I crossed spontaneously on foot, as though traversing my life from end to end.

Everything on the bridge seemed to have been speeded up, the cars, the passers-by, even the birds, as though something awaited them on the other side. Perhaps at the time some of them did not know that what they were looking for might have been left behind. That in truth there was no difference between the two ends of a bridge. The only difference was between above and below.

Only an iron railing prevented the fearful drop that no one stopped to consider. Perhaps because people naturally do not like to consider death too much. The immense drop halted nobody but me. Perhaps because I brought my preconceived ideas and inherited memories with me. Or because I walked that way to be alone with the city on a bridge.

Some stupid mistakes should not be made, like having a date with memory on a bridge. Especially when a story forgotten years before is suddenly remembered. The story of a great-grandfather who threw himself off a bridge, perhaps that one. He was special envoy and confidante to one of the beys. But the bey sought his life after hearing reports that he had treasonously plotted against the ruler with some of Constantine's nobles.

My great-grandfather wasn't strong enough on his own to stand up to this categorical order for his death. He was also too proud to allow himself to be led in humiliation before the bey. So by the time the bey sent for him, my great-grandfather was a corpse at the bottom of a deep gorge like this. He refused to give the bey the honour of putting him to death.

I heard the story once from my father's lips, when I asked him for the meaning of our name. It seemed he didn't like to tell the story. Suicide was a shameful thing and against the religion of pious Constantine. So our family left for the west of Algeria and adopted a name to disguise our origins. We didn't return to Constantine for a generation or more, bearing the name of another city.

I looked down again. What had I come looking for on a bridge suspended 170 metres above solid ground and crossed by speeding flocks of crows? Perhaps I was looking for traces of an ancestor named Ahmed. Supposedly, he was handsome, rich and learned, and one day he threw everything away from here, leaving his sadness and his wound as an inheritance to our family.

That was Constantine, a city only concerned with how she appeared to others, fiercely protective of her reputation and fearful of the gossip she excelled in. She bought her honour with blood at times, with distance and migration at others. Had she changed? I remembered hearing as a boy about a family that suddenly left Constantine for another city, after the rumour spread that a song (still sung by Fergani today) had been written as a love song to one of its daughters.

The question remained, what had I come to do here on the bridge? Perhaps I had a date with memory, or perhaps that morning just with my painting. I stood in front of it that day without a brush or oils, without nerves or fear of the square of blank canvas. At that instant I wasn't its maker, painter or creator. I was part of it, even capable of folding myself into its details.

I could have crossed the iron railing that separated me from it, as though crossing the frame and entering the picture to live in it for ever. I would roll down the deep rocky valley as a human speck, a drop of colour in an eternal landscape painting. One that I wanted to paint, but that painted me. Wouldn't that be the most beautiful end for a painter: merging into the scene of his painting?

I stared into the deep gorge below with its rocky channel carved by the Rummal's churning slowness. At that instant, I knew that the feminine chasm was drawing me down to the depths for a final erotic death. That might have been my last chance for physical union with Constantine and with the memory of an ancestor with whom I suddenly began to feel a puzzling complicity.

Perhaps the longing to fall and shatter gave me vertigo as I stood suspended on that bridge on my own. I suddenly felt ashamed of the city. I almost apologised for it. Only strangers felt dizzy here. When exactly did Constantine put me in that category?

Even so, I admit I wasn't ready to die that day. Not that I was clinging on to life, but because I had linked the deep, sweeping sadness that had overwhelmed me since I stepped into the city with another mysterious and powerful emotion.

In my resentfulness and disappointment I had attained a vague sense of serenity and happiness. I had learned how to make fun of the things that annoyed me and confront memory with bitter irony. Didn't I come here as the result of a crazy decision, possibly in search of madness in a city quite skilled in it? So I secretly began to enjoy the painful game and took care to experience the blows with deliberate masochism. Perhaps that day's disappointment in the city would become the source of my future madness and genius.

Even so, I decided to escape the bridge that had once been the beginning of my mania. I had been infatuated with it for ages and turned it into the backdrop of my life after surrounding myself with multiple copies, and I suddenly fled.

Did that feeling overtake me when from my vantage point I caught sight of the rocky slopes whose green passes were once dotted with poppy anemones and narcissi? The people of Constantine would visit them every year to welcome spring, laden with pastries, sweets and coffee that the women prepared for the occasion. Now the slopes seemed sad, as if the flowers had left for some inscrutable reason.

Or was the feeling the result of seeing the tomb of Sidi Mohamed of the Crow? He suddenly came to mind and I recalled what I had recently read about him in a book on the history of Constantine. I shuddered. What if, without realising, I had been struck by the curse of Saleh Bey, the greatest of Constantine's beys, because of the bridge? He had wanted to crown his magnificent architectural achievements and the various reforms he had made to the city by repairing the viaduct bridge – the only link between the city and the outside world and the only one of the five Roman bridges to survive.

According to folklore, the bridge was one of the reasons for Saleh Bey's tragic death. For on the bridge, he had Sidi Mohamed, a very popular holy man, put to death. When the head of the saint hit the ground, his body was transformed into a crow that flew off towards Saleh Bey's country house, which was on those slopes. The crow cursed him with a no less painful and unjust death than that of the saint he had killed. Saleh Bey could do nothing but leave his house and lands for ever, in flight from the crow, making do with his house in the city.

So the people called the place Sidi Mohamed of the Crow, and it remained a place of pilgrimage for two centuries. Muslims and Jews visited at the weekends or holidays, when they would spend a whole week wearing pink clothes and performing ceremonies passed down from generation to generation. They offered pigeons in sacrifice and bathed in the warm waters of the rocky pool where tortoises once swam. Pilgrims lived off arrack and submitted to bouts of primitive dancing in circles in the open air to the rhythm of the poor women's drums.

Yet Constantine did not spurn her bey, who gave her so much status and luxury. Out of beneficence or madness she put the killer and the killed on an equal footing. The tomb of Sidi Mohamed of the Crow became the most famous of all Constantine's sites of pilgrimage, and that in a city where every street bore the name of a saint. While the name of Saleh Bey alone, among the forty-one beys who had ruled, become immortal. Her most beautiful poetry was written about him, and her most beautiful lament was sung for his tragic death. Although she did not know it, she was still mourning for him today in the black shawls of the women.

Such was Constantine. There was no difference between her curse and her mercy, no divide between her love and her hate, no known measure for her logic. She granted immortality to those she wished and punished those she wished.

Who might make her pay for her madness? Who might make his position towards her clear? In love or hate, guilty or innocent, without confessing that in every situation she was a paradox?

Every day that I spent in the city I became more entangled in her memory. In my evenings with Hassan, during our long, rambling conversations, which often went on very late, I searched for another recipe to help me forget.

In that family atmosphere I had been missing for so long, I searched for a different self-assurance. My presence in the family house, which I knew and which knew me, had an effect on my spirits during those days. Perhaps it was my secret and unexpected prop.

I would return to it every night as if ascending to the far recesses of my childhood to once again become unborn. I hid myself in the body of an imaginary mother, whose place here remained unfilled after thirty years.

During those nights I would remember Ziyad – he had stayed with me in Algiers for a few months when his landlord had refused to renew his lease. At the time I got used to leaving him the bed. I would sleep on a mattress on the floor in another room. Ziyad protested and felt a little embarrassed, thinking I was doing it out of politeness.

I kept stressing that thanks to him I had discovered I preferred sleeping on the floor. The mattress reminded me of my childhood, when for several years I slept next to my mother on the same woollen pallet whose blue colour I still remembered. Every autumn Mother washed and re-stuffed the blue wool mattresses that furnished my bedroom.

I wished I could ask Atiqa to put a mattress on the floor for me in the guest room, like she did with her children. They slept in the other room on a shared mattress that exuded warmth and aroused a desire to slip under the beautiful wool blankets. I was envious, and longed for a time so distant I could no longer recall whether I had really lived it or only imagined it.

But could I reasonably put such a request to Atiqa? She had given me the most beautiful room in her house: the modern bedroom that was arranged more for the benefit of guests than for their married couple's nights of love.

If I had asked, she would have found no explanation for my perversity, and I would probably have embarrassed her. Atiqa sometimes joined in our late nights and tried to appeal to me, as a civilised man from Paris, to persuade her brother to give up that old Arab house with its backward way of life. She practically apologised for all the things I found beautiful and unusual.

Because I was unable to convince her of my view, nor bold enough to disagree with hers, I just listened to her discussions with Hassan. These almost turned into arguments before she backed down and went to bed. Semi-apologetic, Hassan would say, 'You can't persuade a woman who watches *Dallas* on television to live in a house like this and be grateful. They have to stop that soap as long as they can't give people decent homes and a better life.'

I envied Hassan's sense of contentment and admired his philosophy of life.

He would say, 'To be happy, you should look at those worse off. If you've got a piece of bread and look at someone who has nothing, you'll be happy and thank God. But if you raise your head and look at those with cake, you'll never be satisfied. You'll be made miserable by your discovery and die crushed!'

In Hassan's view, living in a house like that, with all its bad points (which at times were annoying) and its minor inconveniences surpassed by the modern age, was still better than what thousands had to endure. Tens of thousands, rather, who didn't have a spacious house like that where they could live alone with their wife and children. No, they often had to share a cramped apartment with relatives for years.

That was Hassan. He looked at things head on. Everything he had learned he had acquired as a boy from the blackboard. He was happy with that way of looking at things, which was also down to his mentality as a badly paid teacher with meagre dreams.

What could he dream about, a teacher of Arabic who spent his days explaining literary texts and relating the lives of ancient writers and poets to his pupils whose grammatical and spelling mistakes he corrected? He didn't have the time, or didn't dare explain what was happening in front of him, to correct bigger mistakes made in front of his eyes in the name of words that had suddenly dropped out of the language and entered the lexicon of slogans and bids.

Deep down there was something bitter about Hassan, apparent in all the details of his life. He kept it to himself, however. He was clearly exhausted, floundering in the problems of his six children and his young wife, who dreamed of a life other than Constantine's straitened existence. Hassan, though, didn't dare to dream or, more exactly, in those days he was dreaming of finding someone with the connections to get him a new fridge, no more!

When I learned of his simple but hard-to-obtain dream, I was sad to realise that we weren't just backward when compared to Europe and France – as I'd thought, and a manageable and understandable matter – but we were also backward when compared to the way we had been under colonialism fifty or more years earlier. Back then, our hopes were more beautiful, our dreams bigger. Today, it would be enough to study people's faces and listen to them talking or look into shop windows to understand that. Back then we were a country that exported dreams at every news broadcast to all the world's peoples.

Constantine alone exported more and better newspapers, magazines and books than the institutions of the nation as a whole did now. Back then we had intellectuals and scientists, poets, wits and writers who filled us with pride at our Arabism. No one would buy the papers and hoard them in the cupboard any more, as there was nothing left in the papers worth preserving. Nobody sat with a book any more to learn something. Cultural despair was a mass phenomenon, an infection that you might catch flicking through a book. Back then books were always right and we could speak as eloquently as those books. Now even books lied, just like the papers. So our honesty had diminished; our eloquence had died, since conversation revolved around scarce consumer goods.

When I said all that to Hassan, he looked at me in shock, as though he'd discovered something that had never occurred to him before. With some sadness he said, 'True. They've set us small goals unrelated to the issues of the day, illusory individual triumphs like finding a small apartment after years of waiting, getting a fridge or being able to buy a car, or just a set of tyres! No one has the time and energy to go further or ask for more.

'We're so tired. The difficulties of daily life have exhausted us. You always need connections to sort out ordinary hassles. How do you want us to think about other things? What cultural life are you talking about? Our concern is just surviving; anything more is a luxury. We've been turned into a nation of ants hunting only for food and a nest to hole-up in with the children.'

Naively I asked him, 'And what do people do?'

Joking, he said, 'People? Nothing. Some wait, some steal, the rest kill themselves. This is a city that gives you three choices with the same justifications and the same grounds!'

That day the city made me fear for Hassan. A dark shudder went through me.

Without thinking, as if asking which of the three prescriptions he had chosen, I asked him, 'Have you got any friends you see and go out with here?

As though he found the question surprising or was happy at my sudden interest in the details of his life, he replied, 'I've got friends, most of them teachers in the same school as me. Apart from that, there's no one. Constantine has emptied. All the old families we know have left.'

He reeled off a list of big families who had emigrated, gone to settle in the capital or abroad, leaving the city to strangers, most of whom came from neighbouring villages and small towns.

Then he said something that didn't strike me at the time, but that years later assumed fateful dimensions. 'The natives of this city only come to visit for weddings and funerals.'

Before I could comment, he continued as if he'd remembered something. 'I'll introduce you to Nasser, *Si* Taher's son. He'll definitely be coming the day after tomorrow for his sister's wedding. You'll see. He's become a man as big and tall as you. He's been visiting me for the past few months since he decided to settle down in Constantine. He's the only one who's migrated in reverse. He even refused a scholarship abroad – imagine! No one can believe that. When I asked him why he didn't leave like all the rest and run away from this country, he said to me, "I'm scared that if I leave, I'll never come back. All my friends who've left haven't come back."'

I laughed when I learned that he was an extremist like you, as if it ran in the family. I felt a desire to prolong the conversation that, in one way or another, was leading towards you.

I asked him, 'What's he doing now?'

'As a martyr's son, they gave him a shop and a van that bring in a nice income. But he's still lost, unconvinced. Sometimes he thinks about resuming his studies, then at others of devoting himself to business. Really, I'm not up to giving him advice. It makes me sorry that someone should give up their university education because they'll always feel the loss. Then again, he says qualifications have no value any more, when he sees young people around him with university degrees unemployed, and other stupid people driving Mercedes and living in mansions. This isn't a time for knowledge, but a time to be smart. Today, how can you persuade your friend, or even your student, to devote himself to knowledge? Standards have been completely upset.'

I said to Hassan, 'What matters is that a person knows his true goal in life. Is money the main problem, or knowledge and inner balance?

226

Hassan responded, 'Balance? What balance are you talking about? We're half-deranged. None of us knows exactly what he wants, nor exactly what he's waiting for. The real problem is the atmosphere the people are living in, the general dismay of an entire nation. It robs you of any hunger for initiative, for dreams, for planning any project. Intellectuals aren't happy and neither are the illiterate, ordinary folks or the rich. Tell me, God have mercy on your parents, what you can do with your knowledge if you end up a civil servant with an ignorant supervisor who's only in his job by chance not by merit, or rather because he has lots of contacts and is well connected! What, for example, can you do with your money in Constantine except pay it as commission to get an apartment that's unfit for habitation most of the time, or hold a wedding where Fergani sings? But if all you have is less than 20,000 dinars, you're left with the choice of spending them on "cups of coffee" for a local official hidden out of sight behind some other petty bureaucrat who is selling passports for the Hajj. Then you can perform the commandment and reserve yourself a small room in the afterlife. Once this world has squeezed you out!'

I said in disbelief, 'What? Is it true? They sell passports for the Hajj for 20,000 dinars?!'

'Of course. The government has set an annual number of pilgrims because they cost so much hard currency. That was after they discovered that most went quite a few times, and for purely business reasons unconnected with the Hajj. How else can you explain why there's been no noticeable effect on the morals or behaviour of people who've been on the pilgrimage half-a-dozen times? I know one pilgrim who's a drunkard who's always got a bottle at home, and another who's a bit of a wheeler-dealer and exchanges currency on the black market. Such people still go on Hajj every year. They can easily get hold of 20,000 dinars. As for me, where can I get that sort of money from and perform what I'm commanded? My income is less than 4,000 dinars a month.'

I said to him, 'What? Are you planning to go on the Hajj?'

'Of course,' he said. 'And why not, I'm a Muslim, aren't I? I started praying again two years ago. Without my faith, I would have gone out of my mind. How could you bear all this wickedness and injustice without faith? Only belief gives you the strength to survive. Look around you: everyone has reached the same conclusion, perhaps young people more than most because they're the chief victims of this country. Even Nasser has started praying since coming back to Constantine, maybe because of that, or because faith is like heresy – catching! I swear to God, Khaled, on Fridays thousands pack the mosques and block the streets. If you saw it, you'd pray with them without wondering why!'

I found I had nothing to add to Hassan's words on that marvellous evening that lasted until two in the morning. Hassan was happy I was there and because it was the summer holiday, which meant he could stay up late talking to me after all the years that had kept us apart.

I let him talk and lay bare the homeland that I had covered up with nostalgia, longing and obsession.

Was he worried in case I was disappointed, afraid of losing the joy that my return to him and the homeland had brought? Did that make him stop talking and move on to another subject? Indirectly he was leading me towards religion, piety and faith. He was tempting me to repent, as though being in Paris was an act of sinful apostasy. Was that Hassan?

At the time I couldn't stop myself smiling when I remembered the two bottles of whiskey I had brought.

That night when I was in bed I wondered about my sins. I tried to summarise and enumerate them. I didn't think they were worse than other people's – in fact, I thought they were far, far fewer. I wasn't a criminal, a gambler, an atheist, a liar, a drunkard or a traitor.

I didn't have a wife and a marital bed to swap for another. Fifty years of being alone, half of which I could call the 'wounded years' and that I spent with only one arm, disfigured in body and dream.

How many women had I loved? I no longer remembered. From my first love for the Jewish neighbour I seduced, to the Tunisian nurse who seduced me, there were other women whose names and faces I no longer remembered who took turns on my bed for purely physical reasons and who left laden with me while I remained empty of them.

Then you came along.

My greatest sin of all was you. The only woman I didn't have, the only sin I didn't actually commit.

My sins with you were what I might call 'sins of the right hand' – the hand with which I painted, and with which I summoned and had you in fantasy.

Would God punish me for the sins of the only hand he left me with?

I don't recall who said, 'Virtue does not mean not sinning, it means not wanting to.' Only on that basis would I say I wasn't a good man.

I shouldn't have desired you and started sinning with you. Loving you had a taste of the forbidden and the sacred that we ought to avoid, but which I slid into without thinking. The really shocking thing about my story with you was that the reasons that made me love you were the very ones that should have stopped me.

Because of this, perhaps I loved you and stopped loving you several times a day, with the same extremity each time. Ultimately, I was only here to find an end to the high and low tides of emotion I went through with you at every instant.

I knew that someone in love was like an addict, unable to decide to give up on his own. Every day he descended a little further towards the abyss. But he couldn't stand on his own two legs and run away before he had reached the ultimate point of hell and touched the bitter depths of disappointment.

I was happy that night. A bittersweet happiness, because I knew that everything would be resolved in the next two days. That one way or another I would finish with you.

That evening, Hassan's wife had been exhausting herself getting ready for the main event of the next day: the procession of women to the baths and the henna party for the bride. She was in constant motion and too busy for us and her children with her woman's concerns. Among these were the clothes she would pack to take to the baths where, as customary, the women would display every-thing, even their lingerie. They would do so to flaunt their wealth, which was mostly false, or just to convince themselves that in spite of everything they were still able to attract a man. Just like the bride they were with and whom they secretly envied.

Let it be. The next day, your marriage rituals would begin, and the time we had stolen from fate would come to an end.

Sweet dreams then, my lady, for tomorrow.

Goodnight then, sadness!

Anti-love woke me up that summer morning and turned me out on the street.

As soon as I was awake, I decided to get away from the house. Atiqa was talking incessantly about wedding traditions, about the important people and families who had come specially for the event, the likes of which Constantine hadn't witnessed for years. She followed me all the way to the door to keep talking. 'You know, they say everything was brought from France a month ago by plane. If only you could have seen the bride's things and what she was wearing yesterday. Like they say, some people have a life and others just keep them company.'

Shutting the door behind me, as if slamming the doors of my heart, I answered her, 'What of it? The country is theirs and the planes too. They can bring as much as they took!'

Where to escape? There was nothing in front of me except me. Unthinking, I fell in with the crowds of pedestrians who aimlessly roamed the streets every day. Here you had the choice between walking, leaning against a wall or sitting in a café to watch those walking or leaning on the wall opposite. I walked.

At some point I felt that we were all walking round this rocky city without quite knowing what we should do with our anger and misery, and whom to pelt with the pebbles that filled our empty pockets. Who was first in line for stoning in this country? Who? The one sitting atop everyone or those sitting on top of us?

The title of a novel by Malek Haddad came to mind: *Zeros Turning Around Themselves*. I wished that I had read it. Perhaps I would have found an explanation for all these nothings that we had turned into.

My thoughts took me to a scene I had witnessed in Tunisia of a blindfolded camel turning endlessly around an open space in Sidi Bou Said to bring water up from a well to the delight and surprise of tourists. What had given me pause that day was the camel's eyes, which had been blinkered so that it would imagine

231

it was walking forwards and die without discovering it had been going around in circles. A whole lifetime spent going around in circles. Perhaps we had become that camel, which no sooner finished one circle than it began another, going around small day-to-day worries in one way or another.

Weren't the newspapers, full of promises of a better tomorrow, just blinkers to hide the shock of reality, the catastrophic poverty and misery that for the first time assailed half this people?

Perhaps I, too, no longer knew how to go forward in a straight line that didn't automatically take me backwards to the nation's memory. The nation's special capacity to take a straight line and twist it into a circle, into noughts, where did it come from?

Memory was an encircling fence that enclosed us from every side. It besieged me as soon as I set foot outside the house. Every direction I went in, distant memories walked alongside me.

I walked towards the past with my eyes shut. I looked for the old cafés, those where every scholar or personality had his own place and the coffee was made on a stone stove and served in a small copper pot. The waiters would be embarrassed to hassle you when your presence was an honour. In those days Ben Badis used to stop at the Benjamina Café on his way to school. There was the Bou Arour Café where Belattar and Bashtarzi held their meetings and where I sometimes spotted my father as I walked by.

Where was that café, so I might drink a cup of coffee in his memory that morning? How would I stumble upon a café that was only as famous as its patrons? How would I find it now that there were many large cafés to match the city's misery, all of which had the same sad look as the people's faces? Nothing distinguished them any more. Not even pride, characteristic of the people of Constantine, whose brilliant white sashes and hooded capes had become rare and faded.

Perhaps the first thing to catch my attention that morning was the uniform dress of that city that woke up sadly, as she had slept. The dark tones shared by both sexes; the women wrapped in their black shawls that only left the eyes visible; the men in grey or brown suits the same colour as their skin or hair, which all seemed to have been acquired from the same tailor. Only rarely did a spot of light or the bright colour of a skirt or summer jacket appear within the crowds.

Perhaps that morning I was taking in that city with the eyes of a painter attuned only to colours, almost unable to see anything else. Or was I just seeing her with the eyes of the past and the frustrations of the present?

I threw myself into the crowds of men, lost like me in the city. For the first time I felt I had started to resemble them. Like them I did not know what to do with my time and my virility. I could do nothing but walk the streets for hours, as they did, burdened with my civilised despair and sexual frustrations.

We were suddenly alike in everything. The colour of our hair and suits, the dragging of our feet and our directionless steps on the pavement. We were alike in all things. You were the only unique thing about me. But did that change anything?

Loving you, which induced me to come as far as that city, also returned me to my backwardness without my realising. It threw me into the crowds of men walking slowly in no particular direction under the summer sun. They did not know what to do with the energy that their heated bodies would accumulate in the daytime and that despairing hands would spend secretly at night in solitary pleasures.

My feet came to a sudden stop in front of the walls of a house unlike the others. It was the largest *maison close* visited by men. It had three entrances leading to different streets and markets. It was, in fact, a planned brothel, designed so that men could creep inside from any direction and exit from any other. Men headed to it from every direction, fleeing the neighbouring towns and villages where there were no pleasures and no women. Beautiful, miserable women also came from all the neighbouring cities to hide behind these yellowing walls. They only left as old ladies to spend their riches on charity, good deeds and the circumcision of orphans at the season of their final repentance.

It was there that my father had spent his money and his manhood. I tried not to stop outside that exceptional house, which for a few years had been the cause of my mother's secret sadness, and perhaps her death from despair.

For a few years of my adolescence, it had also lain behind my secret indulgence and my suppressed dreams. I dreamed about it but didn't dare go inside, perhaps afraid I would meet my father. Maybe, too, I was satisfied with my stolen transient liaisons on the roof or in the storeroom, which was rarely opened.

My father was no longer around for his possible presence in that house to stop me going in. He died after leaving his distinguished history behind those walls, just like any rich and respectable man of Constantine at the time.

To teach my mother patience and get her to accept betrayal with disdain, my grandmother used to say, 'What men do is embroidered on their shoulders!' But my father stitched his adventures on Mother's body. A burning wound he was unaware of.

I had not known what had become of that house. Some said it was closed down, one doorway perhaps remaining. It may have been part of a policy to curtail the pleasures available in the city or to show respect for the dozens of mosques that had sprung out of the mountainside and whose sound would combine several times a day to remind people of the advantages of faith and repentance.

At such a moment, like most men of this city, I stood midway between carnal desire and spiritual chastity. The secret call of the darkened, lustful rooms, where sin was sweet, drew me downwards. While the minarets' call to prayer and invocation of God's greatness, which I had long missed, caused me to ascend. Its power entered my soul and shook me for the first time in years.

In a matter of days I had developed the split personality of this city. I started to be aware that in this world full of opposites there were no innocent cities and no immoral ones. There were just hypocrite cities and those less hypocritical. There were no cities with just one face and one profession. Constantine was the city with the most faces and the most contradictions. It was a city that induced you to sin, then with the same force dissuaded you.

Everything here was a veiled invitation to sex. Something about the city promised surreptitious love: the endless siestas, the warm lazy mornings, the sudden desolate night, the rock-hung pathways, the secret tunnels, dank and pestilent, the wild, mountainous landscape criss-crossed with diverging paths, the forests of laurel and oak, all the concealed caves. But you had to make do with observing the generations-old traditions of hypocrisy and avoid looking this city in the eyes so you didn't embarrass her and throw her into confusion!

Everyone here knew that behind the wide avenues clustered narrow tortuous alleyways, illicit love affairs and pleasures hurriedly stolen behind closed doors. Beneath her staid black shawls the suppressed desire of centuries was dormant. The desire reflected in the singular strut of Constantine women and which gave their eyes behind the *ajjar* that rare flash.

Over centuries women here had grown used to carrying their desires buried in the unconscious and waiting to explode. Desire would remain suppressed until a wedding, when the women would surrender to the beat of the drum and start to dance as if surrendering to love. Shy and coy to start with, they would move forbidden parts of the body to the left and to the right to the rhythm of the chants. Under the weight of their clothes and bracelets, their stifled femininity had been aroused. They had become more beautiful in their inherited seduction. Breasts shaking and hips swaying, the loveless body had suddenly heated up.

The fever unquenched by a man had suddenly flared within. The drum, warmed up by the women beforehand, had become complicit with the hot body. The beats would quicken and intensify. The women's plaits would come loose and locks of hair fly free as they danced like savage creatures writhing in pain and pleasure at a celebration of attraction and intimidation. They would lose all connection with their surroundings, as if they had left their bodies, memories and lives and nobody would be able to bring them back to their former calm.

As at rites of pleasure and torture, everyone knew that the beat of the drum must not cease or its quickening rhythm be broken before the women reached the peak of their trance and pleasure and fell in a faint to the ground. Women supported them around the waist, and others sprinkled them with perfume prepared for such occasions until they gradually returned to consciousness.

In this way women would make love in Constantine, in fantasy! Constantine seduced me with one night of fantasy love, and I accepted her secret bargain in exchange for a little amnesia.

Where was forgetting, Constantine, when a wound lay in wait for me at every corner?

* * *

Is nostalgia a medical condition?

I was afflicted with you, Constantine.

Constantine, our meeting was a prescription I tried as a cure, but that proved fatal. Did I exceed the recommended dose of desire in such cases? I hadn't bought you at some pharmacy, so I couldn't sue the seller of fates who had put you in my path. I had created you myself and assessed all your details by my own standards.

You were a mixture of my contradictions, my sense and my madness, my worship and my apostasy. You were my purity and my sin, all my life's complexes. There was no difference between you and other cities. Perhaps you were just the city that killed me more than once, for a contradictory reason each time.

What divides the dose that cures from one that kills? At times of disappointment memory becomes a bitter draught to be swallowed in one go, while before it had been a shared dream to be sipped at leisure.

Shared memory began here, with the streets inhabited only by history.

Some I walked along with Si Taher, some with other people.

Here was a street that bore his name. Here were streets that remembered his passing. I became one with his steps and continued the path we hadn't completed together.

Arabism walked with me from neighbourhood to neighbourhood. I was suddenly filled with a strange arrogance.

A person couldn't belong to the city if he didn't share its Arabism, which here meant pride and bravado and centuries of bold defiance.

The bearded face and words of Ben Badis still ruled the city, even after his death. He continued to gaze at us from that famous photograph of him in his bearded gravity, leaning on his hand, thinking about where we had ended up after him. His cry to history remained after half a century the only unofficial anthem we all knew by heart.

> The Algerian people is Muslim
>> Part of the Arab nation
> Whoever says they've betrayed their origin
>> Or says they've died, is a liar
> Whoever wishes to assimilate to it
>> Wants an impossible desire.

Your prophecy came true, Ben Badis. We didn't die. Only our hunger for life died. What should we do then, your learned excellence? No one anticipated that we would die from despair. How could a people that multiplies every year die out?

> Youth, you are our hope
>> The dawn is close thanks to you.

The youth he wrote about no longer looked out for dawn, since those enthroned above us had sequestered the sun. They looked out for boats and planes and only thought of escape. Queues of our dead formed at every foreign embassy to obtain a visa for a life abroad.

History had turned full circle and the roles had reversed. France now rejected us, and obtaining a visa, if only for a few days, was the 'impossible desire'.

We hadn't died from abuse, but from subjugation. Only indignity could kill a people.

We used to repeat that anthem in Constantine's prison. It was enough for it to begin in one cell for other cells, whose occupants weren't political prisoners, to pick it up. Its words had an extraordinary power to unite us. We discovered by chance that we had one voice. We were one people whose voice made the walls shake, before our bodies shook under torture.

Had we lost our voice, or was there a voice louder than everyone's, since this homeland became the property of only some of us?

My mind had generated all those ideas as I crossed the street to confront, for the first time in thirty-seven years, the walls of a prison I had once seen from the inside.

Did prison become something else simply because we were looking at it from the outside? Could vision have wiped away memory that day? Could one memory wipe away another?

Kidya prison had been part of my original memory that time had not erased.

Memory stood still before it, forcing my legs to stop. I entered it again as I had that day in 1945 along with 50,000 prisoners arrested after the demonstrations of the eighth of May of grievous memory. I had been lucky compared to those who hadn't entered then. Forty-five thousand fell in demonstrations that shook eastern Algeria from Constantine to Sétif, Guelma and Kherrata. They were the first official batch of Algerian martyrs whose deaths came years before the war of liberation. Had I forgotten them?

Had I forgotten those who went in and never came out? Those whose corpses were left in the torture chambers? Those who died more than one death as comrades of those who chose their own death?

Take Ismail Shaalal, just a construction worker whose mission was to memorise the secret archive of the Algerian People's

239

Party. He was the first person to receive a visit from the General Intelligence Agency, who knocked on the door of his tiny attic room shouting, 'Police! Open up!' Rather than opening the door, Ismail Shaalal opened the only window and threw himself into Wadi Rummal, to die with his secrets in Constantine's deep valleys. Was it possible even decades later, for me to remember Ismail Shaalal without crying? A man who had chosen death rather than give away our names under torture?

Take the voice of Abdel-Karim Ben Wataf, whose screams under torture reached our cell like a dagger plunged into our bodies or like an electric shock. His voice cursed his torturers in French, calling them dogs, Nazis, murderers, words that interspersed his other cries. '*Nazis, salauds, assassins, criminels.*' Our voices would respond with strident anthems and chants. Ben Wataf's voice would fall silent.

Take Bilal Hussein, *Si* Taher's closest friend and one of the unknown makers and victims of history. Bilal was a carpenter, and though not well educated, a whole generation learned patriotism at his hands. His workshop under the Sidi Rachid bridge was a base for clandestine meetings.

He would stop me in the street as I passed by his workshop on my way to secondary school. He would suggest I read *al-Umma* newspaper or a secret pamphlet. Over the course of two years he prepared me politically for joining the People's Party. He set me more than one test in the field, which every prospective member had to go through before going before the membership committee and beginning his activities in one of the cells determined by Bilal.

There was no trace left of the workshop, but it was where the political leadership assembled. Messali Hadj gave his last instructions from there. The slogans raised at demonstrations were composed and written on banners there at night to surprise the French.

The demonstrations would start on Sidi Rachid bridge, as planned by Bilal for tactical reasons, since assembly was made easier when protestors could scatter along the many roads leading there. The French forces were taken aback by the unexpected precision and order of the demonstrations. Bilal was the first to be arrested that day, and he was tortured as an example.

Bilal Hussein did not die like others. He spent two years under torture in prison, leaving his skin on the implements of torture. He spent several days naked from the waist up, unable even to put a shirt on, as it would stick to his open wounds after the hospital doctor refused to be responsible for treating him.

He was released after being sentenced to exile and put under observation. Bilal Hussein lived as a fighter in unknown battles, hunted and sought, until independence.

He died only recently, aged eighty-one, on 27 May 1988, the same month as his first death. He died in misery, blind, without money or children. He confessed to his only friend a few months before his death that his torturers had deliberately made him impotent. In reality, he had died forty years before.

The day he died, a handful of semi-officials accompanied the funeral procession, the very people who had never once asked him what he was living on and why he had no family. They walked a few steps behind him, then got back into their official cars without a trace of guilt.

No one knew his secret, which he had guarded for forty years with the shame of a man of his generation and standing. Was it a secret that deserved to be so closely guarded? Bilal Hussein was the last man in an age of eunuchs. A visionary in an age when the sighted were blind.

Had I forgotten Bilal Hussein?

Here was Kidya prison.

I contemplated it as one contemplates the walls of a prison that one is entering for the first time, like entering a nightmare unprepared.

Many years passed before I entered a different prison. That time, however, the executioners were Algerians. That prison had no known address for Mother's ghost to locate and visit me, as she had done here before, when she cried and pleaded with every guard.

Here was Kidya prison, which held more than one revolutionary from more than one revolution and so many painful and other extraordinary stories. In 1955, exactly ten years after the events of 8 May 1945, the prison came to the fore with a new batch of exceptional prisoners for whom France had prepared an exceptional punishment. In cell number eight, death row, thirty leaders of the Revolution awaited the certainty of execution. They included Mustafa Ben Boulaïd, Taher el-Zubeiri, Mohamed Lafia, Brahim Tayeb, the comrade of Didouche Mourad, Baji Mukhtar and others.

All the preparations were in place for their death. Even the barber to the criminal inmates told the martyr Commander Mustafa Ben Boulaïd in the morning that they had washed the guillotine the previous night, and that he had dreamed they had been 'executed'. The word held a double meaning for Mustafa Ben Boulaïd, who had long been planning an escape from Kidya. Days before he had started digging a tunnel with his comrades, which had reached an enclosed courtyard inside the prison. They resumed digging with the aim of breaking out.

On 10 November 1955, after the sunset prayer, between seven and eight o'clock to be precise, Mustafa Ben Boulaïd and ten of his comrades escaped. They pulled off the most spectacular escape from a cell that no one else left that day unless it was for the guillotine.

Afterwards, Commander Mustafa Ben Boulaïd and some of those who escaped with him fell as martyrs in other battles no less heroic than their escape. Algerian history books have given a prominent place to their deaths, and major streets and facilities are named after them. Those who remained behind in the cell were unable to escape execution. Today only two of the eleven prisoners who escaped from Kidya are still alive. Twenty-eight of the men brought together by cell number eight have died.

The whole time I stood in front of the prison's high walls, my memory was scattered, darting between faces, names and executioners. I longed to open the gates of other prisons that, in the absence of a single writer willing to repay the debt of those who had been through them, were still guarding their secrets.

Once I was envious of the comrade with whom I shared a cell for a few weeks.

Then, Yacine and I were the youngest political detainees. He was only sixteen years old and might have been a few months younger than me. Although I was released due to my age, they refused to let Yacine go, and he remained in Kidya prison for fourteen months. He dreamed of freedom and of an unattainable woman ten years his senior called Nedjma.

I went back to school after six months in prison, but a few years later Yacine wrote his masterpiece, *Nedjma*. The idea of that tragic novel was born in the long night there, in pangs of bitterness and disappointment and in great nationalist dreams.

Yacine was always amazing, full of rejection and the urge to

243

provoke and confront. His belligerence spread from one prisoner to another. We would listen to him, unaware at the time that we were before Algeria's Lorca and witnessing the birth of a poet who would one day become the greatest talent produced by this country.

A few years passed before I met Kateb Yacine in his other forced exile in Tunis. With joy and no little astonishment I discovered that he had not changed. He still talked with the same intensity and aggression, declaring war on all those whose hint of submission to France, or any other country, he sniffed out. He was allergic to polished betrayal and some people's instinctive willingness to comply.

That day he was giving a lecture in a large auditorium in Tunis. He suddenly launched an attack on Arab politicians, the Tunisian authorities in particular. No one could shut him up that day. He carried on speaking and swearing even after the microphone and the lights were turned off and the audience was forced to leave.

That day, in a police interview, I paid the price for being in the front row and for my shouts of 'Long live Yacine!' Nobody paid attention to the faces of those applauding, but someone with an interest spotted my one arm raised aloft in support and admiration.

I learned then the other side of having one arm: you were destined to reject and oppose because in no circumstances could you clap!

I embraced him afterwards and said, 'Yacine, if I have a son I'll call him Yacine.' I felt a surge of energy and pleasure, as though telling him the most beautiful thing that could be said to a friend or writer. Yacine laughed as he patted my shoulder nervously, as was his habit when an admission embarrassed him.

He said in French, 'You haven't changed either. You're still crazy!' We laughed and parted for yet more years.

Perhaps I wanted to be faithful to our common memories, or just wanted to compensate for my complex regarding *Nedjma*, the novel I'd never write, but which I felt in some way was also my story. A story with my dreams and disappointments, with the face of Mother on the verge of despair, running between the prison and the saints, offering sacrifices to Sidi Mohamed of the Crow and bribes to the Jewish prison guard who was our neighbour. She even brought me a food parcel from time to time, which she had made specially. Mother, whom I barely recognised when I left prison six months later. My father's indifference to her and me, busy as he was with his business and his mistresses, made her only ask God for my return to her. It was as if I was the only thing that could justify her existence and the only witness to the motherhood and femininity that had been stolen from her.

Yes, in the end we were a generation with one story combining the madness of mothers who loved too much, the betrayal of fathers who were too cruel, make-believe love stories and emotional frustrations. Some of us turned them into world literary masterpieces, others were turned into mental patients.

Writing this book is perhaps only an attempt to escape being branded a lunatic and be deemed a writer.

Ah, Yacine, how the world has changed since that meeting and that farewell.

You ended your novel by having the hero say, 'Goodbye then, my comrades. What an unbelievable youth we lived!'

You didn't expect then that our later lives would be far stranger than our youthful years.

* * *

245

Tomorrow would be your wedding, then.

It was useless trying to forget it by walking the streets of Constantine. Each alleyway and memory led on to another.

Didn't you say you were mine as long as we remained in this city? So, where were you now? In which alleyway in a city whose streets and lanes were as entangled as your heart? They reminded me of your constant absence and presence and were bewilderingly like you.

You were not mine. I knew they were readying you that minute for your coming night of love. They were grooming your body for a man other than me. I picked at my wound to forget what was happening there.

Your day had been full, like the day of a bride; my day had been as empty as a retired civil servant's.

We had each gone our separate ways a long time ago. Our schedules clashed. One was for happiness and one for sadness. How could I forget that?

All the paths led back to you, even the one I took for the sake of forgetting and where you accosted me. There in all the old schools and *kuttab*s, all the minarets, all the brothels, all the prisons and all the cafés. There, too, in all the bath houses where the women would emerge ready to make love, and in all the shop windows displaying jewellery and wedding dresses. I even took a taxi to the cemetery and hunted for Mother's grave. I sought help from the attendant's ledgers to find the numbers of the passageways leading there, but I still only reached you.

Why did my feet carry me to Mother on the eve of your wedding? Did I simply go to visit her, or to bury beside her another woman whom I imagined was my mother?

Her marble grave was plain like her, cold like her fate and layered in dust like my heart. I stood immobile next to it, and the tears I had hidden from her over the chill years of disappointment set solid.

This had been my mother. Now, a thin piece of ground and a marble headstone concealed all the treasures I ever owned: her ample maternal bosom, her smell, her hennaed strands of hair, her figure, her laughter, her sadness, her constant injunction, 'Take care, Khaled, my son.'

I compensated for Mother with myriad other women and never grew up. I compensated for her bosom with a thousand more beautiful, but was never satisfied. I compensated for her love with more than one affair, but was never cured. She had a fragrance that could not be equalled. She was a painting that could not be copied or forged.

Why at a moment of madness did I imagine you were an authentic copy of her? Why did I demand from you things you did not understand and a role you were not up to?

The marble slab next to me was more merciful than you. If I cried now, it would burst into tears too. If I rested my head on its cold stone, enough warmth would rise from below to console me. If I called to it, 'Mother!' the dust would answer in pain, 'What's wrong, my darling?'

I was afraid that even the dust of Mother's grave suffered, since her life had been nothing more than a succession of tradgedies. I was afraid for her even after she died from pain, and tried to hide my severed arm whenever I visited.

What if the dead had eyes? What if the grave didn't mean repose? What a lot I would have to tell her to explain all that had happened to me.

I didn't cry then, as I stood before her after all that lifetime. We always cry later. I just ran my hand over the marble, as though trying to wipe away the dust of the years and apologise for all the neglect. Then I raised my one hand in prayer and recited the *Fatiha* over the grave. At the time the scene struck me as surreal. My one hand open as I recited the *Fatiha* seemed to be asking for mercy rather than giving it.

I sighed, hid my hand in my jacket pocket and headed out of the city of dust and marble.

In their anticipation and ceaseless preparations for the wedding and their excitement at meeting all the important people who would attend, Hassan and his wife at times seemed like children talking about the circus coming to town. A town neither the circus nor clowns had ever visited before. Because of that, I took pity and forgave them.

Constantine, in the end, was a city where nothing happened except weddings. I left them happily awaiting their circus, and kept my disappointment to myself.

Everything about that day was exceptional. I knew the programme in advance from the talk of the night before. Hassan would go and get ready in the morning, then pray the noon prayer at the mosque. After that he would come by with Nasser for us all to go together to the wedding. Atiqa would probably have taken the children and gone in the morning to accompany the bride to the hairdresser. Then she would stay behind with other women to serve the guests and set the tables.

I felt like staying in bed that morning and not leaving it before noon, perhaps because of the previous night's exertions or in preparation for a late night and other exertions awaiting me that day. Or perhaps just because I no longer had any idea where to go, after having spent a week getting lost in a city that had ambushed my memory in every street. Streets where you lay hidden around every corner.

After a little thought, I found that bed was the only place I could escape you, or at least meet you in pleasure rather than pain. Even so, would I really be bold enough to make you present today, at the very time I knew you were making yourself beautiful for another man? Would I be bold enough to make you present that morning? Would my body truly forgive you, on a whim, for all past and future disappointments? That was madness upon madness!

But in the end wasn't that what you wanted when you said, 'I'll be yours that night'?

I felt like having you that morning. As though I wanted to steal everything from you before I lost you for good. After that day you would never be mine. The stupid painful game, which was never a hobby prior to you, would come to an end.

My encounter with you that morning was painful. Full of ferocity and dark bitterness. Full of resentment and crazed longing.

If only you had been mine. Ah, if only you had been mine that morning. In that large bed, empty and cold without you. In that spacious house haunted by memories of a severed childhood and the suppressed longings of a youth that had quickly passed.

If you were mine, I would have you like I'd never had a woman here. In a moment of madness, I would squeeze you with my one hand. I would turn you into pieces, into raw materials, into the remnants of a woman, a paste fit to mould into a woman, into anything other than you, anything less arrogant and wilful, less tyrannical and oppressive.

I, who had never raised my hand to a woman's face, might have hit you that day till it hurt and then made love to you till it hurt. Then I would have sat next to your body begging its forgiveness. I would kiss every part of you, effacing with my lips

249

the redness of your hennaed limbs and tattooing you with savage kisses. Perhaps when you awoke you would find me tattooed on your body, in that blue colour only ever found on the skin!

Where did all that madness come from? Did I want to be alone with you and have you before him? Or did I know, by intuition or prior decision, that in spending the last shudders of my desire with you, I would cast you out of this bed for ever?

My problem with you wasn't simply desire. If it had been, I would have resolved it that day one way or another. There were plenty of women that a man could easily have. There were plenty of half-open doors waiting for a man to push. There were female neighbours who crossed my path in those shared Arab houses, and whose secret desire for love I well knew. Over time I had learned how to read the looks of coy women, with their excessive decorum and polite words. But I would ignore the looks and their wordless invitation to stray.

Today, I no longer know whether I behaved like that on principle or out of stupidity and a sense of nausea. In truth, I felt pity for them. I despised their husbands who had no justification for strutting like peacocks. Except that they had a plump hen at home, whom probably no one would touch in disgust. Or another, tastier one, domesticated according to tradition, whose master wouldn't expect that her short wings still flapped instinctively.

The idiocy of cocks! If all the women were chaste and all the men guarded their honour, who were they all fooling around with, then? Didn't all the men boast of their conquests when they got together? Didn't each of them make a fool of the others while not realising they were making a fool out of themselves? I really hated the atmosphere of hypocrisy and inherited corruption.

If my gaze should catch a woman's, I would recall something you once said. It was when I expressed my astonishment at the contents of your first novel and started interrogating you for a suspicious memory. You said, 'Don't look too hard. There's nothing between the lines. A woman writer is beyond suspicion because she is open by nature. Writing cleanses all that has stuck to us since birth. Look for dirt somewhere other than literature!'

Inherited corruption was everywhere around me, in the eyes of most of the women, who craved a man – any man. It was in the nerves of men who were taut with accumulated desire and ready to snap in the face of the first woman.

But I had to resist my animal desire that day, and not let that city draw me to the depths. There were principles I couldn't renounce, like having an affair with a married woman. Perhaps that explained my recent sadness. For I knew that that day another reason had been added to all the others that made our relationship impossible. You would never be mine after that day.

My right hand didn't shame me that day. I felt a sense of relief as I discovered that, despite all that had happened, I still respected my body. What mattered in these situations was not to lose respect for the body and give it up to the first tramp. What could we inhabit afterwards if we were to humiliate it and it refused to forget?

I suddenly threw off the covers and went over to the window. I opened it as if to let your ghost out for ever and let light enter the room.

In a city haunted by magicians and *jinn*, perhaps you were a *jinn* who would creep in to bed with me in the dark and tell me tall tales, promising me a host of magical solutions to my tragedies. Then you would disappear with the first rays of the sun, leaving me to my obsessions and doubts.

Did your ghost really leave my bed, my room and my memory that day? Did it escape out of the window? I don't know.

All I know is that Constantine came in through the same window that I rarely opened. The call to prayer from many minarets all at once startled me. I was rooted to the spot as people rushed in every direction. The Sidi Rachid bridge also seemed absorbed in its constant motion, like a woman getting ready for some event, caught up in its daily worries and weekend enthusiasm.

That morning in particular, the bridge seemed too busy for my sadness, which I felt amounted to betrayal and ingratitude. In my turn, I decided not to flatter it and closed the window in its face.

All of a sudden, I was struck by an overwhelming desire to paint, a raging hunger for colour that almost matched the violence and intensity of my earlier sexual desire.

I no longer needed a woman. My body had been healed and the ache had moved to my fingertips. Ultimately, the bed wasn't my pleasure ground or the arena for the rituals of my madness. Only the white space stretched between wooden runners would allow me to empty myself out. I wanted to pour my curse on to it, spit out the bitterness of a lifetime of disappointments.

I emptied out a memory that had developed a penchant for black since I aligned myself with a city that had foolishly been wrapping herself in blackness for centuries and that, in contradiction, had been hiding her face under a white triangular scarf of seduction.

Greetings, impossible triangle. Greetings, city confined between the unholy trinity of religion, sex and politics. You swallowed up so many men under your black robe. Not one of them expected you to match the Bermuda Triangle's desire for victims.

Ashen thoughts multiplied in my mind that morning. My rage

mounted as time progressed towards Hassan and Nasser's arrival to take me to that house for your wedding. Rage and frustration paralysed my arm and even prevented me from shaving and getting ready for the wedding-funeral.

I was pacing up and down the room, as strung out as an addict lacking his shot of heroin.

How had I failed to anticipate my sick need to hold a brush that day, the overwhelming desire to paint? That irresistible desire that became a pain in the fingertips, a bodily tension that passed from one limb to another?

I wanted to paint and paint until I became completely empty and fell down dead or unconscious in exhaustion and ecstasy.

Most likely I wouldn't paint bridges or viaducts. I might paint women in black shawls with white kerchiefs over their faces, and lying eyes promising a certain joy. Black, just like white, was mostly a colour that lied. I might not paint anything and just die standing, impotent before a blank canvas.

Was there anything more brilliant than signing a blank canvas with blankness and withdrawing on tiptoe, as long as we didn't sign anything in the end?

Only fate signs our life and does what it will with us.

So why try to deceive things, then? Why evade them?

Were you not my painting? What would be the use of my having painted you a thousand times if someone else left his signature and fingerprints on you that day, his name on your ID papers? What was the use of the dozens of canvases I covered with you compared with the bed containing your body and immortalising your eternal femininity?

What was the point of what I painted, if as usual someone else's signature appeared in my place?

* * *

At that pinnacle of despair, the telephone suddenly rang and brought me out of my solitary obsessions for a moment. I hurried to a distant room to answer it.

It was Hassan. Without introduction he asked, 'What are you doing?'

I answered, somewhat truthfully, 'I was dozing.'

'That's OK then,' he said. 'I thought you'd be ready and have been waiting for me for a while. I wanted to let you know I might be a bit late. There's a small problem I have to sort out.'

Startled, I asked him, 'What problem?'

'Guess what Nasser's come up with today? He doesn't want to attend his sister's wedding.'

My curiosity growing, I said, 'Why?'

'He's against the wedding. He doesn't want to meet the guests, the groom or even his uncle!'

I almost interrupted with, 'He's got a point,' but just asked, 'Where is he now?'

'I left him at the mosque. He said that he'd rather spend the day there than with those pim—'

For the first time I laughed from the heart and couldn't stop myself commenting aloud, 'Nasser is great! I swear he's one of us.'

Hassan cut me short, however, in a tone of reproach and bewilderment. 'What! Have you gone mad too? It's not done. Have you ever heard of someone not going to his sister's wedding? What would people say?'

'People? People? Let them say what they want. Look man, for the love of your parents, let's—'

Before I could say anything more, he said, 'Stay in the house, then, and I'll come by as soon as I've finished. We'll talk about it later. I'm calling from a café and there are lots of people around.

Understand?' He went on, 'There's some food in the kitchen that Atiqa cooked for you.'

I hung up and went back to my room.

I didn't want to eat. I just had a morning thirst and felt that after the phone call my bitterness had a hint of happiness.

Nasser's stance made me feel elated. There was someone else who, without knowing, shared my sadness and, in his own way, stood with me against your wedding. Nasser was a thoroughbred, worthy of being *Si* Taher's son. I hadn't met him as an adult, but expected him to be stubborn and direct like his father. And if he was truly like his father, Hassan would never succeed in making him change his mind.

I still remembered *Si* Taher's stubbornness, and the absolutely unshakeable decisions he took. Back then, I found something dictatorial about such an attitude and the arrogance of the commander. But I came to realise that the early days of the Revolution needed men like *Si* Taher, stubborn and totally self-confident, able to impose their will on others. This was not out of love for glory or control, but to unify the Revolution and prevent disagreements and personal considerations from holding sway, so that its sparks were not scattered and taken by the winds.

The memory of *Si* Taher returned suddenly at a moment I had not prepared for him. His form came back, painful as the bullets they emptied into his body one day and that claimed him a few months before he could witness Algeria's independence. Where was he on this exceptional day, another one he would miss? Was it his fate to miss two momentous occasions?

He left as he had come, before his time, as if he knew he hadn't been created for the time to come.

255

A bitter realisation struck me: not one of those who loved you would attend your wedding. Many of those you had delighted would be absent – *Si* Taher, Ziyad and Nasser too. Why had the lot fallen on me alone, why had fate led me to you? Why had it lured me here, in the name of memory and nostalgia and that mad, impossible love? I said the words that filled the pockets of dreams: 'I will be yours as long as we are in Constantine.'

How had I believed you and come? I knew you were lying, giving me white clouds for a long summer. But who could resist the beautiful rain of lies? There were lies we tried to believe so as to confound predictions. But when the rains poured inside us, who would dry the tears of the sky?

The truth is you were a sadist and I knew it. One day I said to you, 'If Hitler had had a daughter, by rights she would have been you!' You laughed at the time, the laugh of a mighty ruler confident of his power. With the naivety of a victim I commented, 'I don't know what led me to love you when I'm a fugitive from the rule of tyrants. After all this life, could I have fallen in love with a tyrannical woman?'

You gave a sudden smile and after a brief silence you said, 'You're amazing when you talk. You make subjects to write about spark inside me. One day I'll write that idea.'

So write it then some day; it's certainly good material for a novel!

That morning, I turned to drink to forget my failure with you.

In that room furnished with an empty bed, a window over-looking minarets and bridges and a table with no painting supplies, the only means of deliverance I could find were a few sheets of paper, some pens and one of the bottles of whiskey that

I had brought for Hassan, unaware of his return to the faith. They were still waiting in my bag. I pulled one out and drank a toast to Ziyad and *Si* Taher, and to Constantine.

I recalled a play I had enjoyed once and wrote at the top of the page without much thought, 'Cheers to you, Constantine.' I laughed at the part I was playing in this city where alcohol was forbidden but there was every reason to drink.

At the time, I didn't know that I was condensing my failure into a few words that might do as the title for this book, the idea of which was perhaps born that day.

I felt like defying you and that city and that lying homeland.

I raised my glass, brimful of you. Cheers to your memory, as good at making one forget as this drink. Cheers to your eyes, created to lie. Cheers to a wedding night ready for crying. Cheers to my tearless crying.

You reconciled me with God, and once made me worship Him again. But you would betray me on the eve of Friday, rule shedding my blood lawful and shoot me with a traitor's bullet.

Why shouldn't I get drunk? Which one of us would be more irreligious?

In fact, I wasn't a big drinker. Alcohol was the drink for extremes of happiness and sadness. That's why it was connected with you and your crazy mood swings. Every time I drank, I was recording an event in our never-ending affair.

I opened a final bottle in your honour and committed my final act of madness. I didn't think I would get drunk again after that day, because I was going to wash my hands of you from then on and bid you farewell in my own way.

Only the business with Nasser was of any interest now. Your brother was praying in one of the mosques of the city in order, like me, to forget that everyone would come, one after another, to the reception that night and that there would be someone who would enjoy you out of view.

Really, I was getting drunk as a toast to him, no one else. Yes, Nasser. Me, you and Constantine. A city complicit with us in extremism and madness. A sadistic city whose pleasure was to torture her children. She who would become pregnant without trying and give birth to us like a sea turtle that lays its young on the shore and heads off in indifference, leaving them to the mercy of the waves and the seabirds.

'Think, because God won't do it for you.' So said the sea turtle when abandoning its young. Here we were without thoughts, seeking our fate between the bar and the mosque.

We were turtles sleeping on our backs. We were turned over to prevent us running away, turned over in an effort to over-throw logic.

Birth in ancient cities was very like death. There we would be born and die in the crosswinds.

There were so many orphan turtles in that city.

When Hassan arrived later and caught me sitting writing at the table with a half-empty bottle of whiskey in front of me, he almost gasped in shock. He stared at me in astonishment, as if by opening the bottle I had released a demon or genie into the house.

I tried to tease him and said sarcastically, 'Why are you looking at me like that? Haven't you seen a bottle before?'

But he was in no mood for fun and took the bottle to the kitchen, cursing and talking to himself with words that didn't reach me.

When he came back, he said in a tone tinged with despair and traces of worry for Nasser, 'What is it with you two? The place has gone mad. One of you prays; one of you gets drunk. What are we supposed to do?'

I was drawn to an expression I had not heard for several years, 'the place has gone mad', by which he meant the city was in uproar or witnessing something exceptional. The meaning was, in fact, highly sexual. I smiled as I realised once again the power of the city to insert sexual imagery into everything. And with startling innocence.

I raised an eye towards him and said, 'This is Algeria, Hassan. Some pray, some get drunk and all the while the rest "go mad".'

Hassan seemed unwilling to continue the discussion with me. Perhaps he had spent too long trying to convince Nasser and couldn't face arguing any more. So he interrupted and said, 'I'll go and make you a coffee to clear your head and sober you up. Then we can talk. People are expecting us. Some of them haven't seen you for years. You can't turn up like this!'

When he came back with the coffee a few minutes later, I asked him, 'What did you do about Nasser?'

He said, 'He promised me he'd go by at dinner time, just to please me, but wouldn't stay long. I still doubt he'll actually turn up. I don't understand why he's being so stubborn. After all, he only has one sister, and it just won't do for him not to appear with her at her wedding.'

Madness!

I sipped the coffee to sober up, as Hassan put it. Yet at the same time I felt I was getting drunker, or madder, as I listened to him. I asked him why Nasser was boycotting the wedding and the conversation that ensued touched on a number of matters.

He said, 'He disagrees with his uncle. He thinks he's derived a lot of benefit from *Si* Taher's name but didn't give much thought to what happened to his brother's wife and children. The wedding is self-serving and only about political ambitions. Nasser is against his uncle's choice of a man who has a bad reputation, politically and morally. Everyone's talking about the commission he receives from his various deals, about his bank accounts abroad, about his Algerian and foreign mistresses. Plus, this is his second marriage and his children are nearly the same age as his new bride.'

'Did you think it was a normal marriage?' I asked.

'I don't know on what basis you want to judge it. According to how we think here, it's normal, and won't be the first of its kind, or the last. Most important men here have more than one mistress, and all of them, in one way or another, have got rid of wives and children to marry a younger woman more beautiful and cultured than the first. You can't stop a man whose star is on the rise from adding a woman to his household, or a guy who's landed a position he never dreamed of from seeking the girl of his dreams.

'I just tried to convince Nasser that his uncle didn't necessarily intend to put an end to his sister's future with this marriage. That anybody else would grab it with open arms. It's the only way for him to solve his and the girl's problems in one go. It'll save him a lot of headaches.'

I asked him, 'If you had a daughter, and that man asked for her hand in marriage, would you agree?'

'Of course,' he said. 'Why not? It's a permissible marriage. What should be forbidden is some people's modern way of doing things. They despatch their daughter, wife or sister to get hold of an official document for them or to put in a request for an apartment or trading licence. Yet they know that no one here gives you anything for nothing. The ordinary people have created their own currency to meet their needs. Pay with a woman and take what you will!'

'Is that true?' I mumbled.

'It's happening now in plenty of cities,' he replied, 'especially the capital. There, any young girl can go to some party office and obtain an apartment or some other government service. Of course, everyone knows where to go and whom to see. That person provides apartments and services for women and slogans for the people in equal measure. It's enough to see the look of the girls going in to understand the whole thing.'

I asked him, 'Who told you about this?'

Grumpily, he said, 'Who? I heard and saw it for myself a few months ago when I went to the capital to meet a friend who's a party official. I thought he might help me leave teaching. Imagine, not even the doorman could be bothered to talk to me. I wasted my breath explaining to him that I had come from Constantine especially. Only women were worthy of attention there. When I started to complain to the office messenger, he snapped at me that most of the female visitors were officials in the party unions or activists. When one of them went by I nearly asked him which "member" they were active with exactly. But I kept quiet.

'Come on, man. Now everything goes via women during late nights and special sessions. So, if I had the choice, I'd marry my daughter to someone who could get her anything with one phone call, rather than to someone like me who'd live with her in misery like I do, or join in the corruption and send her knocking at a hundred doors.'

Maybe Hassan noticed the signs of shock and confusion on my face. He added, as if to qualify and ease my disappointment, 'In any case, it wouldn't happen. Even if I offered my daughter to *Si* ——, he would be sure to refuse her. They only get married to each other. So-and-so only wants the daughter of so-and-so, so that "our oil only mixes with our flour!" and they ensure their

261

moves from one position of power to another. In such an atmosphere, how do you expect an ordinary young man to build his future? All the girls are on the lookout for officials and managers, men who've already made it. The men themselves know this and set more and more conditions, while the number of unmarried women gets bigger every day. It's the law of supply and demand.

'If you understood that things were like this, you'd definitely forgive *Si* Sharif. What matters is that he protects his niece and ensures her and himself as happy a future as possible.

'As for the groom being a thief who robs the state, what do you want to do? All of them are crooks and cheats. Some are found out, others just know how to keep up the appearance of propriety!'

I was shocked by what I was hearing.

I almost said that in the end he was right, and maybe *Si* Sharif was too. I didn't know.

But there was something about the wedding I just couldn't accept.

Chapter Six

FOR YOUR WEDDING I wore my black suit.

Black is an incredible colour. It can be worn at both weddings and funerals.

Why had I chosen black? Perhaps because when I fell in love with you I became a sufi, and you became my spiritual order and path. Perhaps, too, because it was the colour of my silence.

Every colour has its language. I once read that black was an affront to patience. I also read it was a colour that contained its own opposite. I also heard a famous fashion designer say that he always wore black because it set a barrier between him and others. Today I could tell you a great deal about that colour. But the words of the fashion designer are enough. I wanted to put a barrier between all those I would meet, all the flies who would come and land at your wedding table, and me.

Perhaps I also wanted to put a barrier between you and me.

I wore my black outfit to silently counter your white dress. Studded with pearls and flowers, it had been specially made for you at a Parisian couturier, or so the rumour said.

Would it be possible for a painter to choose his colour impartially?

I looked elegant – sadness has an elegance too. The mirror confirmed this, and Hassan's looks. He suddenly had faith in me again and said in the Algerian accent I adored, 'That's how we like you Khaled. Knock 'em dead!'

I looked at him and nearly said something.

At the gate, open for cars and the arriving crowds, *Si* Sharif greeted me with an embrace. 'Hello, *Si* Khaled, hello. You bring blessings. Thank you for coming. You are our happiness today.'

Once again, I summarised that absurd situation in a few words and said, 'All things are blessed.'

I masked my face with happiness and tried to keep it up for the whole evening.

The house was filled with trilling cries of joy. My lungs were filled with the smoke of the cigarettes that I lit and that lit me. My heart was full of grief. I learned automatically to put a false smile on my lips and laughed with the others. I sat down with people I knew and those I didn't. I talked about things I knew and others I didn't. That way I wasn't alone with you for a second. That way I wasn't suddenly surprised by you inside me and didn't collapse.

I said hello to the groom, who kissed me with the affection of a long-lost friend.

'So you've made it to Algeria, sir! If it wasn't for this wedding we wouldn't have seen you!'

I tried to forget that I was talking to your husband, a man talking to me out of courtesy, hurriedly, perhaps thinking about the moment he would be alone with you at the end of the night.

I looked at his cigar, extra long for the occasion, the blue silk suit he was wearing – or that was wearing him – with the elegance of one accustomed to silk. I tried not to stop and think about his body. I tried not to remember. I distracted myself with the faces of the guests . . . and you appeared.

You entered in a procession of women, professionals at joy and nuptials as much as I was a professional in painting and sadness.

I was seeing you for the first time after all those months of absence, passing close and distant, like a shooting star. With a heavy dress and heavy steps you walked among the trills of joy and the drumbeats. A song scratched my memory and took me back to being a child running around the old houses of Constantine with other processions of women behind other brides about whom I knew nothing at the time.

I loved those wedding songs so much. Songs to accompany the bride, which I enjoyed without understanding. Now they were making me cry.

'Open the door, mother of the bride.' It was said that brides always cried when they heard this song.

Had you cried that day, I wondered?

Your eyes were distant. The mist of my tears and the throng kept me from them. So I dropped the question.

I made do with contemplating you in your final role.

You approached like a fairytale princess, seductive and desirable, surrounded by admiring glances, bewildered and bewildering, humble and arrogant.

There you were, as usual, every man's secret desire and the envy of every woman.

There I was, as usual, still stunned before you.

There was Fergani, as usual, serenading those with stars on their shoulders in the front row. His voice sweetened and his violin grew louder when he played for the notables, the decision-makers, the generals. The musical instruments reached a crescendo and the singers united in one voice to welcome the groom:

> How sweet the wedding with its ouds
> May God never part them
> Or have them fear the evil eye.

The ululations went up and the banknotes fluttered down.

What strength there was in hired throats. How generous were the hands that contributed as quickly as they had amassed!

There they were then. All of them, as usual. Men with distended stomachs, Habana cigars, and multi-faceted suits. The masters of every era and every time. Diplomats and suspect wheeler-dealers, masters of happiness and misery, those with unknown pasts.

There they were. Former ministers and ministers-in-waiting. Former thieves and thieves-in-waiting. Opportunist administrators and opportunists waiting to become administrators. Former informants and military men disguised in ministerial dress.

There they were. Those with revolutionary theories out for a quick buck. Those with vacant minds and towering villas who talked of themselves in the plural.

There they were. They always gathered like sharks, always swarming around dubious feasts.

I knew them and ignored most of them. 'Don't say "I" until the neighbourhood big shots die!' I knew them and pitied them. How pitiable they were with their wealth and their poverty, with their knowledge and their ignorance, in their rapid ascent and their calamitous fall. How pitiable on the day when no one would offer them a hand to shake.

Until that day came, the wedding belonged to them. Let them

eat, let them enjoy, let them scatter banknotes. Let them listen to Fergani singing, like at every wedding in Constantine, the song 'Saleh Bey'.

The same song had been sung for two hundred years to remind people of the tragedy of Saleh Bey and of the deceit of power and glory, which did not last for anyone. It was being sung that day out of habit; no one paid attention to the words.

> Ministers and sultans
>> All dead and mourned.
> Great wealth they had,
>> But the Arabs said.
> 'What use wealth and glory,
>> Saleh with his money.'

Listening to those words, I remembered the words of a pop song I had heard on the radio: 'Saleh, Saleh, I love your eyes.'

Yes, Constantine, every age had its Saleh, but not every Saleh was a bey, and not every ruler was *saleh*, fit to rule.

Finally the other homeland was in front of me. Was that really the homeland? At every table was a face that I knew too much about. I sat down and looked at them. I listened to them grumbling and complaining. Not one of them was happy, it seemed. It was unbelievable that they were the ones who always had something to complain about. They criticised the situation and cursed the homeland.

A very strange thing! It was as though they hadn't all run scrambling after their positions. It was as though they weren't part of the filth of the homeland, as though they weren't the cause of the disasters.

I said hello to *Si* Mustafa. He had become a minister since the day he visited me to buy a painting, and I refused to sell it to him.

Si Sharif's predictions had come true, then, and he had backed a winning horse.

I asked him politely, 'How are you *Si* Mustafa?'

He launched straight into a complaint. 'We're drowning in problems, you know.'

Quite by chance a phrase of De Gaulle's popped into my head: 'A minister has no right to complain – nobody forced him to become a minister!'

I kept the thought to myself and just said to him, 'Yes, I know.'

Yes, I knew about those vast amounts of money he had received in Canada as commission for refitting one of the large state facilities. But I was ashamed to say that to him, because I knew that those who had preceded him in the job had done no better. I contented myself with listening to him complaining in a way that would have evoked the pity of any wretched citizen.

Hassan was busy talking to an old friend, an Arabic teacher who had, all of a sudden, become ambassador to one of the Arab states. How had that happened? It was rumoured to be a payback. An inheritance and an old friendship linked him with the father of someone important. That wasn't the only diplomatic case!

There was the case of *Si* Hussein, whom I knew well. He had been director of a cultural institution when I was director of publications. Overnight he had been appointed as a foreign ambassador, after his smell turned sour at home. So they kept him under wraps for a few months and then dispatched him abroad with full diplomatic credentials under the Algerian flag.

He was back that day, in his natural environment. After some fraud and deception with state funds abroad, he had been summoned home to take up a party post without any fuss being made. Just in a back seat this time. In such cases there was always a respectable dumping ground!

At another table, someone was still theorising and going on as if he was the philosopher of the Revolution and all future revolutions. One of his personal revolutions involved reaching the top ranks in dubious circumstances, after having supplied female students to an elderly official with a thing for young girls.

Such was the homeland. Such was your wedding to which you invited me. It was a circus whose only acts were clowns and contortionists who jumped the queue, broke necks and trampled on values. A circus where a handful made fun of the masses and a whole people was trained to be stupid.

How right Nasser was not to turn up to that grotesque show. I knew intuitively that he wouldn't appear, but where was he? He might still have been praying in the mosque so as to avoid meeting anyone from the wedding party. But had his prayer, or my getting drunk, changed anything? Ah, Nasser, stop praying, my lad. They also pray and put on a guise of piety. Stop praying. Let's think while the flies land on everything and the locusts devour the feast.

As the night went on, my sadness grew, as did their enjoyment. Banknotes rained down on the important women surrendering to the intoxication of dancing to the most famous popular song:

> When the night falls, where will I sleep?
> On a bed and pillows of silk.
> Some hope!

Yes, Fergani, sing!
The song had nothing to do with the housing crisis, as it might

269

seem at first. It was a paean to the lurid nights and silk sheets that weren't within reach of the masses.

> Those who've died, don't cry for them,
> those who've died.
> Some hope!

I wouldn't cry. It wasn't the night for *Si* Taher or Ziyad. It wasn't for martyrs or for lovers. It was a night for deals, openly celebrated with music and trills of joy.

> She leaves the bath-house perfumed.
> Is it for me or for another?
> Some hope!

I wouldn't ask myself that question. I knew you were another's and not mine. The songs confirmed this, and the procession taking you away with trilling cries to your licit night of love.

When you went past me in the bridal march, I felt that you were walking over my body, not perfumed as the song says, but with your hennaed feet and your gold anklets clinking inside me like bells awaking memory.

Stop.

Easy now, you, dressed in the fashion of Constantine! Poems do not pass by so fast!

Your dress, embroidered in gold and studded with gold coins, was a long poem on red velvet composed by Constantine over the generations. A gold belt, tightly encircling your waist to make your femininity and seduction overflow, was the epicentre of my amazement. The greatest lines of Arabic poetry ever written.

So go easy.

Let me dream that time has stopped, that you are mine. Me, who might die without marrying, without the ululations rising for me.

How much I wished I could steal the song from all those women's throats to bless my taking possession of you. If I were the bride snatcher of legend who runs off with beautiful women on their wedding night, I would have come riding the winds on a white horse and snatched you from them.

If you had been mine, the city would have blessed us, and from every street we passed, a saint would have come forth to light incense on our way. But how sad the night, Constantine. How dejected her holy saints. They alone sat at my table for no good reason and reserved a front seat for my other memory.

So I spent my evening greeting them, one by one.

Peace, Sidi Rachid. Peace, Sidi Mabrouk, Sidi Mohamed of the Crow, Sidi Suleiman, Sidi Bouanaba, Sidi Abdelmumin, Sidi Maseed, Sidi Bumezza, Sidi Shalice.

Peace to you who rule the streets of this city, her alleyways and her memory.

Stay with me, holy saints of God. I am tired tonight. Do not leave me. Wasn't my father one of you?

My father, member of the Aissawiyya Order, like his father and grandfather before him. In the closed circles, at the incredible ceremonies of the Order, he would plunge a red-hot skewer into his flesh, right through his body and then pull it out without a drop of blood on it.

He, who swallowed red-hot iron, putting it out with his saliva and not getting burnt, may he teach me tonight how to be tortured and not bleed. Teach me how to say her name and not burn my tongue. Teach me to be cured of her, he who frequented the Aissawi group in sessions of ecstasy and terror, dancing possessed by the flame, 'I am Sidi Aissawi who wounds and heals.'

Who will heal me, father, who? When I love her.

At that late hour of pain, I confessed I still loved her. That she was mine.

I defied those with distended stomachs, the one with the beard, the bald one, the bearers of innumerable stars and all those to whom she gave so much but who raped her today in my presence.

I challenged them with my lack. With the arm that was no longer my arm. With the memory they had stolen from me. With all they had taken away from me.

I challenged them to love her like me, because I alone loved her without return.

I knew that right then someone was lifting that dress off her in haste. He would take her gold bracelets off with little care and rush towards her body with the eagerness of a fifty-year-old man taking a girl.

My sadness was for that dress.

How many hands had embroidered it? How many women had taken turns for a single man to enjoy lifting it off? A man who would throw it randomly over a chair, as though it were not our memory, our homeland.

Was it the fate of nations to be built by entire generations for one man to enjoy?

I wondered why it was only me who considered all these details. Why only now had I discovered the meaning of all those things that had no meaning before?

Was it perhaps love for the homeland, or distance from it, that had given ordinary things a sacredness that only those deprived of them feel?

Now ordinary life had killed the dream and the sacredness of things. One of the Prophet's companions advised the Muslims to leave Mecca as soon as they had finished the rites of the pilgrimage, so that that city would retain its awe and sanctity in their hearts, and not be transformed into an ordinary city where anyone might steal, fornicate and oppress without dread.

That is what had happened to me since stepping into Constantine. Only I treated her as an extraordinary city. I treated her every stone with love. I greeted each one of her bridges individually. I asked for news of her families, saints and men, individually.

I contemplated her walking, praying, fornicating and putting her madness to work. No one could understand my mad attachment to a city that all dreamed of escaping.

Did I blame them?

Did the inhabitants of Athens feel they were going to and fro over history, over the soil trodden by the gods and many mythic heroes? Did the wretched poor of Giza know they were living by the oldest wonder of the world? That the pharaohs were still among them ruling Egypt with their chambers and tombs? Only foreigners who have read Greek and Egyptian history in books treated these stones with sanctity and came from all over the world just to touch them.

Perhaps I had spent too long in the city and committed the stupid mistake of coming within burning closeness to dreams. Now, day after day and failure after failure, I would be cured of the power of her name over me and lose my beautiful illusions. But not without pain. At that moment, I only wanted the city to provide a bullet of mercy.

So I accepted the cries of joy that arose at that early hour of dawn to bless your petticoat sullied with your innocence, the last shot fired in my face by the city. Without a silencer or a muffled conscience, I received it frozen, with the astonished look of a corpse, while I watched them competing around me to touch your shift on display.

There they were offering you to me as a painting splattered with blood, in proof of my ultimate impotence, in proof of their other crime.

I didn't move or protest. A spectator at a bullfight cannot change the logic of things and side with the bull. If that were so, he should have stayed at home and not gone to the *corrida*, which existed to praise the matador.

Something about the atmosphere evoked the bullfight. The ululations and the elegance, the music to mark the 'consummation' and the cries directed at a slip smeared with blood reminded me of its rites. A beautiful death would be arranged for the bull who entered the arena to dance music and died to it under deadly, decorated swords, entranced by the colour red and the elegance of his killer.

Which of us was the bull? Was it you or me who was colour blind and saw only the red colour of your blood? Which of us was the bull circling the ring of your love with the pride of a creature only conquered by deceit, who knew his death was preordained?

In truth, your blood embarrassed me and made me ashamed. I felt torn.

Hadn't I always been desperate to know the end of your story with him, the one who took you from me? Perhaps he had taken everything from you.

The question had occupied and haunted me to the point of madness since the day I put Ziyad in front of you and put you before your other destiny.

Did you open up the gates of your fortress to him, lower your high towers and surrender to his masculine seduction?

Perhaps you left your childhood to me and your womanhood to him?

The answer had come to me after a year of torture. There it was at last, a sticky, fresh red rose, a moment old. There it was, the answer I didn't expect, intruding, shaming. So why the sadness?

What hurt me most that night? Was it knowing that I had wronged Ziyad with my doubts, and that he, the most worthy of you that night, had died without enjoying you? Or was it knowing that you were just a city taken by military force, like every Arab city?

What annoyed me most that night? That I finally knew your riddle, or that I knew I would know nothing more about you after that day, even if I were to spend a lifetime talking to you and read you a thousand times?

Were you still a virgin, your sins merely ink on paper?

Why had you made me believe all those things? Why did you give me your book as though giving me a dagger for jealousy?

Why did you teach me to love you line by line, lie by lie, and to violate you on paper?

Let it be.

My consolation now was that among all my failures, you were the most beautiful.

'Why are you sad this morning?' asked Hassan.

I tried not to ask him why he was happy.

I knew that Nasser's absence and boycott of the wedding the day before had spoiled his mood. But it didn't prevent him from getting into Fergani's songs, laughing or talking at length to people he had not met before. I was observing him and quite happy at his naive happiness.

Hassan was happy that doors so rarely open to the common people were finally opening for him, that he had been invited to the wedding, which he would now be able to talk about for weeks with his friends, describing the guests, the food and what the bride was wearing to those who asked.

His wife could also forget that she had borrowed the clothes and jewels she had worn to the wedding from neighbours and relatives. She in turn could start boasting to everyone about the opulence she had seen, as if she had suddenly become part of it just because she had been invited to gawp at the wealth of others.

Suddenly he said, '*Si* Sharif has invited us for lunch tomorrow. Don't forget to be home around noon so we can go together.'

In an absent voice I said to him, 'I'm going back to Paris tomorrow.'

He cried, 'How can you go back tomorrow? You must stay at least another week with us. What's waiting for you there?'

I tried to make him believe I had a number of commitments and had begun to tire of my stay in Constantine.

But he pressed, 'That's wrong, brother. At least stay for lunch with *Si* Sharif tomorrow and then leave.'

I replied in a firm tone that he didn't understand, 'It's finished. I'm going tomorrow.'

I liked to talk to him in the accent of Constantine. With every word, I felt that a long time would pass until I might say it again.

As though convincing me of the need not to refuse the invitation, Hassan said, 'I swear, *Si* Sharif is a good guy. Despite his position, he's still true to our old friendship. You know that some people here say he might become a minister. Perhaps God will grant us some relief through him that day.'

Hassan said the last sentence in a barely audible voice, as though to himself.

Poor Hassan! My poor brother to whom God gave no relief after that. Was it just naivety that made him ignorant of the fact that the wedding was nothing more than a deal, that *Si* Sharif would have to get something in return? We wouldn't marry our daughters to high-ranking officers without prior intentions.

Any benefit Hassan might derive from *Si* Sharif's prospective post was simply an illusion. The believer starts with himself, and years might pass before he got around to giving a few crumbs to Hassan.

I asked him in fun, 'Have you also started dreaming about becoming an ambassador?'

As though the question had somehow hurt him, he said, 'What misery, man! Too late for that. All I want is to get out of teaching and land a decent job in any cultural or media organisation. A job to support me and my family in a half-normal way. How do you expect the eight of us to survive on my salary? I can't even afford to buy a car. Where would I get the millions to buy one? When I think about the luxury cars lined up at the wedding yesterday, I feel sick and lose the desire to teach. I'm tired of that profession; there are no material or moral rewards. The times of "the teacher almost being a prophet" have changed. Today, as one of my colleagues puts it, "the teacher's no more than a rag".

'We've become everyone's rag. The teacher goes on the bus just like his pupils. He has to insert his ticket and stamp it just like them. People curse him in front of them. Then he goes home, like that colleague, to prepare his classes and correct homework in a two-room flat that eight or more people live in.

'At the same time there are people who own two or three flats thanks to their job or connections. He can meet his mistresses in them or lend the keys to someone who'll open other doors for him.

'Good for you, Khaled, that you live far from these worries in your high-class neighbourhood in Paris. You don't have to worry about what's happening in the world!'

Ah, Hassan, when I remember our conversation that day, the bitterness congeals in my throat. It becomes a raw wound, tears of regret and grief.

I could have helped you more, Hassan, that's true.

He would say, 'Ask for something, Khaled, while you're here. Weren't you a fighter? Didn't you lose your arm in the war? Ask for a shop, a piece of land or a van. They won't turn you down. It's your right. Give it to me, if you want, to support myself and the kids. You're known and respected. No one knows me. It's crazy for you not to take what's rightfully yours from this nation. It's not charity they're giving you. Plenty of people can prove they were fighters, but they did nothing during the Revolution. Your body is your proof.'

Yes, Hassan. You didn't understand that that was the only difference between them and me. You didn't understand that it was no longer possible, after all these years and all the suffering, for me to bow my head to anyone, even if in exchange for a patriotic gift. I might have done that right after independence, but today it was impossible.

There's not long left now, my brother. Not long left now for me to bow my head before I die.

I want to remain like that before them, plunged like a dagger in their consciences. I want them to be ashamed when they meet me. For them to lower their heads and ask how I am, in the knowledge that I know all about them and am a witness to their baseness.

Ah, if only you knew, Hassan! If only you knew the pleasure of walking the streets with your head held high, to be able to meet anyone, an ordinary person or a VIP, without feeling shame.

Today there are people who can't walk the streets, when before, all the streets were reserved for them and their convoys of official cars.

I said nothing to Hassan. I just promised, as a preliminary step, that I'd buy him a car. I said, 'Come with me and choose a car that suits you. Take it with you from France. I don't want you to live feeling like this any more.'

Hassan was as happy as a child that day. I felt that was his great dream, one that he had been unable to fulfil and unable to request from me. But how could I have known that, as I hadn't visited him for years?

When I remember Hassan today, only that gesture brings a little joy to my heart, because I made him briefly happy and gave him respite for a few years. A few years I never imagined would be the last ones.

Hassan returned to the subject. 'Do you really insist on going tomorrow?'

I said, 'Yes. It's wiser that I go tomorrow.'

'Then you must call *Si* Sharif today and apologise to him. He might misinterpret your leaving and get upset.'

I thought a little and found he was right. I said to Hassan, 'Call *Si* Sharif for me and I'll apologise to him.'

I expected that would be that, but *Si* Sharif was welcoming and embarrassed me with his kindness. He insisted I come and visit him, even if right then.

He said, 'Come and have lunch with us today, then. What matters is seeing you before you go. Plus you can give your present to the newly-weds yourself this evening before you leave.'

There was no way out of it. Once again I had to face my fate with you. And I had decided to hasten my departure so as to escape an atmosphere which, in one way or another, centred around you.

There I was, once again putting on my black suit and carrying a painting that you stood before one day and that became the reason for all that happened to me afterwards. I went to the lunch with Hassan.

My legs carried me, once again, towards you. I knew I would meet you that time. I had an intuition that we wouldn't miss that date.

What did *Si* Sharif say that day? What did I say, and whom did I meet? What was put in front of us to eat? I no longer remember.

I was living the last moments of loving you. Nothing interested me right then but seeing you and ending it with you at the same time. But I feared your love. I feared it would reignite from the ashes once more. Grand passion remains frightening and risky even in its death throes.

You arrived.

The most painful, the most crazy, the most ironic moments were those when I stood to say hello and give you two innocent pecks on the cheek. I congratulated you on your marriage using all the right words for such an incredible situation.

How much strength I needed, how much patience and dissimulation, to make the others imagine that I had not met you before, other than one passing encounter, and that you weren't the woman who had turned my life upside down. The woman who had shared my empty bed for several months, and who had – until the previous day – been mine!

How good an actor I had to be to give you that painting

without any further comment, without any explanation, as if it wasn't the painting that marked the start of my affair with you, twenty-five years ago.

You gave an admirable performance too as you unwrapped it and looked at it in wonder, as if seeing it for the first time. I could only ask in the secret complicity that had once joined us, 'Do you like bridges?'

A brief silence enveloped us, which seemed as long to me as the wait for a death sentence or a pardon. Then you lifted your eyes towards me to pronounce judgement. 'Yes. I love them!'

How much happiness you gave me at that moment with your words. I felt you were sending me the last sign of love. I felt you were giving me ideas for future paintings and nights of fantasy and that, despite everything, you would remain faithful to our shared memory and to a city that was complicit with us and extended all these bridges to bring us together.

But were you really my beloved? At that moment another man was next to you, devouring you with two eyes not sated from a whole night of making love. At that moment when all the talk was about the cities you would visit on your honeymoon, I said my farewells in silence for your final departure from my heart.

That was your first defeat with me. So, everything was over. I had finally met you, but had the meeting been worth the wait and the pain?

My dreams of it had been so beautiful. Yet, that day, incredibly, it fell flat. So full of waiting for you had it been, that in your presence it proved hollow, painful.

Was the half-glance we exchanged worth all that pain, longing and madness?

You wanted to say something to me and words failed. Looks failed.

Your eyes had forgotten how to talk to me. I no longer knew how to decipher your hieroglyphs.

Had we reverted to being strangers that day without realising?

We had separated.

Two final kisses on your cheeks, a glance or two, lots of pretence and a secret, voiceless pain.

We all exchanged polite words of congratulation and a final thank you.

We swapped addresses after your husband insisted on giving me his phone number at home and in the office in case I should need anything.

We went our separate ways, each with their own illusions and mind made up.

When I arrived back at the house, I stared a long time at the card that I had handled all the way in shock and with a funny taste of bitterness. It was as if you had moved from my heart to my pocket under a new name and telephone number.

Without much hesitation or deep thought I decided to rip it up right away while I still had strength to do so and while I still had the resolve to end everything there in Constantine, as you had once wanted and as I had come to want that day.

What did you want that evening when you called out of the blue and pulled me out of the blur of my contradictory thoughts and feelings?

When Hassan passed me the telephone saying, 'It's a woman who wants to talk to you,' you were the last thing I expected.

'Haven't you left yet?' I asked.

You said, 'We're leaving in an hour. I wanted to thank you for the painting. It made me unexpectedly happy.'

'I didn't give you anything,' I said. 'I returned a painting ready for you for twenty-five years. It's the gift of our fates that crossed one day. I have a different present for you that I expect you will like. I'll give it to you some day in the future.'

As though you were afraid someone might hear you or steal that present, you spoke in a low voice. 'What will you give me?'

I said, 'It's a surprise. Let's assume I'll give you a gazelle.'

Surprised you said, 'It's the title of a book!'

'I know,' I replied, 'because I will give you a book. When we love a girl we give her our name. When we love a woman we give her a child. When we love a writer we give her a book. I shall write a novel for you.'

I sensed joy and confusion in your voice, amazement and vague sadness. Then you suddenly said in a voice full of desire that I wasn't used to from you. 'Khaled, I love you. Do you know that?'

Your voice suddenly cut off and fused with my silence and sadness. We remained speechless for a few moments before you added with a touch of hope, 'Khaled, say something. Why don't you answer?'

In bitter irony I said to you, 'The pavement of flowers no longer responds.'

'Do you mean you no longer love me?'

In an absent voice I answered, 'I don't mean anything in particular. It's the title of another book by the same novelist!' What I said after that I don't remember. Most likely that was the last thing I said to you before hanging up. We separated for several years.

'Don't keep knocking at the door. I'm not here any more,' Malek Haddad wrote.

Don't try and come back to me via the back doors and holes

283

in memory, the folds in dreams, the windows blown open by storms.

Don't even try.

I abandoned my memory the day I made a shocking discovery: it was not *my* memory, but one I shared with you. Each of us had a copy of it even before we met.

My lady, don't keep knocking at the door. I no longer have a door.

Walls dropped on me the day I dropped you. The ceiling fell in on me as I tried to smuggle out my possessions that were scattered in your wake. Don't circle like that around what was my house. Don't look for a window to climb through like a thief. You've stolen all I have and there's nothing left worth venturing.

Don't keep knocking so painfully at the door.

Your phone call rings in the caves of memory, empty without you, and the echo resounds painfully and fearfully.

Don't you know that after you I live in this valley like the stones live at the bottom of Wadi Rummal?

So, easy now, my lady. Easy now as you cross Constantine's bridges. Any slip of the foot will send me down in a landslide of rocks, and any inadvertence on your part will send you down to be crushed with me.

Woman disguised in my mother's clothing and perfume and her fear for me, I am as tired as the bridges of Constantine. I am suspended like them between two rocks and two paths.

Why all this pain? And why are you the most lying of mothers and why am I the most idiotic of lovers?

Don't knock on Constantine's doors one after another. I don't live in this city. She lives in me.

Don't seek me on her bridges. They never once supported me. On my own I supported them.

Don't look for me in her songs, and come rushing to me with old-new news, and a song for sadness now sung in joy:

> The Arabs said, they said:
> > We didn't give Saleh money.
> The Arabs said, look:
> > We made Saleh Bey of Beys.

I know by heart what the Arabs said, and what today they dare not say.

I know that Saleh was your first mourning garb, even before you were born. He was the last bey of Constantine, and I was his last testament: 'Ah, Hamouda, ah, my child, take care of the home for me.'

Which house, Saleh? Which house do you mean?

I visited the Asr market and saw Saleh's house, empty of memory. Even its stones and iron windows had been stolen. They had destroyed its passages and ruined its inscriptions. Yet it still stood, a yellowing skeleton where drunks and tramps pissed on its walls.

What nation is this where they piss on its memory, Saleh?

What homeland is this?

Here is a city that donned mourning for a man whose name it had forgotten. Here you are, a little girl whose kinship with these bridges remained unknown.

Take off your shawl after today. Lift the veil from your face and don't keep knocking at the door.

Saleh is no longer here and neither am I.

So we had split up.

Those who say that love never dies are wrong.

Those who write love stories with happy endings, to fool us into thinking that Majnoun, the crazed lover of Laila was an emotional exception, know nothing of the rules of the heart.

They didn't write love, they only wrote literature.

Passion can only be born in the middle of minefields, in danger zones. For that reason the triumph of desire doesn't always mean a sedate and happy ending. It dies as it is born, in beautiful destruction.

So we had split up.

Farewell, my beautiful destruction. Farewell, volcanic rose, jasmine sprouting from the fire.

O, daughter of earthquakes and cracks in the ground, your destruction was the most beautiful, madam. Your destruction was the most horrific.

You killed an entire homeland within me. You slipped into the recesses of my memory and blew it all up with a single match.

Who taught you to play with fragments of memory? Answer!

Where have you come from this time, yet again, with all these burning waves of fire. From where have you brought all the devastation that has come since that day?

So we had split up.

You didn't lie to me, or really tell the truth. You weren't a lover, or a cheat really. You weren't my daughter, or really my mother.

You were just like this homeland, the thing and its opposite.

Do you remember that distant, early time when you loved me and searched me for a copy of your father?

You once said, 'I've been waiting a long time for you. I've waited so much, like we wait for the holy saints, or the prophets. Don't be a false prophet, Khaled. I need you!'

At the time I noticed that you didn't say, 'I love you.' You just said, 'I need you.'

We don't necessarily love the prophets. We just need them, at all times.

I replied, 'I haven't chosen to be a prophet.'

You said as a joke, 'Prophets don't choose their mission, they just carry it out!'

'They don't choose their followers, either,' I replied. 'So if you should discover that I'm a false prophet, perhaps that's because I was sent to especially faithless followers!'

You laughed and, with the stubbornness of a woman tempted by the challenge, said, 'You're looking for a way out of your probable failure with me, aren't you? I won't give you such an excuse. Give me your Ten Commandments and I will obey.'

I stared at you that day. You were too beautiful to obey the commandments of a prophet, too weak to bear the weight of heavenly teachings. But you had an inner light I had not seen in a woman before. A seed of purity I didn't want to disregard.

Isn't the role of prophets to find the seed of goodness within?

I said, 'Put the Ten Commandments to one side and listen to me. I have only an eleventh commandment for you.'

You laughed and said, with some truth, 'Let us have it, you bankrupt prophet. I swear I shall follow you!'

At the time I felt like taking advantage of your promise and saying, 'Just be mine.' But those weren't the words of a prophet. Without realising, I had started to play the role you had chosen for me. I searched my mind for something a prophet new to his vocation might say. I came up with, 'Carry your name with greater pride. Not with arrogance, necessarily, but with a profound awareness that you are more than a woman. You are an entire nation. Do you know that? Symbols have no right to fall to pieces. These are mean times and if we don't stick to our values we'll find ourselves numbered among the rubbish and waste. Stick to your principles and flatter only your conscience, for in the end it's your only companion.'

You said, 'Is that your commandment to me? That's it?'

'Don't treat it lightly. It's not as easy as you imagine to fulfil. You'll discover that for yourself some day.'

You should never have mocked the commandment of that bankrupt prophet that day and treated it so lightly.

A half dozen years have passed since that trip, that encounter and that farewell.

During those years I have tried to close my wounds and forget. I tried upon my return to put some order into my heart, restore things to their former place without upheaval or complaint, without smashing a vase, without moving a painting or rearranging the old set of values that had been gathering dust inside me for a long time.

I tried to turn time back, without resentment or forgiveness either.

No, we don't so easily forgive those who with transient happiness make us realise how miserable we were beforehand. Even less do we forgive those who kill our dreams in front of us without any sense that it is a crime.

So I haven't forgiven you, or them.

I have just tried to deal with you and with the homeland with less love. I chose indifference as the sole emotion for both of you.

Your news would reach me by chance as I listened to someone talking about your husband, his continuing ascent, his secret deals and public business that was all the rave at gatherings.

News of the homeland would also reach me, at times in the newspaper, at times at other gatherings, and when Hassan came to visit me, for the last time, to buy the car I had promised him.

Every time, I treated all I heard with the same indifference that could only have arisen from ultimate despair.

I began to be attached only to Hassan, as if I had suddenly discovered he existed. He was the only thing that mattered to me once I realised that he was all I had left in the world, and once I discovered the miserable life he led, which I had known absolutely nothing about before my visit to Constantine.

I took to calling him on the phone regularly. I would ask how he was doing and about the children, about the house, which he was intending to fix up and which I promised to pay for.

His spirits would fall and rise from one call to the next. One time he would speak about some project and the calls he had made to be transferred to the capital. Then he would suddenly lose all his enthusiasm.

I knew this when he asked me during his final call, 'When are you coming, Khaled?'

At the time, I felt he was like a sinking ship sending out an SOS to me.

Even so, I just humoured him and kept promising that I would visit the following summer. But deep down I knew I was lying. I had burned the bridges with the homeland until further notice.

In reality, I had become convinced that there was no hope. The train was going in the opposite direction, and at a speed we could do nothing about. Nothing, except await the disastrous crash in dismay.

I packed the suitcases of my heart and also went, without realising, in a different direction, away from the homeland.

I furnished my exile with forgetting. I made myself a new

homeland out of exile. Maybe an eternal one that I would have to get used to living in.

I started to reconcile with things. I formed sensible relationships with the Seine, Pont Mirabeau and all the landmarks visible from that window, which I had treated as enemies for no reason.

I chose more than one transient lover. I furnished my bed with insane pleasures, with women whom I amazed more and more as I used them to kill you more and more, until not a trace of you remained.

This body has forgotten its longing for you. It has forgotten its passion and folly, how it went on strike against every pleasure except fantasies of you.

I set out to strip women of their primary symbolism. Those who say 'woman is exile' or 'woman is homeland' are liars. Women have no domain beyond the body. Memory is not the path that leads to them. Today, I can state categorically that there is only one path.

I have discovered something I must tell you now. Desire is all in the mind, the exercise of the imagination, that's all. It's an illusion we create at a moment of madness. We become slaves to one person whom we judge in total awe for a mysterious reason outside of logic.

Desire born like that from the unknown may lead us back to another memory, to the scent of another perfume, a word, a face. To a crazed desire born some place outside the body, from memory or perhaps the unconscious, from mysterious things that you infiltrated one day to become the most awesome, the most desirable and all women in one.

Do you understand why I automatically killed you when I killed Constantine inside me?

I wasn't surprised, then, to see your corpse laid out on my bed.

In the end the two of you were only one woman.

You will say, 'Why did you write this book for me, then?' And I will reply that I'm just borrowing your rituals for killing and that I decided to bury you in a book, that's all.

There are corpses we must not preserve in our hearts. Love after death also has a foul smell, especially when it takes on the aspect of a crime.

Note that I didn't use your name once in this book. I decided to leave you nameless. Some names don't deserve to be mentioned.

Let's assume you're a woman called Hayat, who perhaps has another name. Is your name really that important?

Only the names of martyrs cannot be forged. It's their right that we remember them by their full names. It's also the right of this homeland to reveal who betrayed it and built their glory on its ruins and their wealth out of its misery, as long as nobody holds them to account.

I know it will be rumoured that this book is yours. Let me confirm for you, madam, this rumour.

Critics who practise criticism in compensation for other things will say that this book isn't a novel, but the ravings of a man who knows nothing of the norms of literature.

I confirm to them in advance my ignorance and my contempt for their norms. The only norm I have is pain. My only ambition is to amaze you and make you cry when you've finished reading this book.

There are things I haven't said to you yet.

Read this book and burn the other books in your cupboard by half-writers, half-men, half-lovers.

Literature is only born from wounds. Let all those who loved you rationally, without bleeding, without losing weight or their balance, go to hell.

Leaf through me with some shyness, as you would leaf through an album of yellowed pictures of you as a child. As you would look through a dictionary of old words at risk of extinction and death. As you would read a clandestine pamphlet you found in your letterbox one day.

Open your heart and read.

Once I wanted to talk to you about *Si* Taher, Ziyad and others, about all you were ignorant of. But Hassan died. There's no time left to talk about martyrs. We're all martyrs in waiting.

I'm sad that I haven't given you a gazelle. 'Gazelles are only gazelles while they live,' wrote Malek Haddad. I have nothing left to give you today.

You took from me all those I loved one after another, one way or another. My heart has turned into a mass grave where all those I loved are sprawled. It's as though Mother's grave had expanded to hold them all.

All I am now is the gravestone for *Si* Taher, Ziyad and Hassan, the gravestone of memory.

I knew a lot about the foolishness of fate, about its oppression and stubbornness when it insists on pursuing someone. But could I have imagined that something like that would happen?

I thought I had paid enough to this fool destiny. That after this life and the years that followed the tragedy of Ziyad and the tragedy of your marriage, the time had come for me to finally find rest.

How could fate come back and take my brother from me? My brother, whose death had no logic. He wasn't in any Front, or on the battlefield to be shot dead like *Si* Taher or Ziyad.

That day in October 1988, news of his death struck over a telephone line full of static and Atiqa's voice choked with tears.

She kept sobbing and saying my name as I asked her in torment, 'What's happened?'

I was aware of the events that had shaken the country. The French media competed to pass on in-depth details and images with a gloating prurience. I knew that the events of the second day were still restricted to the capital. How, then, could I have expected what happened?

Atiqa's voice kept repeating in broken fashion, 'They've killed him, Khaled. They've killed him.'

My voice repeated in shock, 'How? How have they killed him?'

How did Hassan die? Did the question matter? His death was as foolish as his life, as naive as his dreams.

I read all the newspapers to understand how my brother had died, between one dream and another, one fantasy and another.

What had taken him to Algiers when he only rarely went to the capital?

He had gone at the weekend looking for his own end.

He'd had enough of Constantine. Her many bridges had led him nowhere.

He had been told, 'You'll have strings in the capital. They'll give you a shortcut there that the bridges here never will.'

Hassan believed it and went to the capital to meet so-and-so through another so-and-so.

He was destined finally to solve his problems this time, after several years of connections and interventions, and finally leave the teaching profession by moving to the capital to take up a job in the media.

But it was fate that decided his case this time.

Between so-and-so and so-and-so, Hassan died, a mistake by a stray bullet on the path of his dreams.

Dreaming isn't for all, my dear brother. You shouldn't have dreamed.

Is it true, as Malek Haddad said, that 'misery knows how to choose its ingredients'? Is that why it chose me, and all these shocking disasters for me alone?

Me, who only dreamed of giving you a gazelle.

How could I have done that when you gave me so much destruction, so much ruin?

An old conversation we had comes to mind.

A conversation that went back six years to the time when you saw a similarity between me and Zorba, the man you loved most, as you put it. You had dreamed of emulating his novel or loving a man like him.

Perhaps because you couldn't write a novel like that, you were content to turn me into a copy of him. You made me learn, like him, to get over the things that I loved by consuming them to the point of nausea.

You made me love beautiful destruction and learn to dance in agony like a freshly slaughtered chicken.

Here were the beautiful ruins, which you had once told me about with a zeal that didn't arouse my suspicions. You had said, 'It's amazing that someone's disappointment and tragedy can make him dance. He stood out in his defeats as well. Not all defeats are available to all. You have to have extraordinary dreams, joys and ambitions for those feelings to become their opposite in that way.'

My lady, if only you knew!

How grand my dreams; how horrific the destruction that the television stations raced to air!

Such horrific destruction. How sad my brother's dead body on the pavement, hit by a random bullet.

How sad his body, as it waited in the morgue refrigerator for me to identify and then accompany to Constantine.

Once again Constantine. The tyrannical mother lying in wait for her children, sworn to bring us back to her, even as corpses. She has defeated us, brought us both back to her. At the very moment we believed we had got over her and cut the tie of kinship.

Hassan would not leave her for the capital. I would not run away from her again.

We would go back to her together. One of us in a coffin, the other, the remains of a man.

You have given your judgement, rock, mother of rock.

Open your tombs and wait for me. I'm coming to you with my brother. Give him a small space next to your holy saints, your martyrs and your beys. Hassan was all of that in his own way.

He was a gazelle.

While waiting, come, madam, and see all this beautiful destruction!

Soon, Zorba will appear to take hold of my shoulder for us to start dancing.

Come here. You mustn't miss this scene. You'll see how prophets dance when truly bankrupt.

Come here. I'll dance today like I never have before, like I longed to dance at your wedding but didn't. I'll leap as though my feet have grown wings and my missing arm has grown back again.

Come here. May my father forgive me for never joining him at the Aissawi rites. At sessions where he would sway and dance madly and plunge that skewer right through his body in the ecstasy of pain that transcends pleasure.

Grief has many rituals and pain has no particular homeland.

May the prophets and the holy saints forgive me. May they all forgive me. I don't know exactly what prophets do when they grieve, what they do in the age of apostasy. Do they cry or pray?

I decided to dance. Dance also reached out, was also a form of worship.

Look, Almighty, with one arm I dance for You. How difficult it is to dance with one arm, my Lord. How horrific it is to dance with one arm, my Lord.

But You will forgive me, You who took away my other arm.

You will forgive me, You who took all of them away.

You will forgive me, because You will take me, too!

Was the believer really afflicted? Or was that saying created just to teach us patience. To market us delight in a certificate of piety instead of our afflictions?

So be it.

Thank you, Almighty, You who alone are praised even in affliction. You who only bestow Your affliction on Your faithful and righteous worshippers.

I confess I never expected such a certificate of good behaviour.

I emptied of you, my lady, and filled with a Greek melody.

Zorba's music came over me as an invitation to utter madness.

It came from a cassette I was used to hearing with strange pleasure. Coming in the midst of ruin and corpses, now the melody assumed its true, original aspect.

The music hit, and I leapt up from my seat and shouted, like in the novel, 'Come on, Zorba, teach me to dance.'

This was the beautiful destruction that you had made me desire. I didn't think it would be so horrific, so painful.

Theodorakis' music stole towards me. It penetrated me note by note, wound by wound.

Slowly. Then fast, like a storm of tears.

Shyly. Then bold, like a moment of hope.

Sadly. Then ecstatic, like the musings of a poet over a drink.

Hesitant. Then certain, like the march of soldiers.

I surrendered to it and danced like a madman in a vast room furnished with paintings and bridges.

I stopped in the middle of the room, as if on the towering cliffs, to dance in the midst of ruin while the five bridges of Constantine shattered in front of me and rolled like rocks towards the valleys.

Yes, Zorba! The woman I loved and who loved you got married. I wanted to make her a copy of me, but she made me a copy of you.

Ziyad died, that friend who bought this tape, perhaps because he, too, loved you for her sake, or perhaps because he anticipated a day like this for me, and prepared for me, in his way, all the details of my sadness to come. Perhaps it was her gift to him, which I've inherited among all the grief.

Hassan has died, my brother who cared little for the Greeks or their gods.

He had but one God and a few old albums.

He died and only loved Fergani, Umm Kalthoum and the voice of Abdel Baset Abdel Samad.

His only dreams were to obtain a passport for the Hajj, and a fridge.

He finally achieved half his dreams. The nation had given him a fridge where he was calmly awaiting me to bid him a final farewell.

If he had known you, perhaps he wouldn't have died this idiotic death.

If he had read you closely, he wouldn't have looked at his killers with such amazement, wouldn't have dreamed of a job in the capital, a car and a nicer house.

He would have spat in his killers' faces in advance, cursed them like he had never cursed another, refused to shake their hands at that wedding, would have said, 'You pimps and thieves and killers, you won't steal our blood too. Stuff your pockets as you like. Furnish your houses as you like and fill your bank accounts with any currency you like. We will keep blood and memory. We will make you answer to them, we will haunt you with them and rebuild this homeland with them.'

Ah, Zorba. Ziyad died and now Hassan has also died of betrayal.

Ah, my friend, if only you knew that neither of them deserved to die.

Hassan was as pure as quicksilver and good to the point of naivety. He was even afraid to dream. Once he started, they killed him.

Ziyad was a bit like you, Zorba. If only you had seen him laugh or heard him talking, rebelling, cursing, crying, getting drunk. If you had known them, you would have danced in grief for them tonight like you've never danced before.

But it didn't matter. I knew that you wouldn't turn up tonight either. Perhaps because you had died, like in the novel, after cursing the priest who came to administer the last rites. Or perhaps because you had never existed at all, but were just a mythical hero for a time when people were seeking a new Greek mythology to teach them madness and defiance and the absurdity of life.

Did it matter that you were absent tonight when everyone was absent?

I didn't blame you, my friend. You weren't responsible for all the stupid mistakes that could be made because of a novel.

Just answer me this. You killed Turks, and they killed many of your comrades. Was there any difference between killers?

Si Taher died at the hands of the French, Ziyad died at the hands of the Israelis, and now Hassan has died at the hands of Algerians.

Were there degrees of martyrdom? What if the homeland were both killer and martyr?

So many Arab cities had a place in history because of massacres, the graves of which still remained secret.

The inhabitants of so many Arab cities were martyred before they even became citizens.

Where should we file them? Under victims of history or under martyrs?

What to call death when it is by means of the Arab dagger?

As soon as Catherine saw me that morning, she cried out, 'You look as though you were drunk last night!' Then she added, with some wit and a clear hint, 'What did you get up to last night, naughty boy, to be in such a state?'

I said, 'Nothing. Maybe I didn't sleep well.'

Casting a curious, woman's eye around the living room in search of clues as to the kind of person I spent the evening with, she said, 'Did you have friends round last night?'

I smiled at her question and felt like saying yes. When sadness verges on madness it can turn sarcastic on its own.

She continued, 'Did they spend the night here?'

I said, 'No. They left.' After a brief silence, I went on, 'My friends always leave!'

Perhaps I wasn't convincing or I just increased her curiosity. She resumed looking for something in the disorder and the two open suitcases.

Women are like that. They see no further than their bodies. So Catherine was unable to discover the traces of Ziyad, Hassan and Zorba in the house.

In truth, Catherine always lived on the fringes of my sadness, so she had convinced herself in a few words that I was awaking from a night of passion.

She asked me, as if all of a sudden she could find no justification for her presence with me at that moment, 'Why did you ask me to come round straight away?'

'For many reasons,' I said. Suddenly I added, 'Catherine, do you like bridges?'

In a tone not devoid of astonishment, she said, 'Don't tell me you brought me round this morning to ask that question!'

'No,' I said. 'But I'd like you to answer it.'

'I don't know. I've never asked myself such a question before. I've always lived in cities without bridges, except for Paris, perhaps.'

'It doesn't matter. In the end, I'd prefer you not to like them. It's enough that you like my painting.'

She replied, 'Of course I love what you paint. I've always thought you were an exceptional painter.'

'That's settled then. All these paintings are yours.'

She shouted, 'Are you crazy? How can you give me all these pictures? They're of your city. You might miss it one day.'

'There's no need for nostalgia after today. I'm going back. I'm giving them to you because I know you value art and that they won't get lost with you.'

Catherine's voice acquired a new mysterious note of sadness and joy, 'I'll look after them all. No man's ever given me anything like that.'

I gave her body, hidden as usual under light, baggy clothing, a final glance, and said, 'And no woman before you has given me a more delicious exile.'

She said, 'I'm afraid you'll regret it and miss one of them one day. Know that you'll always find them with me.'

300

'That might happen,' I said. 'We always regret something.'

She interrupted me, as though suddenly discovering the seriousness of the situation. *'Mais ce n'est pas possible.* We can't part like this.'

'Oh, Catherine, let's part hungry. For various reasons, history has condemned us never to be completely satisfied with one another, not to completely love one another. Now you have more than one copy of me. Hang my memory on your wall, even if it's an antidote to memory. You were also party to it!'

Catherine was unable to understand the reason for all the symbolism.

Why this mysterious talk that I had not conditioned her to?

Perhaps she did understand, but her body refused to. Her body was always off topic. Her body was a French employee, always protesting, always asking for more. Overdoing freedom of expression and the right to strike.

But where would I find the words to explain my sadness to her?

Where would I find the silence that would speak to her without my saying that Hassan was waiting for me in the morgue in another city, and his six children had no one but me?

How would I explain to her my cold feet and the chill creeping up on me as the hours advanced and her hands started to open the buttons of my shirt without warning, out of habit?

'Catherine. I don't feel like making love. I'm sorry.'

'What do you want, then?'

'I want you to laugh like usual.'

'Why laugh?'

'Because you're incapable of sadness.'

'And you?'

'I will wait till you've gone to be sad. My sadness is only deferred, as usual.'

'Why are you telling me this today?'

'Because I'm tired and because I'm leaving in a few hours.'

'But you can't leave. They've cancelled all travel to Algeria.'

'I'll go and wait at the airport for the first plane. I have to travel today or tomorrow. Someone is waiting for me.'

I could have said to her, 'My brother is dead. My only brother, Catherine,' and broken down crying. I needed to cry in front of someone that day.

But I couldn't do it with her. It might have been an old complex. Sadness was a personal matter that sometimes became national.

So I kept my wound to myself and decided to keep talking like normal. I might tell her another day, but not today. Silence today was greater.

I suddenly felt I had mistreated the butterflies.

I said, 'Catherine, we had a beautiful thing, didn't we? A bit complicated maybe, but beautiful all the same. You were the woman who was always about to become my beloved. Perhaps separation will bring about what all the years of being together couldn't.'

'Will you love me when we split up?'

'I don't know. I'll definitely miss you loads. That's the logic of things. I had more than one habit with you, and someday I'll have to change my habits.'

'Will you come back?'

'Not for a long time. I have to learn the other side of forgetting now. Exile is also a mother, and it's not easy for us to cross the bridge that separates us from her.'

'Khaled, why do you surround yourself with all these bridges?'

'I don't surround myself with them. I carry them inside me. There are people like that, born on a suspension bridge who come into the world between two tracks, two paths, two continents, born in the currents of crosswinds. They grow up trying to reconcile the contradictions inside. Perhaps I was one of those. Let me tell you a secret. I've discovered that I don't like bridges. I hate them in the way I hate all things with two sides, two faces, two possibilities, two opposites. That's why I'm leaving you all the paintings.

'I wanted to burn them. It was a tempting idea, but I don't have the courage of Tariq ibn Ziyad. Perhaps because a sailor burning his ship in battle is easier than an artist burning his paintings in a moment of madness.

'Even so, I want to burn them to cut off any path back for my heart.

'I don't want to spend my life walking the bridge both ways.

'I want to chose a final place for my heart.

'I want to return to that city perched on a rock, as if reconquering her, just like Tariq ibn Ziyad conquered Gibraltar and gave it his name.

'Since leaving her, I've lost my bearings. I've severed my link with history and geography. I've stood for years before a question mark, outside lines of latitude and longitude.

'Where is the sea, and where is the enemy? Which is in front and which behind?

'Over the sea there is only the homeland. Before me is only the raft of exile. Only I stand between them.

'Who shall I declare war upon when there are only the regional borders of memory around me?'

I looked at Catherine. She understood nothing.

Our relationship had always been the victim of misunderstanding and short-sightedness. We split up as we had met more than one century before, without really knowing each other.

Without completely loving each other but always with the same mysterious attraction.

You said, 'What happened to us was love. Literature was all that did not happen.'

Yes, but.

Between what happened and what didn't happen, other things occurred, unrelated to love or literature.

The outcome in both cases was for us to produce nothing but words. Only the nation created events and wrote us as it willed, as long as we remained its ink.

I had left the country at a time when there was no air. Now I was going back at a time of curfew.

As I, alone this time, confronted the airport of this city draped in mourning, I remembered something Hassan said years earlier, which had made me pause for no obvious reason. He had said, 'The natives of this city only come to visit for weddings and funerals.'

The discovery stunned me. I had become a legitimate son of this city that had summoned me by force twice. Once to attend your wedding and once to bury my brother. What was the difference between the two?

My brother had actually died while I had been dead since your wedding.

Our dreams killed us.

Him because he was infected with vast, empty dreams.

Me because I abandoned my fantasy and went into permanent mourning for my dreams.

An edgy customs officer, about the same age as independence and not put off by either my sadness or my one arm, shouted in my face. He had the tone of someone convinced that we only went abroad to get rich and always smuggled something back with us. 'What do you have to declare?' he asked.

My body raised memory before him, but he didn't read me.

It can happen that a nation becomes illiterate.

At the same moment, others were entering through the VIP channel with elegant diplomatic bags.

His hands rifled through Ziyad's modest suitcase and fell upon a bundle of papers. A proud tear in my eye almost answered him, 'I declare memory, my lad.'

But I kept quiet and gathered up the draft of this book scattered in the suitcase. Chapter headings, the headings for dreams.

A NOTE ON THE AUTHOR

Algerian novelist and poet Ahlem Mosteghanemi is the bestselling female author in the Arab world. She has more than 2.6 million followers on Facebook and was ranked in the top ten most influential women in the Middle East by Forbes in 2006. The Arabic original of this title (*Dhakirat al-Jasad*) was awarded the 1998 Naguib Mahfouz Medal for Literature (founded in honour of the Nobel laureate). It is the first in a trilogy of bestselling novels and has since been translated into several languages and adapted into a television series. Ahlem lives in Beirut.

A NOTE ON THE TRANSLATOR

Raphael Cohen studied Arabic at Oxford University and the University of Chicago, and now lives and works in Cairo.

A NOTE ON THE TYPE

The text of this book is set in Bembo. This type was first used in 1495 by the Venetian printer Aldus Manutius for Cardinal Bembo's *De Aetna*, and was cut for Manutius by Francesco Griffo. It was one of the types used by Claude Garamond (1480–1561) as a model for his Romain de L'Université, and so it was the forerunner of what became standard European type for the following two centuries. Its modern form follows the original types and was designed for Monotype in 1929.